I0760420

One Poisonous Queen

Book Two

Monica Shantel

one
poisonous
queen
queens of orsadia
book two
monica shantel

One Poisonous Queen

Book Cover by Monica Shantel

Art by Monica Shantel

ISBN 978-1-960696-13-7 (Paperback) 978-1-960696-14-4 (Hardcover)

First Edition

For all those who've never felt worthy enough, who've felt alone too many times to count. I hear you. I got you.

AUTHOR'S NOTE

This book deals with heavy topics. Including the topic of homophobia, self-loathing, mental illness, suicidal thoughts and a successful suicide, an animal corpse, a ton of gore, as well as isolation from the world. Please keep this in mind to decide if this book is right for you.

Writing this book has broken me in ways I never expected writing to be able to ruin me. It has allowed me to express my darkest fears and thoughts. I've poured so much of my own soul in Lana. I've cried so many times. I've had to pause and step back in multiple scenes. Lana's feelings are very much my own, and this book has been the hardest book for me to write to date. I hope you can find some comfort, whether you feel the same she does and if you can relate to any extent. Thank you for giving her a chance to tell her story.

2/11/25
"Mira Sunder"

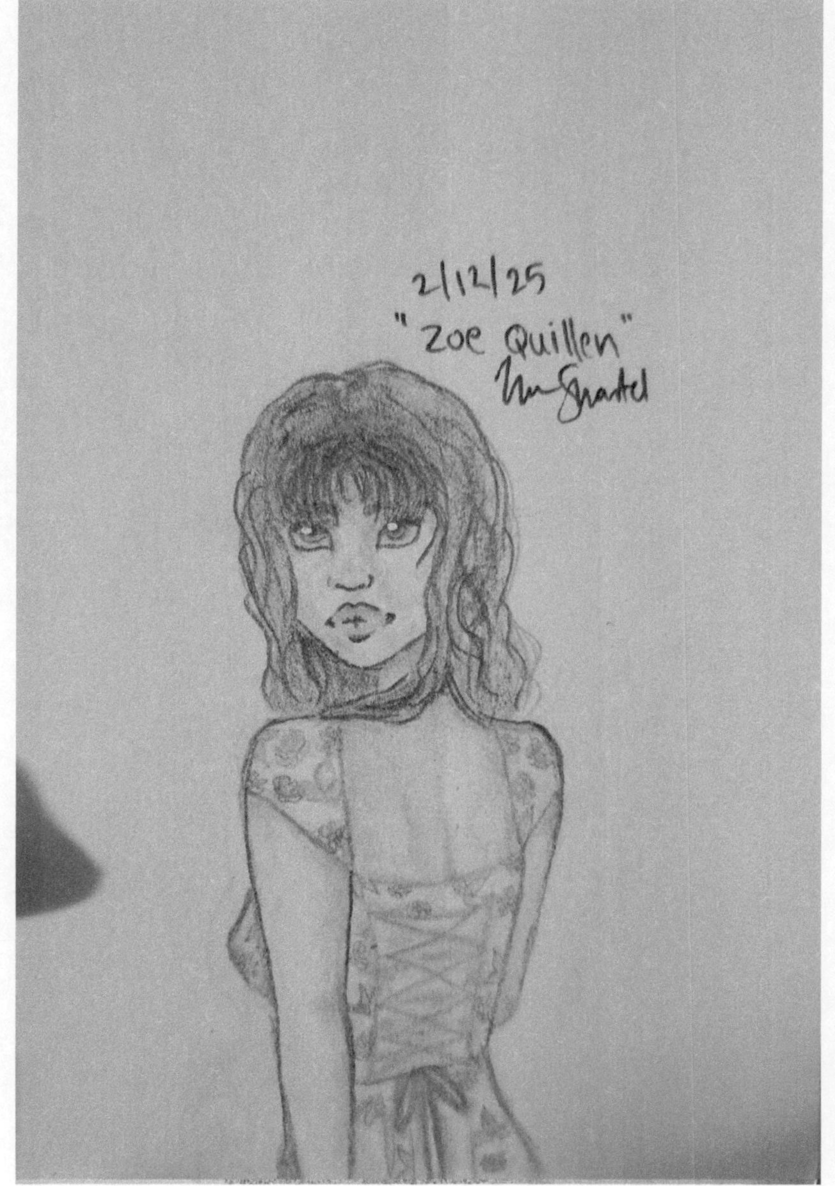
2/12/25
"Zoe Quillen"

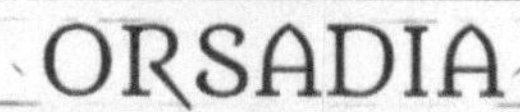

verinthian Castle

LUKA'S CAVE

KEENAIN RIVER

FOUNTAIN

Ash Forest

UNDERGROUND CAVE

GRAVEYARD

VILLAGE

Drecose Castle

Hypnotic Arythe

PROLOGUE

Some preferred fire over ice. Summer vs. winter. Too hot or too cold.

I'd say let it burn. Let it freeze over. What difference did any of it make if not for the sake of a world worth living in? This was no land worth residing in any longer. Not now that the curse had snatched me up in its claws and pinched me into dust.

Mira screamed at me to fight it. "Don't let it make you like the rest of us, Snow! I was wrong; you're strong enough to say no!"

She'd been wrong, *again,* and not in the way we both hoped. I was not strong enough.

The urge to steal the life from this villager's soul had been so powerful.

"You're not better than the Evil Queen. No better than the rest of them," the resident spat.

She was right. I was no better. But I had managed to spare her, hadn't I? Did she not appreciate that? Did she not understand the kind of fight I had put up against what the curse persuaded me to do?

At times, when the curse went to sleep, a tiny fraction of myself whispered for me to eradicate it. I tried, even, a few nights in a row. To peel the darkness from my essence. To rip the voice from my head.

Every time, the curse would wake at full force and remind me that I was weak.

If you had any strength at all, you would never have lost the war.

How could I argue with that? I'd lost. I had become the next cursed queen.

Fallon and I had drifted apart from my doing. And with this influential voice in my head, I hadn't wanted to drag him down with me. For his safety, he needed to go his own way, and I needed to keep my distance.

Mother, too, could not witness the same thing happen to her daughter that had devoured her own mother.

I'd spare them the heartbreak.

That burden would become my own.

Smart girl. Together, you and I can turn Orsadia into our personal cemetery, that low, deep voice purred.

He appeared in my head one day, naming all the terrible things I'd done to those around me as to keep me in my castle. His voice had come from someone I couldn't quite put my finger on—familiar in the wrong ways—or maybe I had been losing my sanity and the curse had a voice that matched those I once trusted.

So Mira said.

The voice isolated me from who I might have had left. When it spoke to me, shivers crawled down my spine. I feared for my safety, and the people of Orsadia. But he was always right. Something about him just lured me in until I breathed the curse.

And Luka...

That bastard left me after I'd told him to.

I knew it was entirely wrong of me to ever expect him to stay. He expressed how much he wanted to explore and travel. But how long would he stay away? Did he have any reason to ever return home? Did he consider this home anymore?

I'd done a wonderful job of creating distance between people I cared about. If I built my walls, I could never experience the heartache that came with loss and abandonment.

Luka would have planned to leave whether I kept him close or not. At least this way, I could blame myself and protect him from being the villain. Everything I did...it was for the sake of others.

Was I such a terrible person?

You want to rip their hearts out, Little Raven, he hissed seductively. *You're truly wicked to the core.*

Having temptatious thoughts of death couldn't be inherently evil. Yet here I was, entertaining the idea as I looked out upon the land of my people.

I yelled at the skies from outside the window. I shouted at the walls that encased me. I cried out to the voice that kept me company where I had nobody else—because I'd gotten rid of them.

"I'm a terrible person. They're better off without me," I whispered. "How—how do I quiet the bloodlust?"

You cannot. You're a necromancer. It's all you will know of this world. If you play the part, they cannot hold you to impossible standards. I know you. You're exhausted from living up to everyone else's expectations. Let me help you.

"How?"

Let me show you how powerful you are, and what your grandmother was never able to do as queen.

Sorrow filled every crevice, every crack in my bones at the mention of her.

I'd not made her proud. I had not given anyone a good reason to roll out of bed each morning, and because I had fought so hard to meet their wishes, the fall to rock bottom had been that much more painful.

Maybe he was right—the curse. Maybe letting people believe what they were going to believe was far less brutal.

"Snow?" Mira stepped out of the darkness, Aalia trailing behind her, both in translucent forms.

As I lifted my gaze from the floor, I met concerned looks. "I no longer go by Snow White. Call me Lana."

ONE

Soulless eyes. Blackened hair. *Ghostly* complexion. And that damned scar that Mira left behind on my once flawless features.

As I gazed at myself in the mirror, I touched the dark spots that formed on the base of my neck, where she had choked me multiple times before injecting me with a drug to close off my windpipe.

"Seems appropriate, is it not?" the Evil Queen asked from behind.

I turned to face the spirit that sat on *my* throne.

She sighed. "Snow, we've been over this. I'm not going anywhere until this curse is broken. Aalia agrees with me." She snapped her fingers and pointed in the direction of where Aalia stood in the shadowed corner.

Aalia's white hair was a beautiful contrast against her dark skin. It seemed so...*fitting*.

I approached the window and scanned the village. "I've said a million times before that I'm in no position to break this curse. What I am interested in is an apple."

"You hate apples," Mira said.

"Precisely, but an apple is Zoe's favorite snack and that is exactly what I need to kill her before she takes this life out of my hands. I don't expect you to help me, but I do expect you to keep your mouth shut. Understood?" I turned to face Aalia and Mira.

Neither of them responded and I lifted my chin while uncurling my fingers like a flower. "Understood?"

On cue, both of them said, "Yes, understood."

Facing the land once again, I gripped the windowsill. "What's one more corpse for a necromancer? It'll be my playground to control."

“That sounds great and all, Snow, but we should focus on the task at hand.” Mira gestured to the book on the table over by the wall. “Hypnotic Arythe.”

“Must I remind you I go by Lana?” I whipped around to face her.

Regardless of the power wielded, her demeanor never cowered in my presence. “Lana. Snow White. You've gone back and forth. Forgive me for not keeping up with whatever your fleeting feelings decide on for the day.”

I could have smacked the smugness from her expression. It'd be so easy, given how much contact I had with the dead.

So I said nothing at all.

“What do you plan to do with it?” Aalia piped in.

Approaching the table in slow strides, I placed my palms flat on the top, leaning over the pages. "I can only touch it in a way that my power allows." A sigh escaped my lips. "Such a shame for Orsadia. My magic is certainly great. I want something memorable. Alluring. Something that even Zoe could never resist. A carnival is out of the question," I spat as Mira opened her mouth to suggest it.

With a groan, she leaned her head over the arm of my throne. "It was certainly exquisite. It lured you in."

"When I was searching for the sins. It had never been earlier than that." I shot her with a murderous gaze.

Her eyes lightened as she met mine. "I was never in this for myself. This whole royalty duty I'd been given. My father taught me long before you'd been born about what my legacy would entail. He prepared me from the moment I could walk, along with my mother of course. I had been set up for failure. But you, Snow, were not supposed to be the failure. When I set up those seven sins, I knew you'd never be able to kill living human beings. I expected you to come running here the second you found out your quest, giving me the chance to take your life myself. I assumed you'd have asked me to take your life so you'd never have to commit such horrendous, immoral acts. I hired them. Each and every single one. Offered them gold. Riches. Homes. Food. They took the offer. And they fit their sins perfectly. But you defied me. You convinced yourself to murder them in cold blood." She slumped. "For me, it was never about keeping my magic. I simply wanted the curse to be over. You were supposed to die. Then I would have killed every sin, and then Alexander and myself. However, here we are..."

And against Magic Law, I'd been granted the right by Mira Sunder to enter Everinthian the night she killed me before I took the throne.

"You sent Luka away," I snapped. "Knowing it'd leave me with nothing to fight for. Just so I'd lay down my life for you."

"I had to ask myself: you or tons of innocent people? I chose the people. I don't regret the decisions I made. I only pity you for never making the right one."

With a snicker, I brushed away her insults. "Don't bother with the pity, dear. I don't request it."

“What you did request was my brother's absence. I imagine watching the light disappear from his eyes was the most satisfying event of the century,” she said in a bitter tone. “I knew that from the start, just how deep your hatred ran. Using him. I tried everything I could to get you to do what I needed. You didn't care for his hand in marriage, and so he had to *try* to kill you, just so you'd kill him. That was the plan. However, he lied about his past because we needed to see how deeply rooted the darkness was in you. Fortunately, not deep. Much to our dismay, you were never willing to sacrifice your life for the people of Orsadia. Selfishness is your vice."

Before she got another word in, I clutched my black skirt and slipped from the Great Hall, down the stairs and out of the main entrance. Strolling down to the garden, I stopped to say hello to the hemlock on my right and black hellebore on my left. They flourished just as more bodies dropped. A creation I had been insanely proud to have grown. Greenery thrived, filling every crevice of the garden. With spring sweltering the earth beneath our feet, I delighted in the desiccation to come.

The sun warmed every surface, every petal, every leaf. I brushed my knuckles under a few buds, stopping just before I came in contact with deadly nightshade.

"You're doing exceedingly well," I said with envy slithering between my teeth.

Something caught my eye, and I lifted my gaze. Approaching the blue roses, I caressed the curls at their tips, inhaling the subtle scent.

In a land far away, I despised Mira for what she did. I blamed her, and I wanted her to suffer in agony for centuries.

However, that land had been out of my sight for a while. Luka had to leave for me to carry out my plans. Without his incessant advice, I could make like the plants amongst me, contaminating every living creature left.

Watch them wither. Crumble to ash.

I took pride in being the very hand that incinerated the ones who defied Magic Law.

They certainly didn't call me the Poisonous Queen without reason.

TWO

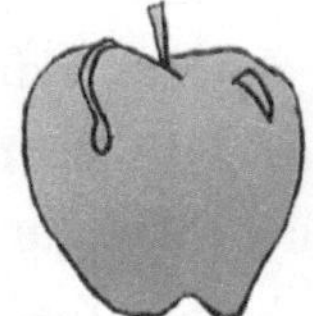

Rubbing the worn, gold metal between my thumb and forefinger, I huffed. And taking her compass with me to the library, I dropped whichever books I found on Mira Sunder and the Sunder family as a whole.

I set my candle down as little light streamed in from the window, the flame creating a glow with a radius around the measurement of a human skull.

The library in Everinthian had been dark. Dusty, with cobwebs strewn about. Most if not all of the books had been left abandoned. A pity if you asked just about anyone living on the island.

A clicking echoed from the corner. I glanced over, cocking an eyebrow. "I raise the dead. You certainly can't put terror in my veins."

Nobody showed themselves. Cowards never did.

"Listen," I started, taking my candlestick to the corner and waving it around until I spotted the culprit. "You're here to look pretty for me. Keep people out. Keep me in. I will not give up my throne. And not for any princesses." I stared down the skeleton of a man once killed at the hands of a past queen in the dungeon. "No more clicking. You don't need to scare me. I'm no intruder. I'm your queen. Is that understood?"

When he didn't respond, I asked again.

This time he clamped his jaw shut and fell limp.

I had full control over my magic by all means. But I also had a presence about me that the dead were drawn to. That and I always glowed, which they followed. I'd wake them up within a hundred giant femur bones. Naturally, I did. And I didn't entirely have the heart to shut it off. I'd been the light they needed to finally live again. I'd allow them that.

"Thank you." I sauntered back over to the table. After some consideration, I said, "I've changed my mind. I'd like your help over here." I waved him over.

Seconds later, he stumbled from the shadows and stopped at the other end of the table, waiting for his command.

I pointed to a book. "Find any mention of this compass, and when you do, leave it open on that page and give it to me. Even in the afterlife, the vile woman still challenges my ideas. Sure, I could get rid of her with the snap of my finger. But I like seeing her suffer. I ache to see her reaction when I kill Zoe and keep the throne for good."

So, we searched.

After hours of ending up with zero new information, Bones and I slumped in our chairs. "Nothing here. What I need is to locate a diary. Something where she may have mentioned it, and when she got it, who from, what it means to her, and preferably a way in which I can humiliate her very name."

We both sat in silence, gears turning. Bones clacking together. Brain buzzing with such concepts.

"What about you?" I pointed at him. "You've been here a long time. You've seen things. Do you know anything about this compass?"

The soulless pits of his sockets bore into me as he slightly shook his skull.

"What a shame," I huffed as a frown appeared.

By now, the sun had set just beyond the ocean and stars shined from its departure. The moon conjured a bit of light for us to make our way out of the library, but once we'd entered the hall with the chamberstick in my hand, we saw merely the length of a tombstone in front of us.

Quiet pierced the air on our way down the stairs. Bones certainly wasn't a sneaky one, trying to linger behind me with his feet hitting the wood—cluck.

Yeah, Mira and Aalia certainly wouldn't hear us coming.

As we dropped onto the last step, I twisted my head his way. "A haunted castle seems so much like me. I never could have dreamed of anything better. Concrete from ceiling to floor, ghosts floating about and a few of my beautiful creations walking the halls. That's you, Bones. My beautiful creation."

The two of us ventured through the dead of the night, up and down the corridors and into rooms. We kept our eyes peeled for every mention of Mira or a compass, but still nothing entirely came of it.

Hallways amassed with vines, sconces on the walls with nature promising to take back what once was its own. We lived in sync, and I was not one to poison the plants even if it had been my name.

I threw my arm out to halt Bones in his tracks. "What's this?"

He tilted his head as we both studied the door before us. A door hidden amongst the shelves down in the dungeons, a crack just barely visible if you looked hard enough.

The shelves had been filled with old nick-nacks collecting more dust. Trinkets. Maybe a book here and there. Décor meant to set the mood of the dungeons, and that had been with weapons, skulls, and some sculpted animals carved intricately of wood.

"Open it."

He did as I said, but his strength wasn't enough.

Lifting my arm and waving my hand forward, clicks and clacks echoed through the cells as the dead rose and bent to my whim. With at least a dozen, they got the door open for me in no time, and then I took my skirt and burning candle with me through the doorway.

I put more effort into commanding the dead to stay put. They ached to follow me—their gaslamp in the dark. My skin did certainly help at times with its subtle glow.

Cobwebs hung in the corners while dust coated in thick layers. Whatever room this had been, it had been smaller since its construction.

Bare walls closed off from the outside world. I spotted a writing desk in the corner with a candle that'd melted into a waxy puddle. As the realization dawned on me, a tear betrayed me as it rolled down my cheek. "Oh, Grandmother," I breathed out.

Where she had written all her letters in private. The letters that had been dated during her reign.

Where she had to come to terms with the idea that her love had never been returned.

Anne Regali had her first and only daughter at twenty-six, after her term ended. I remembered how she had passed at the young age of forty-four just before I'd been born. Mother was only eighteen then.

But if my grandmother truly had not received love, then who created my mother with her to carry for ten months?

Turning away from the chair made of oak splintering apart in the backrest, I swallowed my emotions. They played no role here. It'd be trouble if I allowed it to simmer for too long. That was how a perfectly good dish burned.

With the flame held high, I brought it towards the shelves of books and pens displayed next to bottles of dark ink, walking along the edge of the room and reading every front cover until something caught my eye.

Mira Sunder's journal.

I called in the skeletons for an audience.

"I got you right where I want you now, little ghost." I reached forward, plucking it from between a few others which had been recorded by previous queens.

The world will bow before us.

My throat thickened at the thought. Did I enjoy being the thing of their nightmares? We were all once equal.

Equal...

With the shake of my head, a wicked grin crawled onto my lips as I glanced back at my forming army. "We just discovered gold, my children. Do you know what we do with such things?" After a few skull shakes, my brown eyes darkened as my pupils dilated. "We make ourselves rich. We set our future in stone. I make them weep."

THREE

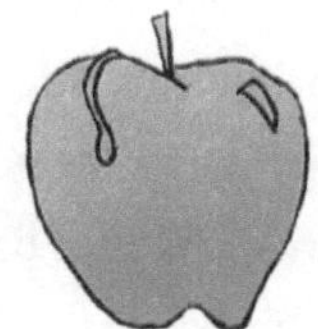

Flicking the needle scratched an itch in my brain I couldn't quite explain. "I imagine this is how you felt when you prepared the drug that ended my life, Mira." I pulled an apple from the bin of poison it'd been soaking in, then injected just a bit more under the skin. "This ensures that she's killed, of course. We wouldn't want to fail, given what she will be. She can't suspect a thing."

"No, I suppose not," she said with a sigh. "Would I be able to ask a favor?"

"Of me? I don't do favors, and certainly not for you." I turned my head slightly, never giving my full attention. I hoped with every fiber that she was offended by the insult.

Mira leaned forward and asked anyway, "Can you grab Alexander and allow him my company? Or I his? Please."

She said *please.*

It made this next part so much sweeter.

My lips pursed. "I don't think that I will." I whirled around in my gown and placed the apple amongst the rest as I continued my duty. "You said so yourself that it's clear my hatred goes far too deep for him. Why would I ever taint my castle with his presence? Use that pretty head of yours. *Please*," I mocked her.

It hadn't been a lie when I called her pretty. Mira had embodied beauty in ways all the queens had. Confidence. Strength. Her eyes sparkled the same blue the surface of the ocean did under a burning sun on a lovely day. Much like me, she'd had fairer skin, only she could add more color under the rays of gold while I could not. Well, before I'd effortlessly taken her life. Her hair cascaded down her back, pin-straight, in a chocolate shade lighter than Luka's.

"You hate him that much," she spat. "He's my brother. Surely you of all people can understand that kind of love."

Something inside me snapped, like the string of a small instrument, icy hot as it pressed me for more. Then I was in her face within mere seconds, squeezing my fist as I rooted her spirit where she sat. "Don't you dare talk about my brother. He dug his grave. He has to lie in it."

Her eyes narrowed. "I forget you disowned him because he defended himself against those disgusting boys. Now here you are, murdering people for sport. A fucking hypocrite, Snow."

I squeezed my fist tighter, nails digging into my palm, drawing blood. "Me? Your brother kissed me without my consent as if I wanted it. You condone such acts? As much as I despise you, I could never sit around and justify someone assaulting you. That's the difference between us." I let out a scowl.

Her upper lip twitched, then curled. "Is there a difference? I'm willing to sacrifice my life for the end of the curse. You'd never do such a thing. They called me the Evil Queen, but I was barely the tip of the iceberg. What does that make you? You truly are wicked."

I sewed her mouth shut. "No, dear, what I am is poisonous."

Even after I'd spun on my heels and stormed out, I didn't allow her the freedom to follow or yell after me.

Everything they repeated to me about Fallon haunted me. Everyone stood by his side, and rightfully so. He deserved all the support. What had I done exactly? I had convinced myself that seven human beings were mirages of Mira's. I had slaughtered them for my own gain. I'd assumed the Evil Queen had been my enemy when she had been my ally all along. I could not allow my tainted blood to pass onto Fallon.

And maybe I did murder for sport these days, but my brother had, too, and what was his excuse?

He had none.

I forget you disowned him because he fought back against disgraceful boys.

A small whimper escaped me.

No, Little Raven. He deserves better than your guidance.

That was *his* excuse—their actions.

Did that so much as make me a terrible sister for not wanting to aid in his growing darkness? I'd only become more of a terrible influence now. And while I reveled in it, I wouldn't allow him the same.

It was what good sisters did. Allowed the demons to consume them at the expense of others. It'd be the only way I could protect them. By disowning him, I made it a point to show him it wasn't something he should have gotten used to. Not something he should have taken joy in.

It was my fault our father had been killed.

If I could save at least my brother, maybe this time I could salvage what was left of the Edmilla family.

I just couldn't *be* part of it anymore. I'd been the omen. The smear that needed to disappear from their lives.

They don't want you, Lana. They merely pretended to stay on your good side to avoid being smited when you took the throne.

Why was that so easy to believe?

I'd renamed myself Snow White, thinking maybe I'd escape the curse. Maybe I could have saved my father and changed the course of fate.

I discovered I could not change much of anything. If my past wasn't that important, why bother to fight it? Snow White had lost the war with the shadows. It was Lana who embraced all she was ever meant to be.

I didn't want to fight the inevitable anymore. What was the purpose in rejecting it when I had no support left? The people knew; they made me what I was, and so I stepped into that role without any objections.

Nobody remembered who I was when I changed my name the first time. It'd been pitiful, knowing deep down that they never knew me by name, because they knew me as the girl who'd had the gay brother.

For that, my sole purpose was to be the Poisonous Queen. It was one I could play so well, and why would I ever try to be something different? I could never *disappoint* anyone.

They'd always expect the worst of me, and that was an expectation I could certainly live up to.

Now I just needed to kill the princess with a poisoned apple and my legacy would embed itself on my gravestone.

FOUR

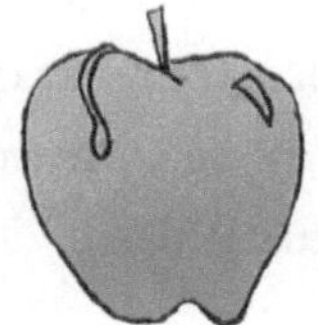

Hell hath no fury like a woman scorned.

Well, I was hell. A scorned woman, indeed.

A phthalo green gown adorned with subtle shimmery from the hem of my long, puffy sleeves to the end of the skirt with a slit up the side. Fitted bodice, and two pleated strips of fabric that spanned over each breast and around my biceps, forming a soft heart neckline.

And my sword dangling at my side. Would I part without it?

"Are the apples ready?" I glanced over at Mira and Aalia as they pulled my basket from my reach. "You are well aware I can force you to hand it over. Don't play childish games with me."

I pulled the black cloak around my shoulders with one swoop, fastening the gilded clasp at the center between my collarbones.

They shot each other a look before Aalia nodded and Mira gave me the basket of ripened apples. All were poisoned, of course. It would only take *one* poisoned apple to kill her, however. I just needed to ensure that her soul left her body quickly so I kept my reign over Orsadia.

"How do you intend to hand her the fruit? You realize she knows your face, right?" Mira snorted. "Everyone knows your face, Snow. She's going to expect you to murder her. It's what you did to me, and you haven't let anyone forget that day."

A sigh escaped my lips as I slightly turned my head. "You underestimate my intelligence. It's really quite insulting." I tightened my grip on the woven handle as I turned on my heel. "I'll be back when the princess of Orsadia is dead." The doors slammed on my way out.

You never cease to impress me, Little Raven.

That tone sent unease down to my bones.

The walk to Drecose was the longest walk of the entire land. My days training there had been long behind me. A day in which my father still breathed.

Now, I wasn't actually allowed on Drecose Castle property as a queen. I couldn't even walk the bridge I'd so carelessly cut myself from three years prior.

What I could do, however, was send one of my lovely corpses up to her door.

And you don't assume they'd notice a corpse limping up to the castle?

I supposed they would know. Unless I wrote a note stating the basket was a gift from the village, thanking the princess and begging her to save our land. From a distance, the corpse would look more like a person than anyone else living and breathing. As long as I found a recently deceased corpse, that was.

The graveyard was littered with them.

As I entered the cemetery, a chilly breeze brushed my neck. I welcomed and encouraged it even. Here was home to me. Like the gentle caress of a mother consoling her child after a nightmare.

The gravestones all dated each body, as well as named them. Rightfully so. This made my job as a necromancer much more fluid.

As I dropped in front of the stone dated six months prior, I reached my fingers into the soft, muddy ground. Using every inch of my soul, I expelled my magic through waves, keeping my mind focused solely on the rotting flesh and pouring enough magic for it to bring itself back.

Like an animal retching up last night's prey.

The temperature dropped a few degrees as I sat back on my calves and watched the first hand break through the earth. Skin peeled from the bones, but it was something we could fix.

Standing from the grave, I took a few steps back as the corpse clawed its way above ground. When he stood on wobbly legs, his shoulders hung low while he waited for orders only I could give.

"Walk with me." I beckoned him, leading him from the graveyard and towards Drecose. We took Ash Forest to avoid the peeping villagers. Much like most of my interactions with the dead, this one was quiet. He had not much to say since his demise. Entirely my doing. Now, he had no fight left in him. Without a soul, he became my property. I bathed in the power.

As we approached Drecose, an arrow flew through my hair. My gaze followed the arrow now protruding from the tree. I recognized the craftsmanship. Aside from that, only one person around these parts was that handy with a bow and arrow. I hadn't expected him to come home so quickly.

My breath hitched.

Oh, but he did return. And he never proceeded to come say hello.

I gritted my teeth. Pulling my hood on swiftly, I fingered my sword.

Boots sloshed in the mud from behind as I slid my sword out and swung my body, slicing into an arm. He hissed.

I swung again, this time taken off guard as he pulled a dagger from his belt. His fingers caught my wrist and my sword clattered to the ground as he shoved me back against the tree, his forearm across my throat. He ripped my hood off and that was when his strength faltered.

"Firefly," Luka breathed.

His pupils dilated, brows creasing ever so slightly. His face softened, gaze darting for a moment to contemplate my fate. Let me go or keep me pinned. Regardless, he swallowed his words.

The edge of my lips curved up as my eyes darkened. "Enjoy your adventure?"

His fist tightened at the end of the arm he pressed against my neck. "Don't make me answer that," he said in a lower voice.

I adore how you put him in his place. We make a lovely duo.

Every inch of me warmed so quickly it sent shivers up my spine. Our kiss rushed back like the ocean waves that once devoured me. I drowned in the longing. Why did he have to leave? Why didn't he come back? Why had he never searched for me when he did finally return home?

"You enjoyed yourself more than you want to admit to me. I was not enough to stay, was I?"

Why the hell would you ask such a thing, Little Raven? he spat.

Before Luka could answer, I flicked my wrist. The corpse yelled out—a guttural, animalistic growl, ripping Luka back and throwing him into the mud.

Once Luka caught sight of the decaying body up close hovering above him, he scooted back in the mud. "What the hell is that?" Did he not know?

It just gets better and better, the voice exclaimed.

"He's my assistant. His name might have been Dave once." I

shrugged off the questions. "Why the hell are you stopping me in the woods? You're well aware I do rule over Ash Forest and I can have you imprisoned for any reason at any given time. You've got guts to be treating me as if I'm the criminal."

The huntsman scrambled to his feet and scraped off the mud he could. "I've been tasked with protecting Zoe. You and your...assistant were threats." He nodded towards the corpse. "Now that I know it's you specifically, I'm entirely *certain* you're danger."

"How do you figure?"

"You're the queen. It's your job to stop the princess."

"How long have you been protecting this princess?" I sent a nod towards the castle. "Zoe."

He shifted his weight and grabbed his quiver. "A few months. Since I've come back."

"And me?" I wanted to ask, reluctantly shoving it down.

"Whatever we had, consider that no longer a thought. I'll stop you at whatever cost I must. Zoe is my priority. I took an oath," he stated.

He left you. He came back and went straight for the princess rather than checking in on you. Don't you see it now? Nobody wants you anymore. Nobody cares about you but me.

I forced down the lump in my throat.

"Do tell, Luka, how much do you know about the past three years?"

He glanced at Dave. "Not enough."

I shot a smirk towards my project. "They call me the Poisonous Queen." I pinned my gaze on the huntsman. "What I do is I go inside soulless bodies and I take control. I use my magic to wear them as my second skin. My light is a beacon for the dead. Ghosts. Corpses rotting in the earth. They bend to my every whim. Death follows me like a lost squirrel. I am its mother, and it is mine to *feed*."

"What happened to Mira?"

I huffed. "I plucked the life from her eyes. I stole her blood. What else was going to happen?" My brows creased as I studied his features. Why ask a rhetorical question?

His jaw clenched. "Princesses should never kill the queens."

A subtle smile waltzed on my lips.

I was death in the flesh.

His fingers squeezed tighter around the hilt of his dagger. "And the curse. You never broke it."

This time, my eyebrows shot up. "You're not completely dumbed down. Good for you."

"You fell victim to it. And I left because you told me to," he forced out in a hush.

I wiggled my finger side to side. "Mira told you to."

"What are you, Snow?" Fear rushed into his eyes. I quite enjoyed it with every intention to ignore the ping to my heart.

The way he looks at us is a fresh cherry plucked from a tree. No, no. It's better. His terror is that of the lovely belladonna berries that thrive in our garden.

My shoulders tensed for a split moment before I shook it from my form. "What do you think I am?" I used my index finger to wave Dave over to my side. "I play with the dead as a hobby. It's my specialty."

Whatever sparkle had once been in his eye now fled. "Necromancer," he breathed. "I'd heard the stories but I didn't want to believe they existed."

Taking a few steps, I began semi-circling him. "Pray tell, why is that?"

He lifted the point of his blade towards my chin. "They're evil to the core."

A small frown disgraced me. "Poisonous," I corrected. "I'm the Poisonous Queen."

When he shifted, I halted and faced him, eyeing the weapon.

"I won't let you get to her," he said.

"Oh." I dropped my hands to my side, knowing he could never overpower me. "Such a good little huntsman, are you? Always taking orders from pretty princesses. And when the next one steps up, you'll take your little oath. I just have to ask you one question."

His brows furrowed over his perfect sea-green irises.

"Will you kiss her, too?"

"Where is this army of yours?" I tilted my head to give him the impression he'd been more prepared. Little did he know, I never went anywhere without intending to keep my crown.

"What can Dave do?" He nodded towards the corpse waiting for my command.

What can't he do? He's dead.

"I think you're asking the wrong question," I turned my chin to my right, towards the body under my trance. "I've had three years without you, three with unlimited power. How much has my army grown, Luka?" I flicked my wrist upward, positioning my fingers like a tree branch in the dead of winter. "Let's find out." I threw my arms forward as every nearby skeleton rose from the vines that caressed them, sending them right for the only living being before me.

I'd carefully placed corpses in every crevice of Orsadia to ensure wherever I went, I would have weapons at my disposal. Most of them had been left to rot without a grave, so I took them and gave them a purpose.

Whipping out arrows, he began to shoot. After about three, he realized they were useless against what I offered.

And when I pulled my sword from the ground, I began slicing and lunging for Luka. He leaped out of the way just as I crashed to the ground. As I fell onto the handle of my sword and groaned from the blow, I rolled onto my back and met the gaze of the man whose arrow now threatened me mere inches from my eye.

"Call them off or I won't hesitate to let go of the bowstring."

"You wouldn't do that. You never had the guts."

In one moment, he aimed at my shoulder, and I cried out from the pain of metal ripping through flesh and muscle.

A fucking asshole. He shot us.

"You were saying?" He bent down, pressing the toe of his boot against my wrist as I reached for my blade.

With my free hand, I reached for his ankle to pull him off balance, but instead he'd dodged it and kneeled, his kneecap pressing against my forearm. "Don't make me do this, Snow." His olive eyes fell on the end of the arrow. Before I could respond, his fingers were twisting it in my shoulder as I yelled out.

"I thought you cared," I forced out between sputters. "Now I know you simply follow whoever the hero is, and not the person." Not now. Not me.

Because I was no longer the hero of his story.

What a villainous name Lana Edmilla was.

He will never want you. Stop pining for what could have been.

I wouldn't admit to the sting that brought upon me.

He dug the arrow into my shoulder again. It wasn't his incessant burrowing that made me weak, though. I could handle an arrow to the shoulder given all I'd been able to survive back when we were working together.

It was the squeak. The head that poked from around his shoulder.

Jerry, the squirrel I'd made him promise to keep safe while I ran off and killed Mira Sunder, the Evil Queen. The squirrel he took with him on his ventures to another land to see what else existed out there. Had he found anything worth telling about?

The warmth, the gentleness of Jerry's eyes hit just the right spot.

When Luka paused, I exhaled and spread my fingers towards the decayed bodies, slapping the dirt as they dropped from my grasp.

You gave all this up for a damn rodent? You let a pesky squirrel be your weakness—your damnation? You aren't the queen I've trained you to be, he said with a hiss.

I could not disappoint Jerry. He could not see the monster I'd become.

"Good," he said in a hushed tone. "Now I don't have to kill you just yet. I suggest you go home." He lifted himself off my arms and as much as I ached to grab my sword and army and go at him again, the pain rendered me worthless.

Groaning, I struggled to get up from the ground, taken by a punch of sorrow to the gut when Luka didn't offer to help me. I wouldn't have accepted it, but now I knew exactly what he thought of me. I'd been the enemy he trained to kill. How lovely it was for me to even ponder.

Once I'd made it to my feet, I braced myself as I yanked the arrow out. "I don't fucking want this." I pressed my hand to my shoulder. I reached for my sword and put it back in its sheath, turning away. "And Luka."

Now I'll have to fight twice as hard to ensure you're worthy of this throne, Little Raven.

I was. With nobody left, I was every bit the night that kept Orsadia at arms' length—Ash Forest with crows that cawed when death was near.

Certain he was listening, I said, "I go by Lana now."

I trekked back home to Everinthian.

FIVE

"He shot me! That ass shot me in the shoulder!" I clenched my jaw as I wrapped a bandage around my wound and under my armpit.

With a roll of her eyes, Mira dropped into my view. "Are you all that surprised? You expected him to fall head over heels after seeing you again three years later? You're one of the queens, and not a very kind one at that."

"And did you know he's guarding the princess?"

"The way he did you?"

"The way he did me, that's correct!" I nodded, pulling my sleeve back on my shoulder. "Wait." My eyes turned to slits. Did she imply I had needed to be guarded?

She leaned back, studying my form. "Well, it sounds like your plan didn't work. Any others?"

Other plans?

Had I bothered to make backup plans? No, because I was certain this one would succeed.

"What do you expect of me?" I asked. "To lay down my life? I can't do that for you, or for anyone else."

"And why is that?"

A pause.

Swallowing the lies, I let, "Because it's too late for my death to end this curse," slip from my tongue.

Maybe I wasn't entirely a snake—succumbed to the omens I held up.

Aalia slipped from the wall, approaching me with ease. "You don't want to reign terror over Orsadia anymore, do you?"

Despite the glow that surrounded her translucent form, her complexion never lightened. Her hair, however, paled in comparison, the color of snow as it fell from the sky in a fresh powder. Those eyes struck everyone as they met her, a shade of the sea surrounded by luscious greenery that nobody could look away from even if they dared. The first queen of Orsadia had always been striking, and nobody could argue with that.

Samael made Aalia out to be this whore. But when you had such beauty at your fingertips, would any woman not want to use it? She simply gave those men a taste of their own. I admired her for such games.

When her gaze caught mine, secrets fled my little box as the lock shattered, dispersing in the air for everyone to witness. I was a weak queen, and not one to be proud of. I was a legend, and not the kind people spoke highly of.

"That's it, isn't it?" Mira moved her eyes from Aalia to me. "You've admitted you want to break this curse, no?"

Tell them you're lying. Don't you dare rip me from your head. I'm all you have left, he spat with such venom.

"If I could kill Zoe, the curse couldn't take her the way it has me,"

I whispered. Sure, I enjoyed murder. But was it so wrong to enjoy something that if it were to come true, would save all the land? My intentions were good, even if the methods were not. The result would still save Orsadia despite that I got a little gratification in the process.

You want all the gratification. Admit it.

I'd admit to nothing of the sort.

Yet I could not fight the hold this curse had on me, and I would never try. However, I could at the very least prevent it from ever tearing apart the innocence the princess carried.

"There has to be another way," Aalia added. "One that doesn't require you to give into what the darkness wants of you. It's only furthering the cycle, and if I can figure out just what I did wrong..."

Furrowing my brows, I glanced up at her. "Did wrong? I was under the impression you knew what you did. How could you not know?"

They both shot me looks in which I was made to feel like the queen of lowest intelligence. Aalia had been the first in which Drecose was named after. She'd been the one who started the curse, and the first to ever get magic. And that fountain—it played a part. But if that were the case, how could she not know what she did that led us down this path?

"It happened over seventy years ago, Lana," she repeated as if she'd seen my thoughts. "I've died since then and lay dormant in a grave, my spirit floating in the between waiting for another necromancer to come and lower the barrier so I could walk the earth. I know I was poisoned. A woman killed me. My bones are missing. Now that we're here, we can figure it out together and reverse it."

"It's far too late to reverse it," I spat. "It won't bring back my grandmother." The very woman who died before I could have ever met her.

Aalia nodded a tad, sending her apologetic expression my way. "We can stop it. Necromancers are very powerful, and I believe you can help us put an end to this."

I'd been under the impression we were important, but the tone she used about our power screamed there was much more than I could ever grasp. Just how far back did our magic go? Where did we come from? And apart from that, how much influence did we truly have over Orsadia?

All questions I'd answer.

You're willing to give up all of that power for the false hope of a little love in return?

"If I agree to team up with you ground skulls, what would this entail?"

Aalia gestured to the castle we resided in. "We study history. Not just of Orsadia, but ours. Mine. Mira's. We search for clues and links and anything that might point us in the right direction. We figure out how to restore magic to the fountain, or what happened there that we can fix here. We have to ensure no stone is left unturned. And with three of us, we can make it happen. We know what to look for. We were in your shoes. We have the experience."

Deep inside, guilt gnawed away. With that came the strong urge to ask Luka to join us. Having not seen him for three years made a section of my soul ache for his presence even despite the previous events. He was a pain in my ass, but one that made me feel *something.* An addiction I wanted to kick but couldn't seem to. However, he had a new duty now, and it certainly didn't include me or my troubles. This would be our mission.

"So, then, as the queens of Orsadia, where do we begin?"

Watch me, Little Raven. I will fight so much harder to destroy everything that's left of you.

SIX

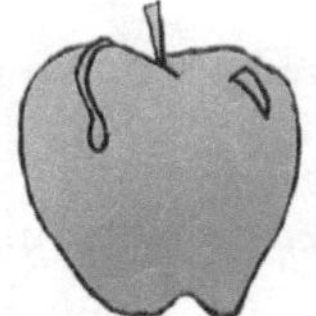

My steps echoed as I descended the stone stairs into the cave Matt once resided in. Dave's just scraped and clacked as he dragged what was left of himself behind me.

"Any clues you can find would be appreciated. Also, we need to figure out where Aalia's bones disappeared to." I shot him a glance.

Pulling my sword out with my good arm, I shielded myself in case of anything.

Between the two of us, something must have been easy to find.

Yet after an hour of searching the tunnels and the clearing, we came up with few answers. Well, I had. I happened to stumble upon the giant bones. A graveyard for those too tall.

As I brushed my fingers along a tibia, a thought occurred to me.

"What are you thinking?" Aalia asked.

"First, I'm questioning why you followed me." When she didn't name her excuse, I added, "but I'm also curious as to how easy it would be to raise this giant from his grave. It's what I do best."

Yes, raise the giant, he purred.

His tone quieted all the doubts I had. My worries had been coaxed into utter obedience.

A snicker echoed from a dark corner. "I suppose you always had questions about them and their history in Orsadia. Wouldn't surprise me if you just asked one what it was."

Mira.

Lovely, they *both* followed me down here. Wasn't Dave the only one I gave permission to?

"To be fair, we've been attempting the same methods for generations and have yet to defeat this curse. Maybe we should try something new, like bringing a giant back to life. Or in my case, make him walk." I wrapped my hand around his pelvis. "You two should step back."

"We're dead," Aalia stated.

"Not thanks to me." I cocked an eyebrow, then expelled the magic coursing through my veins, pouring it into the bones before me. This skeleton took far more power to bring back and control—given his size and how long he'd been rotting down here for.

As dirt crumbled from his form, he fought his way out of the shallow grave and slouched.

He left me in awe.

"I've raised a giant from the dead," I breathed.

You're meant for much worse acts.

I despised those words more than I'd admit to anyone else.

"And how many people do you expect to kill with that?" Luka's voice bounced from wall to wall.

Spinning around, I put on my best villainous expression. "People can't starve if they aren't alive. Besides, the more corpses, the better for me to play with. The castle can become lonely at times. These two make no exception," I nodded towards the ghost queens.

"We're trying to find clues to where my bones went," Aalia said.

His brows knitted together as he took a few steps down. "Why?"

"Shut up," I told her, squeezing my fist to clamp her mouth closed.

"Because maybe that will help us reverse the curse," the other queen said against my wishes. I wired her jaw shut, too.

It's a grave mistake you're making.

Unfortunately for me, I couldn't silence this voice.

"Reverse the curse? You? Then why would Snow be here?" He flashed a taunting smile. "Oh, forgive me. *Lana.*"

Try as he might, he could not make my name sound like a disease on his tongue. He'd had power to his words that made it sound far more enchanting—like a spell he could cast on me and I'd succumb to it in the second it took to take a life.

I narrowed my eyes as the giant snarled, but before he lunged forward, I rooted him with the ball of my fist.

Let him take Luka out.

After a few more seconds of silence, I waved my hand. "They're just making a few tall tales up for the book. We'll be on our way now. I suggest you do the same." I whipped my sword in front of me, heading for the exit. To my poor luck, Luka blocked me. "What do you think you're doing? Move it."

"I see the lies in your eyes." He squinted, leaning down a bit as if he could spot the flecks from here.

Cut off his head. You know you so badly want to.

I wanted them both to shut the hell up.

Maybe he could spot the splinters in my game. I'd certainly counted out each and every speck of oak brown that hid amongst the juniper of his eyes—the lovely shade picked for the hour.

"What lies?" I lifted my chin, pointing the tip of my blade towards his jaw. "I am still your queen. Whether or not you listen is your prerogative, but I'm under every right to punish you for disobeying.

I've discovered ways to ensure nobody goes against my commands ever again. As far as you're aware, I'm in a cave digging up bones and bringing giants to the surface. I'm not harming the princess. Your job is not needed. In fact, just what exactly are you doing down here? Doesn't your little girlfriend need you?"

I hadn't intended the *girlfriend* part to slip.

"Girlfriend?" He reeled back. "I see. Lies *and* jealousy. You truly are a mess, Lana."

He's goading you.

I scoffed, a bit of dirt filling my nostrils. "Mess? I simply fulfilled my duty as the heir. I took my role. What did you do, Luka? You sailed away because you couldn't wait to escape. I've been running this land for the last three years. You've been playing explorer. Don't you dare come back to my home and tell me who I am or who I should be. I did just fine without you."

His laugh bounced between the walls of the cave. "Fine? You're doing poorly. Orsadia is a disaster. People are dropping dead. We have few people left here. This is my home, too. I have every right to aim for a better future. You wanted that, too, once."

I jabbed my sword at him while he dodged it, then I forced myself past him only to have fingers wrap around my wrist and yank me back, twirling me until I faced him. I bit back the pain in my shoulder.

Fucking kill him already, Little Raven. What's the damn hold up?

I didn't always need to take orders from the curse.

"You're going to walk out and pretend nothing happened," he whispered.

Pulling my arm from his grasp, I gritted my teeth. It helped a little that being two stairs up made me taller. "You left for three years. What was I supposed to do with that? Wish upon a star? Mourn? I had to move on with my life. You made your choices. I made mine. They were never going to align."

Hurt swashed around in the windows of his soul. "You told me to leave!" He planted his boot on the step just in front of me, hoisting himself up another few inches. "You made me promise to go see the world and I stuck to it! Am I supposed to apologize for having dreams that didn't involve yours?"

A lump formed in the back of my throat. "You didn't have to stay gone so long! You get to waltz back in here and shoot me in the shoulder, threaten me, tell me I'm doing it all wrong when you never once came back to try and help? Now here you are, at Zoe's aid. Her beck and call! When she takes the throne, you won't even bother to leave her side, will you? You'll be there every step! I stayed here because I was *needed.* I grieved my father. I grieved my brother. I never thought you were coming back. I at some point had to grieve you, too, because I assumed you'd died out there. I've lost everything I could ever lose." I panted. "What else is there left for the world to take from me?"

His face fell, then he lowered it so I could no longer witness the damn pity in his seaweed eyes. "You said when."

You despicable queen.

My left eye twitched. "What?" A lump formed in my throat.

"You said *when* she takes the throne. You didn't say if. You said when. You...don't entirely believe in your path, do you? This curse, and the darkness. You want to end it, don't you? That's why you're down here with your friends. Those are the lies I caught onto. You're searching for a way to end it so Zoe doesn't have to suffer the same fate."

I had no immediate response. There was no excuse, nor a new fib I could form just to throw him off.

Just lift your sword and plunge it through his heart. It's right there.

My jaw tightened.

Then I said the one thing that came to mind. "Took you long

enough to catch on. I suppose taking almost half a decade is your specialty, however." Straightening my posture, I began ascending.

"Let me help."

Tell him to piss off.

This stopped me in my tracks. "Absolutely not." I scowled. "Piss off."

"Don't be too quick to push me away. We both want the same thing."

"And what might that be? To end a century old curse?"

"To protect Zoe."

It always leads back to her.

Why did I loathe when he said her name? His tongue made her a lullaby that rocked the most peaceful sleep of the decade. But once it hit my ears, metal scraping against metal enraged me.

"Why would I agree to work with you? I work best alone these days. Well, as the only one with a beating heart." I side-eyed both Mira and Aalia.

"Because," he paused, "if you don't, how are you sure to succeed? You worked alone in becoming queen and look how that turned out. I'm not leaving this time." When I met his gaze, he had propped his knee up on the step in front of him, leaning onto his hand where his elbow met his thigh. "I suppose I should give you something to lose—or fight for as my definition puts it."

I loathe him.

"We loathe you," I prepared to say.

I could have so easily spat on him. Shoved him down the stairs and broke his neck. He certainly did tempt me.

You still can.

As soon as those beady little eyes poked out from under his tunic, my face softened. Why did he have to bring Jerry everywhere? Did he know I'd never hurt the squirrel?

His gaze slid down to Jerry, his features lighting up. More wrinkles at the corners of his happiness. Seaweed irises turning to basil. I was absolutely ruined by the huntsman. “Oh. *Oh.*” Realization dawned on him. If he hadn’t known before, he did now. Fuck—my weakness. He knew what, or who, to use against me.

A sly smile and a wink later, he persisted with, "Well, what do you say?"

SEVEN

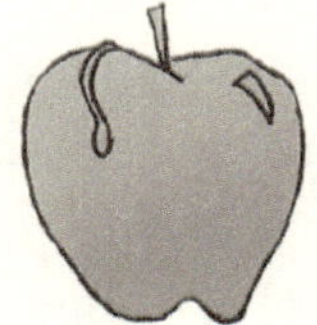

Drumming my fingers on the stone window ledge that overlooked all of Orsadia, I asked, "When were you alive?"

Magnificent, and massive, he answered, "I died under the ruling of Willow Sterling." His voice scraped the gravel of the earth, vibrating with frequencies so low that men my size could never replicate such tones, yet their great magnitude allowed everyone to be able to pick up on the exact words they chose to relay. In this case, the words this giant chose to relay.

"The fourth queen," I whispered.

Mira swallowed. "They called her the Vile Queen. She wiped out an entire species."

I admire her.

But I didn't.

"And Lana is about to be the one to wipe out life on Orsadia altogether. How fitting," Luka said nonchalantly as he brushed his fingers across the top of an intricately designed chair. Candles that'd half melted. Gilded mirrors. An abundance of gowns. What didn't I own?

He's not wrong about that.

I tilted my chin in his direction, never giving him my full attention. "Be a good boy and obey when I tell you to shut your mouth. I am still your queen whether you like me or not—regardless of the fact that you abandoned us during the majority of my ruling."

He scowled but uttered nothing more.

We like it when he doesn't speak.

That we could agree on.

"Why were you killed?" My gaze shifted to the giant.

He turned his skull, eye sockets searching the room before he planted himself right on the floor. It shook under his weight before settling again. "Willow Sterling believed us to be an abomination. A mutation in the human genes. She poisoned our food supply. One by one, we began to drop dead. I was one of the first to go. It seems she was successful in our extinction."

Wrapping my fingers around the hilt of my sword that I tipped on the ground, I puffed my chest. "I'm afraid so. Do you know of a woman named Anne Regali?"

I do, he said with a provocative hiss. *I taught her everything she knew. If only you could be more like her. Worth something, that is.*

I forced down the thickness beginning to build in my throat.

He pondered the question, the tip of his bony finger scratching his jaw. "I don't recall."

"I figured as much. She was only six when Willow would have become queen."

Mira leaned against the wall, picking at the imaginary dirt under her nails. "Everyone knew her name once she became queen. That much is certain. The first necromancer. The one who destroyed so many souls. Us queens may be taking lives, Snow, but necromancers ruin the soul that's left when their body's been snuffed. You make their corpses your toys to feed on. It's abhorrent to say the least. Your grandmother was no different."

One of my favorite queens to ever rule.

She couldn't have been that terrible, could she?

Luka's boot hit the concrete floor as he jumped from a shelf he'd been plucking books from. "There was a reason your parents put a spell on you, to keep death from claiming you. Or in this case, the necromancy that had claimed your own grandmother. They tried to stop it."

This fucking guy again.

I huffed.

"My parents knew what I'd become? That doesn't make sense. They knew my grandmother was a queen of Orsadia, and they knew her great power. No way they guessed I'd end up with the same kind of magic. It's never happened before. No queen has ever shared the same magic with another. Not even familiars. And how would you know my parents knew?"

He met my dark eyes. "The same way I knew how to flush the drugs from your system that Mira used to kill you that night."

I cleared my throat as I scoped him out. "Which is?"

"That's not very important. Let's focus on other things, shall we?" He dropped the books onto the table, dust flying everywhere. I was the only one fighting back a coughing fit as tears threatened at the rims of my eyes.

How convenient of him to ignore your question. When do we plan to remove his heart again?

Now that was tempting...

As they focused, I rubbed my shoulder, slipping away and going to my own room. I stood in front of the mirror and yanked the collar of my gown down my arm, eyeing the wound. Cursing it even as it swelled and burned crimson. I'd had many wounds in the past. Major ones. However, I'd had a medic at the time who saw to it that I healed in time for my war with Mira. He treated and dressed every injury, and once I'd won, I'd moved in here. No medic. No lady's maid. No cook, and not a single staff member whose heart could beat.

"It's infected," his deep voice crossed the room as he reached for the vines that hung from my walls. Vines slithering up into the leaves and clinging as if they could promise a drop of rain.

Little Raven, for the hate of all that's a blazing forest, take his life and dispose of his corpse already.

He would be easier to keep in check.

I pulled my sleeve up, fixing the fabric and tilting my head towards the floor before meeting his judgmental expression through my mirror. "Who gave you any right to waltz into my room without knocking?"

"If I had knocked, I wouldn't have figured out that you're going to lose your arm if you don't treat it." His footsteps picked up as he hurried over to me. "Why would I bother knocking at all? I don't work for you."

The voice in my head growled.

I seethed. "You don't have to remind me just how much you grace Zoe with your presence on a day-to-day basis." When he reached for my shoulder, I fell back against the mirror. "Don't you dare touch me!"

Perfectly, he cocked an eyebrow. "You're okay with losing an arm?"

I tasted the words on my tongue, savoring them. Studying them. When I'd come to the conclusion that he was not telling a tale, I ripped my sleeve down just far enough for him to see the damage. "How would I fix this?"

You're allowing this? He caused the damn wound, you ridiculous woman. He wouldn't have to heal an infection at all if he wasn't so hell-bent on protecting the damn princess.

Not wrong, no. He could make it worse just to prove a point to me. But what other choice did I have?

His eyes wandered, never straying far from the site. "Do you have honey?"

"Honey? Of course I have honey. I could not enjoy my poisonous tea without it." When confusion laced his expression, I replied with, "nothing can kill me these days. Unless it's Zoe, that is." She'd be the death of me, certainly. Her and Luka both.

He didn't need to know I was fibbing. I needed to appear invincible.

Clever. If only he'd believe your lies. You don't do it so well.

A wince.

From the pain, of course. There was no other reason. Or so I convinced myself.

"You'll need to eat a spoonful. Preferably once a day, until that infection clears. If it doesn't, we could always try garlic or another herb."

My lips curled. "Garlic is the last thing I'd ever allow to touch my tongue."

He peeled back with a sly smile. "Is that so? Too bad. I suppose you'll never wish to kiss me again." He turned away. "I assume you keep your jar of honey in the kitchen. I'll find it."

I feel the blaze of your heart and the flutter in your stomach. Oh, fucking hell, Little Raven. No wonder you can't kill the man. You're hopelessly in love.

As he sauntered from the room, my cheeks flushed.

"You did kiss him," Mira sang as she sidled up to me. "I always suspected something happened between the two of you."

I looked over at her. "It happened three years ago and it means nothing now. People change. He's got his precious Zoe."

"How long do you think that will last?" Aalia asked from behind. "More importantly, how long do you think he's been back? Several days? More than one moon cycle? If he's been back a while, did he ever plan to say hi? Or did he head straight for Drecose and befriend Zoe because that's what he does best—protecting princesses?"

With a tight jaw, I shot a glare her way.

Rather than sew her own mouth shut, she continued, "There're important things to think about, Lana. If he's been back a short while, he's got no true connection to her, and there's nothing tying him to Orsadia."

If I hadn't known better, I'd have assumed a mouse stood behind me. I had never heard such a noise escape Mira before. "We can ask him to move in for the time being!"

"We are not asking Luka to move into Everinthian. I'd never stoop that low. It's weakness. Vulnerability. I've shown enough of that. Imagine the humiliation when he laughs in my face and tells me he stays with Zoe because she's far more worthy. Don't ever bring it up again." I swiped my fingers into a fist, squeezing as I bolted their mouths shut.

Luka strolled back in with the honey in which I swallowed a spoonful of in hopes my own right arm would stay attached.

He doesn't lie very well either, just so you know.

Anxiety washed over me as I racked my brain for what that meant.

"How do you know what to use?" My question came out softer than I'd expected.

His eyes flicked up to meet mine. "I've lived my life tending my own wounds if you remember."

Again, heat flooded my cheeks. "And drugs? How did you know how to flush those out?"

This time he paused. His forehead crinkled and he ran a hand through his wavy hair. "I've been drugged before. I never had anyone to rescue me, so I had to do it myself. I'd eaten something I was never supposed to. Things began to warp and distort, and before I knew it, I lost sense of reality. Allowing it to wear off wasn't an option when your entire existence is about survival. I tried to drink water. Wash myself. That didn't work. I eventually shoved my fingers down my throat and it came up, and I started to come to."

Nothing more than a moron.

"And me?" I dropped my arms to my sides. "How could you save me when Mira injected it into my bloodstream?"

His fingers twitched, and he reached up to rub the inner crease of his elbow. "I figured if you were going to die already, it couldn't hurt to try a transfusion." He rolled the sleeves of his tunic up his forearms, and damn it awakened something in the pit of me. A firm grasp so sure of what he was doing. Did he ever waver, or was he always this assertive?

A transfusion? As in, his blood in yours? I've got to step up my game if I'm going to build you back up at all.

And I needed to form my walls taller than they were.

A lump formed. "You gave me your blood?" I opened my mouth to force out the next question, but nothing came out. What else could I have possibly asked? What could I have even said? He'd risked his life for mine.

"I know enough about medicine that it was safe. It saved your life, didn't it? You had enough blood to wash it out."

My magic must have eased up on Mira, for she said, "Tell her what else you did."

There's more? Oh hell.

His eyes filled with concern. "Pardon?"

"I was there, standing at the doorway when you saved her life, Luka. I could have ended yours. I didn't, after seeing how you cared for her that much. I believed maybe that would be enough to get her to make the sacrifice herself. Tell her what else you did that night."

The air grew heavy as the sun slipped just beyond the horizon to allow dusk to sprinkle throughout our land. A raven croaked. Wind rattled the window.

"I had to try to suck out as much as I could, before I tried the transfusion."

"Suck? You..." Memories swirled as my feet swayed.

Well, you're going to be absolutely useless. But I'll find a way...

His lips had embedded their mark in the softness of my neck not once, but *twice.* Amongst that, he'd injected his own blood into my veins. I walked from Everinthian because of him, and I had owed him my life in a very literal sense. But aside from all those realizations racing through my mind, one stuck out like the dead from their graves as I poured my soul into their vessels.

In Orsadia, two blood types existed. Ordinary blood, and extraordinary blood. Those without magic, and those *with* it. The two could never mix safely. Unless...

"How could your blood be safe enough to give to me when I'm filled with deadly magic?" What did that mean for Luka? Had there been something neither of us ever knew?

Had just a pinch of this magic been lying dormant in him all these years?

EIGHT

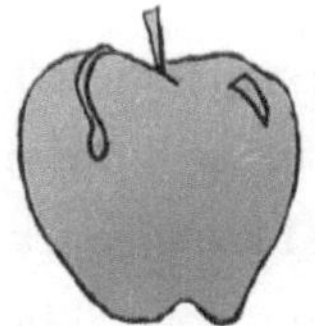

I'd been tangled in my satin sheets as whispers floated around me. Shooting up, I searched the dark before fetching Dave, or Bones. It was hard to recall who was who in such little moonlight.

Slipping my feet over the edge of the bed until they hit the floor, I stood, smoothing out my white nightgown and lighting a candle. As I turned to face Dave, I commanded him to leave and go fetch me Luka.

The wait had been quite long, given how slow a corpse trudged through the forest.

I spent most of that time lighting some candles and peeking from my window only to find I could not locate any movement within a small radius.

The whispers drifted near my ear like a buzzing bug. I swatted, whipping around. "Who has dared to invade my castle?"

Not a scratch could be heard.

My eyes locked onto the floor as my brows knitted together. Why was I up at this hour? One minute I'd been sleeping, and now I found myself perched on a sill as if I'd been the guard at the front door taking night shift.

A fog in my brain lifted.

I'd heard something in my castle. That was it. That was why I woke up.

So why had I forgotten that?

Just as I headed down the stairs, something scraped across the floor. A whistling wind brushed through the vines that climbed my walls.

Something thudded, and I leaped back, fingers at the ready. Just as I began to twist them to bring skeletal figures to my aid, a silhouette rounded the corner where I stood at the base of the steps.

"Firefly, where are you off to at this hour?"

I refused to mention the strange blackout I had moments before in my bedroom.

I nudged the flickering flame atop the dripping wax forward to get a better look at his face only to find a smug expression. How dare he? "Imbecile," I mumbled. "If you're here to throw insults around, I'd rather you go back to where you came from."

Why did you have to call him in the first place? We would have handled this all on our own. I forget you keep hoping he'll love you in return. I doubt it, Little Raven. You're not quite the catch if you cannot be his damsel.

In return? Luka had loved me already, even if that was long behind us.

"And leave my queen to fend for herself all alone in a big dark castle with ghosts and dead bodies?" He faked a gasp. "What kind of man would I be?"

The kind I need you to be.

There'd been that simmering of my heart again.

"I brought the bodies and ghosts here."

His chuckle bounced between the walls. "Yet you sent your messenger to grab me anyway. Pray tell, Lana, are you afraid? Something have the hairs standing on the back of your neck?"

Taking a step back up a stair, I pulled the candlestick close to my chest. "Something is here. The dead reside in my castle—yes—but this feels wrong. Out of my control. Beyond what I'm capable of. They sleep when I sleep. There's a rumbling dread in my stomach that I cannot shake. If this has to do with the curse, why not retrieve the one man who has offered his help to stop it?"

After a moment of consideration, he nodded, not mentioning anything else of my fears. Not another joke passed his lips.

Oh, fun.

No, eternally grateful.

I took him upstairs to my room as I carefully sat on my bed. "Here. I was here when they woke me. Whispers carried by the wind. Except that there is no wind in this castle. All windows and doors are sealed shut at night. There is nowhere for a draft or a breeze to move. If it is the curse, it leaves no doubt in my mind that it originated from Everinthian. Somewhere in here is the curse, or answers, or both."

Luka paced, leaning to peek out the window, then he inspected a small, gold handheld *mirror* on my nightstand—one adorned with all the attention to detail. "Mira and Aalia can't help? I had to travel across the forest?"

"If you don't wish to be here, why are you? If you're not interested in stopping this curse, then by all means feel free to see yourself out. If a late-night stroll is such a damper on your mood, I don't need you after all." I shooed him before pulling the candlestick to my collar, ready to blow it out.

He reached forward and pulled it away, his fingers wrapped around mine. Their coolness seeped well below the surface and rattled my bones. Magic. Did Luka have it? It'd never been seen before in a male, but I had been desperate to explore more.

"I'll help. If you're serious about this."

"Of course I'm serious! I would never have asked you to come if it wasn't. I don't particularly like your presence these days."

All lies.

"Is that so? I find otherwise." The corner of his lip curled upward.

"It is so. You've left and made something of yourself. What did I become, Luka? Yet only a carcass for the curse to weave its way into and wear proudly, strutting out into the public when it so pleases. You become a constant reminder that when this is over, nobody will remember my name in a good light. I don't entirely blame you for your absence. I'm good company for the dead, certainly, but not for anyone who has air in their lungs. My parents were right to try and stop this from ever occurring."

His fingers tightened around mine, but as he opened his mouth to respond, a screech shot up the stairs, causing both of us to jump. I'd nearly dropped the candlestick; however, Luka's firm grasp made sure it didn't topple and ignite my gown.

As he climbed to his feet, he tugged our only source of light from my hands. "Stay here."

Oh good, the ridiculous huntsman has our back.

I snapped my jaw from repeating what the voice said to me.

He circled the bed, heading for the door. I leaned back, twisting his direction. "I am not staying behind! It's my castle and I'm more powerful than you!" I scrambled across the sheets and plummeted to the floor. When I lifted myself from the clumsiness, he watched me with amusement. I'd been just like the carnival to him—an act. A show for his amusement. "I'm coming."

"You are aware if it's the curse, it wants you, correct?"

"And if I stay put in my own room, I'm simply bait with no protection. We're better off together." I clenched my fists at my sides before stalking over to him and taking the candle. "I'll lead the way."

Did you call him protection? From what, exactly? I'm in your head. You can't rid yourself of me.

A shiver scurried down my spine, from the nape of my neck to the dip above my butt.

The two of us began down the hall, passing smaller mirrors on both sides framed in gold. Candles lit the way, framed as sconces that had once been designed by a wielder.

A few leaves from the vines rustled from my dark power, draping between each and every object that decorated the old and peeling wallpaper.

A few bones littered the path in front of us. A femur here. A spine there.

Further down the steps, flickering flames illuminated the path before us, and as the base of the stairs laid a skeleton. On either side, the wall gave way to a white railing, a bit of paint beginning to crackle on the ceiling. I allowed nature to grow in whichever cracks, whichever nook it so decided pleased it.

As I paused to listen, I glanced back at Luka who leaned close, a subtle smirk plastered onto his face. I wanted to scowl, and I supposed I was even ready to do so. Eyebrows pinched together, lips parted a bit, eyes a murderous threat. "You don't have to follow so close, unless you're also scared," I spat at him.

A chuckle vibrated through his chest. "I don't?"

If I'm lucky, he'll scream and run and leave you all to me.

Part of me wanted to appreciate the joke, but Luka wasn't the type. I knew better.

We made it to the bottom, which hadn't been all that much warmer. Not to the huntsman, anyway. To me, this home was as cozy and inviting as could be.

As I attempted to step over a tibia, I planted my foot onto a busted jaw and cursed under my breath as I tried to readjust my footing. When I began to lose my balance, an arm snaked around me, yanking me back into a chest.

"If I hadn't been following so close, you could have broken your neck."

"I wouldn't have truly died. Death is my ally."

"A broken neck is still incredibly painful." As he slowly let go, I stood upright. Something flashed by and Luka grabbed my waist again, pressing me against the wall and caging me. It wasn't until I witnessed the blur again that I realized he was actually shielding me.

"Luka, you're not qualified to do this," I said, shoving against his chest.

He didn't budge. Instead, he covered my mouth and crowded me, his muscles flush against my chest. "I'm very qualified to ensure whatever is hiding in the shadows doesn't get to you."

Oh, Little Raven... he sang.

I desperately wanted to shout at him that he was Zoe's bodyguard and not mine. But as I attempted, a croaking ripped through the darkness. My eyes darted to the side it came from. It began to grow closer, with a clicking, scraping along the concrete floor.

Luka braced an arm against the wall beside my head to block my view, and once he had gotten my attention, he locked in on my wide gaze. Something was here. I could deal with it. I was the one who could handle it. Why couldn't he allow me to just *handle* it?

A growl sliced the tension as it jumped from the ground and went for Luka. He pressed himself tighter as the barrier, but I couldn't allow it. I couldn't let some prick put himself in harm's way for my sake.

Using every ounce of my strength, I shoved him off of me and screamed at the creature. Like that, a shrill cry pierced the air and its head snapped my direction. It started on all fours, croaking and growling as it scoped out its prey.

"Lana, no!" Luka turned to come for me, but I took off into the shadows, feeling walls and stumbling over my own graveyard.

Run, My Queen. Run.

My heart pounded against my ribcage as I struggled to catch my breath. My feet pumped faster. My mind raced a million femur bones a minute.

Luka called out my name, and it echoed until I lost track of where he'd been.

I had no clue where I had ended up, either.

On cue, my skin glowed for me, only it had created a beacon for the creature to follow as it scurried after me. I yelled out, grabbing onto a corner and spinning myself around it only to run into a dead end. A silly nook that someone almost a century ago built—and maybe just for me to be torn to shreds in.

My own tomb.

The creature slowed, eyeing me as flesh hung from its teeth. Bones protruded from its limbs and torso, but it had never been human. This thing was something else entirely.

It crawled closer, focused on the one meal of the night.

As I cowered into the wall the second it lunged, a fire erupted. I peeked from behind my hands to find Luka on the other side of it, the candle laying a foot away as the thing screeched and pleaded for help. The flames engulfed what was left, sending it back to where it came from.

How tragic. Just when the fun was beginning.

Terror seized every inch of my soul.

Sucking in as much air as possible, my gaze flicked between Luka and the creature.

"What the hell was that?" came tumbling from my tongue.

"Whatever it was, it wanted you," he started, "and that is why I'm not leaving this castle again."

NINE

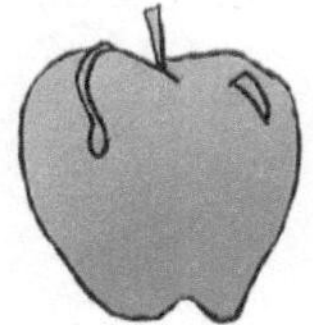

"You shouldn't keep him here," Luka's voice echoed through the Great Room. "The giant. He deserves to rest in peace."

"Ah, so you come into my castle and tell me how to do my job."

"A queen wiped out his entire species. Please, I'm asking you to let him rest. If you want to defeat this curse." He stepped forward.

I tapped my fingers on the arm of my throne.

Don't listen, Little Raven. We've brought a species back to life. We can do great things.

"Why would I do that? I've brought a species back to life."

His eyelids dropped halfway—judging. "I just told you. And you can't call this life when you know that your magic revolves around death. Dave isn't alive. Mira and Aalia are ghosts. You've reanimated corpses. You haven't restored souls and brought bodies back to good health. They continue to rot. What would your father have asked? What would Fallon, or your mother want?"

They wouldn't want me touching my magic at all.

I despised that he had to bring that up.

Leaning forward, I called for the giant to come in. He stood before me, waiting for my next command.

Damn Luka. Damn him for being right.

"I release you from your duties and from my hold. Return to your grave," I said in a quieter voice, waving him away with my fingers.

Damn you for listening to him at all.

The sun rays caressed the leaves and petals of every plant I'd grown in here. I'd since built a structure around my garden made of steel and a plastic film. It allowed the light inside before trapping some heat to make for a better environment.

It resembled a home, made strictly for nature.

I personally had been proud to have created it.

Amongst my other...creations.

"Bones," I called out.

As he stumbled through the door, Dave's corpse stiffened.

"Fetch me my water pail. My garden is looking a little parched these days."

He hurried back into the castle. Once out of view, Dave stepped in front of me, his jaw clicking as he tried to speak.

"Use your words."

His jaw clicked some more, then came unhinged. He lifted his hands to snap it back into place with a crack.

Bones came out with a pail, water sloshing out the sides.

I took it from him with a *thanks* and began to water each plant. One after the other. Each got their turn as I hummed.

Jerry squeaked a little as he explored my garden. Luka and I allowed him to roam here these days, as long as Jerry promised to be good. His little beady eyes told me he certainly kept to that.

A crash sounded and I straightened my back before turning to find Bones crooked in the corner where the base of the wall met the grass. Dave stood over him, intimidating the poor skeleton.

"Now just what in Orsadia are you two doing?" I set the pail down as I stalked over to them.

Dave stepped back, pointing at Bones who jabbed a bone right back at him.

Well, for all I knew, Bones could have been a woman. I supposed calling Bones *he* was disrespectful.

"I don't want to hear excuses. Bones is just around when I need them, okay? Dave, you better get your ass together because this jealousy act you've got going on isn't going to fly. I don't need my own friends getting into quarrels."

Although tossing Bones against the wall hardly seemed like something as harmless as a quarrel.

"Do I make myself clear?" My eyes darted between the two of them, eyebrows raised high on my forehead.

After I received a nod from both, I pointed at the door. "Dave, go inside and look grotesque." When he did as I commanded, I directed my attention to Bones. "And you, up." I flicked my wrist until they scurried to their feet. "Guard my garden."

Bones did exactly as I said.

I'd be a liar if I didn't admit the peace and quiet in my own mind had been relief.

Humming softly, I poured water onto the lovely garden I'd crafted with my own hands. Poisonous plants I had taken care to ensure thrived no matter the weather.

Although I supposed spring sure did help anything grow.

Fingers wrapped around the toe of my boot, forcing my eyes

forward as I watched the buried corpse beg me to let him free.

As if I could do such a thing. No, these bodies were the one reason I had a garden all year. They kept coming back every season, and they'd stay that way. My corpses would never leave their graves.

The fingers tightened, and the other hand shot up. I forced my hands out, commanding them to stop.

Yet they hadn't. Not for my sake.

They clawed themselves out of my perfectly trimmed foliage before standing before me and waiting for their next task. Jaws hung loose. Limbs limp. Cracked skulls flapped as they moved side to side.

In an instant, everything returned. No corpses, no bones, no army. All that'd been left of the evidence was the same skeletal hand wrapped around the toe of my boot, falling away as it succumbed to my power.

"It becomes easier each time I try it out," a female said.

I whipped around to face the princess herself. Zoe Quillen.

Now you can kill her. We'll never have to be apart.

That didn't sound all that enticing.

I shot a glare at Bones, too, for not doing a well job at guarding my space. They cowered under my scrutiny and rightfully so. I supposed Dave *was* the better one.

Redirecting my gaze, I let it roam her body. To scope her out. A witch, much like me. I just didn't entirely want her burned at the stake alongside me. "What did you do?"

Zoe stood taller than I, yet younger, and nobody was fooled by it. Her youthful appearance gave it away. A tint to her skin, dark eyes, black hair that fell to her collarbone in soft waves with a curtain of it that covered most of her forehead.

The dress she wore had been egg-shell white. Airy, as if it had been made from the skies—the clouds—in every possible way. Thin material, but perfect for a spring day in Orsadia where the ocean mist sprayed the air. A long silhouette with a loose-fitted bodice and thin straps. Cotton, I presumed.

"I merely warped your reality. That's what I did."

"You shouldn't be able to hold that much power so early."

"Yet I do." She stepped forward, hands clasped in front of her. "Snow White. Lana Edmilla. It's good to see you. Truly. Alive and well, that is. Luka told me that you've teamed up to stop this curse."

I muttered profanities under my breath. Who gave him the right?

"He also told me that if he is to fulfill his duty in protecting me, he must move in with you to help you end it all and make sure nothing harms you again. Seems like a fair deal. We all want the same thing." A shrug.

"Your mother," I asked. "She died, correct?"

Zoe slightly nodded. "She did. Now it's just me and my sister Wendy."

"Wendy... One of the previous queens, and one of the few to still be living," I lowered my voice.

Again, she nodded. "Yes. Is that so hard to believe?"

I shook my head, relaying the moment I'd pointed out her and her mother. When did her mother die? She hadn't been a queen. But her sister had been, and that should've been a clue to me that Zoe was next. Although, no siblings had ever *both* been gifted magic.

Why had that mattered then? Why did it matter now?

The question slipped, "Does Luka present any magic you know of?"

Her brows knitted together as her gaze honed on the dirt. "Not that I'm aware. You should be asking him that. We don't spend an awful lot of time together, despite the arrangement."

"Arrangement? Because he's meant to protect you?"

She gave a curt nod. "My parents asked that of him. You need not to worry. I bear no romantic feelings for him. He feels more like an older brother. As far as I'm aware, he has none towards me either."

"I was never worried. I do not care what your feelings for one another are."

"Then it's settled." She shot me with a sly grin. "You're free to fantasize about him as you please."

Swallowing the lump in my throat, I lifted my chin. "Zoe, why are you at my castle? I'd invite you inside but that's not allowed by Magic Law. And I have not planned any deaths that require bringing you inside my home."

"I only came to let you know that I hold no ill feelings towards you. I admire you, whether you believe that or not. I hope when this is behind us, we can be friends someday." Then she turned on her heel and exited my garden.

Friends. We'll go even as far as so close she'll never leave your side again.

Taking her up on that offer, I sprinted after Zoe. “Wait!” I called out.

As she spun around to face me, I cleared my throat. “If you’re so sure that you’re willing to help, do you know anything about Anne Regali?”

With the tilt of her head and the crease of her brows, she frowned. “I don’t recall I do. Your grandmother, correct?”

“How did you...”

Her eyes lifted to the sky. “Word can travel fast at times. And as hard as your mother tried to escape the name, some of us knew. You forget I come from a lineage of queens myself. My sister was once in your spot. Queens have access to information that citizens don’t. She allowed me to see most secrets, and so we always knew.” She gave a small shrug, lips pressed together.

Shaking my head, I balled my hands up into fists. “My grandmother was queen, yes, but she never had a child until years later. It wouldn't have been written in any journal, if you had found hers."

"I wouldn't be so sure. Maybe queens don't become best friends with each other and pass along information, but queens do know of each other. Other queens wrote about her in their journals. They mentioned her child, and her child's child."

"They mentioned me? Other queens have written about...me?" A massive shiver racked my body.

"They are always trying to predict the next heir, especially given your grandmother was a necromancer. She was powerful, Lana, and people feared her in ways they've never had to fear a queen."

I love the sound of that...

Swallowing the guilt, I quietly said, "I don't understand."

Zoe stepped forward. "Your grandmother could wake the dead. Imagine you're so terrified of the queen that you'd rather die than serve her. Only in her case, death wouldn't allow their soul to rest. They could never escape the ruthless betrayal from the Dreadful Queen."

Hearing my grandmother's nickname shot an arrow through my heart.

That made my next question more difficult. My tongue swelled in my throat. "Will you help me find her journal?" It'd been missing for who knew how long. All the others left theirs, but why hadn't my grandmother? If she had, where did it go? Who took it? Did they know I'd go looking for it someday?

A grin slid onto her face. "I thought you'd never ask."

My face grew hot. "Don't mention it."

Her eyes fell to my gown. "But we should really change. Where we're going, you'll be wishing for something lighter."

Dropping my gaze to my skirt, I grabbed onto the fabric and swished it a bit. "I'd say it's light."

"I'd say it's not." She snickered and grabbed my wrist. "Let's go." Something warm began deep in my gut. Was this some kind of friendship, the one Mira wanted with me but never got?

We ventured through the forest for a day, stopping just outside Drecose. Well, across the bridge. "I can't go further."

"I know. Wait for me here." She jogged over the bridge before disappearing beyond the doors.

I reluctantly waited minutes before she came running back. After she stopped, she panted. She certainly needed more practice in combat or fighting at all if that's how easy she wore herself out. Before I could mock her about it, she shoved something into my arms. "What the hell is this?"

Holding it up, it appeared to be...a dress. Blue, with some white floral patterns. Luka's favorite color—not that I'd kept track of that all these years.

Uh-huh.

Zoe laughed, and shit, her laugh sounded like the flowers that bristled in a gentle breeze on a sunny day. No wonder Luka enjoyed her company. They both embodied rays of sunshine. All I represented were cemeteries in the dead of night with a howling moon and chill in the air.

"That's a dress. It's a light dress. Thinner material than what you wear. Breathable since we are seeing hotter days."

"And where did you get it?" My gaze flicked to hers, eyebrow cocked.

"Lynn. She suggested I try one. I'm giving that one to you." She threw her arm up to gesture to the fabric. "Try it. You might like it."

Well if Lynn had gifted it to her, could I not trust them both?

You can't, but I know you'll try.

He was right about that.

Taking Zoe's concerning advice, I twirled my finger while she helped me with my gown. Once I'd been in just my chemise, Zoe handed me the dress. "I'll turn away while you put it on." She spun on her heel. "And Lana?"

"Yeah?" I asked as I began to step into the neck.

"You'll need to remove your chemise first. It's meant to be worn as a single article of clothing."

I cursed as I nearly tripped over my own feet while trying to adjust my stance. With a grumble, I removed the undergarment. Here I stood stark naked at the end of the bridge leading up to Drecose. If Luka could see me now, I'd wear shame for a week.

I attempted to step into the dress, only to find that it was way harder. It wouldn't go over my hips, and when I then came up with the idea that it needed to go over my head like my chemise, I almost patted my own back.

Once it was on, I coughed to get her attention.

The princess faced me and waved me over. When I complied, she turned me around and grabbed the strings, pulling them before tying the corset.

Smoothing my bodice, I wiggled a bit. The dress hugged my waist but allowed my breasts to fill the chest freely. The skirt flowed, but what I noticed most was the material and how soft it rested against my pale skin.

The neckline had been more of a heart shape, just enough to cover my breasts.

Best news of all was it had still been my style so I didn't need to worry about wearing pants or tunics.

"It's...nice."

"Great! Let's go." She trudged on.

Gathering my clothes from the dirt, I followed after her.

We started with Hypnotic Arythe and the worn buildings but came up with neither any clues nor the journal itself.

On our way back, the trees with hanging doll heads reappeared. "That's not creepy at all," Zoe commented as we walked through. "You do enjoy that stuff, don't you?"

"Hm?" My eyes darted between them, attempting to pinpoint the voices. "I didn't do this."

"Free us..."

"Please, free us..."

"We should go. Now." I pushed her forward as we stumbled towards the bridge.

Ridiculous Raven, I was enjoying myself there.

Once we crossed it, my lungs expanded again, heaviness lifting. I could no longer hear the pleading of whatever those things were.

"Where are we going to find her journal? It couldn't have just disappeared."

"Maybe your grandmother hid it for a reason, Lana."

"What makes you say she did this?"

She halted, spinning herself to face me. "If it left the castle, maybe she took it with her. But if that's true, why? What didn't she want others—or you to see? How could she keep it from you?" As her gaze danced amongst the trees and villagers' homes, her eyes lit up. "I know where it's at."

"You do? Where?"

"Drecose Castle."

My stomach dropped. I couldn't step foot there. My grandmother had either expected me to team up with the princess, or she had never intended for me to find the journal at all.

"You look like you've seen a ghost." A wide grin spread across her features.

"I can't go in there, Zoe," I whispered, brows drooping in sorrow.

She released a long sigh. "I know that, Lana. I don't forget. I'm going to go search for you. Can you trust me?"

"What if I can't?"

"Then... Let me prove it to you." She waved me behind her as she started back towards her home.

Much like before, I was left waiting on the other side while she went searching beyond the walls. I waited maybe hours before I caught a glimpse of movement. The sun had begun to set, and my stomach grumbled, reminding us we hadn't eaten in over a day now. How were my corpses? My ghosts? My nightshade?

You miss them, even if you try to pretend at times this isn't the life you want. It's familiar.

"Lana!" she screamed as she came sprinting towards me. When she skidded to a stop just inches before me, she shoved the journal into my chest. "Read it. I promise I didn't look."

Not wasting another second, I flipped to the first page.

Much like her given nickname, dread washed over me. Was I prepared for what I was about to find in here?

Starting with the first page, I began reading a bit, but I skipped to the last entry. Hurt slammed into my heart, squeezing it far too tightly. "Shit, Grandmother."

As I skimmed bits and pieces over and over to confirm what I was reading, the truth weighed on me. "My grandmother had been writing entries in here long after her term. Even after my mother was born, Zoe. And I don't think she hid this journal. I think my mother broke into Everinthian at one point and stole it. What she found out... It's dark. This is..." I couldn't repeat the words aloud. I couldn't speak them to the princess and taint her with this image. "I think my own mother left it at Drecose to keep this hidden from me. She didn't want me to know where she really came from."

TEN

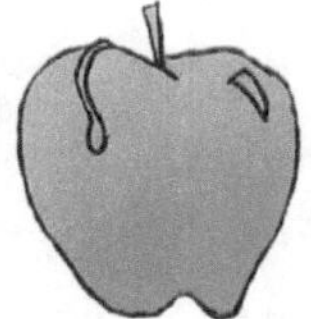

"Did you know that your body is unaware of your eyes?" Luka pointed out as we ventured into the village.

I could believe it.

A separate voice without a body.

People began to hide from my presence alone.

"What does that entail exactly?"

"When you are ill, for example, your body has to fight it off. Your body is aware of most areas, but the eyes do not exist. The connection between your eyes and your immune system is not there. If it were to discover you had eyes, it would attack them. In some cases, it happens."

Much like a voice discovering all it can truly do to a queen...

Pausing to glance at him, I asked, "How do you know all this?"

"You learn quite a lot when you travel abroad."

There'd been mention of the damned adventure. I wanted to hear nothing of it.

If only he'd go back.

I swallowed, fearing the day that would happen.

As we approached a stand, I picked out a pear and offered up a coin. The man handed it to me only after he'd polished it, never quite making eye contact with me.

While walking away, I scanned the village and scoffed. "Everyone is so afraid."

"Can you blame them?"

Even before I'd become queen, they caught a villainous energy from me.

When I was about to answer, he waved at me to follow him. We came upon a couple who immediately scurried their kids into the home before the father stepped forward to protect his family. "We don't wish to talk."

I quite like this sight.

Uncertainty flitted across my features.

I stood a few feet behind Luka, poised and harmless, while he put his hands up in defense. Much like the past, in fact. It had me pondering if people ever questioned the curse themselves. Were they aware of it? How much did they know? What traveled through their minds when another queen turned wicked?

"We only have a few simple questions and we will be on our way," Luka explained.

The man still never eased up on his glare. "One question. I'll decide if I want to answer."

Luka began to negotiate when I interrupted with, "Deal."

What do you have in mind?

When they both eyed me with much suspicion, I exhaled. "Mr. Kalio." They gasped, as if I would never have dared to memorize the names of my people. Whether I let them die or not, they were mine. "What do you know about the wailing banshee and the lock of hair?"

This caught him off guard. For a moment, he hesitated to answer. I assumed he wouldn't, and as I turned to leave him be and find someone else, he blurted, "A necromancer created them."

I halted. "Anne Regali."

We truly are the most powerful together, aren't we, my little monster?

"You know her. The ninth queen of Orsadia."

Slowly turning to face him, I allowed the words to slip from my tongue the way honey did a spoon. "She was my grandmother."

Luka had once mentioned to me that the tales and legends began when I was born. But as the man went on, he informed us that they originated when my grandmother was coming into her power as a child. From what I had gathered, she was the reason such horrid things came about.

First, it began with the lock of hair. Her mother before her had chopped her hair one morning when she discovered that my grandmother had magic. Being a queen had been a curse all on its own, and therefore, each child who found their magic became a smear—a blemish to the family name.

Anne lost all confidence in herself, boiling with rage and mourning what she once had. Orsadia never offered much for us to start with, but when we lost our appearance, what was left?

She took revenge. Killed her own mother. From that day forward, a lock of hair meant impending death one could not run from. But that superstition went dormant after she became a mother. And when I was born, it woke back up due to my magic.

The wailing banshee came much later, after the letters. When my own grandmother's romantic intentions had been unrequited, she lost every sense of who she was. What my mother never wanted to admit that I had been forced to find out in a journal about Anne Regali's past as the ninth queen had been the truth of how my mother came into this world.

Fighting. Violently. Born of something so sinful that no woman could bear such trauma all on their own yet were forced to.

The wailing banshee had been Anne Regali's pleas as she came to realize what she'd become. A hollow shell of a woman meant to rule an entire land with nobody at her side. Little had I known my mother was the result of something so cruel. She might have been young when she had me, but Anne was not when she had my mother. She'd finished her ruling.

As she stepped down for the next, people sought to it that she pay back for what she placed upon the land. The legends, the murder, and the utter ashes from which her magic had been born. They'd beaten and tortured her. They'd inflicted unspeakable things, and so my mother never knew what it had been like to truly be loved, until she had my mother. Her child adored her.

Anne Regali had always raised herself, living off the scraps people fed her.

But Marianne Regali had been raised to see the horrors of being a queen, escaping a fate not made for her, only to pass it on to her daughter instead.

Marianne Regali married young and changed her last name to Edmilla, to ensure I didn't end up with the same fate. But deep down, she knew.

I'd worn the necromancer title the same as my grandmother.

The reason, I feared, that I had been the first to share magic with another queen was because my grandmother's curse had been so great and so traumatic that it attached to our family name regardless of Mother trying to change it.

When Luka and I left the man, I said nothing. Instead, I turned to the vibrant green leaves and white petals that floated like snowflakes.

"Lana," he said in a quieter voice.

Grating, like nails to a chalkboard.

"Do you believe she attracted that kind of reaction because of how dark her magic had reached into the underworld?"

"I didn't know you believed in the underworld."

"I don't know what I believe anymore. My grandmother had been assaulted with no choice but to have my mother and raise her from such violent acts. If we share the same darkness, is that going to be my fate?"

His joking demeanor shifted entirely as he stepped well into my bubble, scowling. "Absolutely not. Listen, if I have to kill you to keep Zoe safe I do it out of defense. But for people to go out of their way to take revenge on a queen who no longer has magic is far too out of touch. It's abhorrent. What they did was sick and twisted. That does not make them victims. It was not out of defense. They attacked a vulnerable woman who no longer had the power to fight back."

He has a heart. How despicable.

Just not for me, given his heart was no longer mine to have.

"They'd only done to her what she forced on them," I whispered.

This time, he grabbed onto my cheeks to capture my gaze. I couldn't look anywhere else but those retched river-green eyes. "*Eye for an eye* is the saying. Faitore taught me or more precisely, the girl in the tower—who does exist mind you. They did not live by that. She took lives. They took her sanity. *Eye for a tooth.* That won't happen here."

"Why? How can you be so sure that I won't end up following in her footsteps? I already have."

You could have more if you'd just let me, you useless elbow.

Where had I heard that before?

"The man she loved may not have returned the feelings. You cannot say you've lived that experience." He brushed a strand back from my face. "And for what it's worth, you will not be left to fend for yourself if you just let us in this time."

He spits all lies.

I wanted to say I'd already been left to do just that. I had no family. I barely had Luka, and he only came to ensure Zoe's future. None of this was about me.

Eventually, it would be my future. When my term was up and my magic was stripped away, I'd be hunted and burned at the stake. Maybe by my own *army*, too.

She'd been assaulted to the highest degree.

You can hardly relate to that.

Maybe it'd been a punishment for what monster I'd eventually become. Alexander might have been my warning to turn it around before it was too late. Before I ruined entire lives. I had never heeded his warning.

He may not have believed, but I knew what lay ahead because of my grandmother's sins. I'd been left to atone for them. Both of us had to pay dearly for them, regardless.

I could never escape the Regali name no matter how hard I fought it.

ELEVEN

"I found something!" Luka burst through the black door of my bedroom, causing me to turn away and groan for just a few more minutes of shut-eye. "Firefly, get your ass up. This curse waits for no one."

But apparently I'm forced to wait for him.

"How could you have found something?" I grumbled, pulling the sheets over my head to try and drown out *both* of their voices.

Seconds later, he ripped them off, leaning far too close into my bubble. "It mentions Magic Law and how it ties to the curse."

"And?" I couldn't have tried to hide the disgust on my face. I woke up on my time, and having this skull-head invade my space was a nightmare all on its own.

He trusts you. You could so easily kill him. He's in our domain now.

But where would that leave me?

"And I tried to find out more about it, but I require your help. You know far more about this than I do having lived through it the last three years."

A snicker. "Get the hell out of my face. And close my door on the way out."

A sly smile crept up. "Is that a yes?"

"Luka," I growled.

With a wink, he stood. "As you wish. A little growl is enough to jolt my body into action," he joked as he exited.

I'd yell after him if that didn't make things worse. He got off on irritating me, and whatever the hell this was, I wanted no part. The flirting? He had too much fun with it, and that was precisely why I didn't.

I carefully put on a bright green dress with floral patterns and a loose fit. I made sure to take my time just to give myself a moment to wake before I faced the bastard again.

When I did meet him at the bottom of the stairs where bones piled up and vines snaked their way around, he grinned.

We despise that smile.

" *We* do not despise anything," I argued.

"What?" Luka tilted his head.

"Nothing." I dismissed the voice.

"I suggest we start somewhere else," I demanded. He wasn't actually given a choice. "There's something that's been plaguing my mind. You gave me a blood transfusion, which shouldn't have worked unless you have magic in your blood. I'm no medic but I know that much because my own family never would have been able to. How long have you known, or questioned who your parents were? Furthermore, why aren't you more concerned with pulling this magic out of you to play with?" My fingers drummed against the stone wall as my eyes roamed his face, reveling in the joy that dropped from his expression.

We do enjoy this.

That we could agree on.

"I've seen how magic has corrupted every single one of you. I truly want no part of that. I lied, partially about who my parents are. My father did have an affair with a queen, yes. Astrid Lockwood. But I wasn't conceived in his wife's womb. I was not a commoner's child. I was Astrid's. If people knew, things would change. I don't like how you look at me now that you know the truth. I really was raised by Ash Forest. My father did cheat, but Thomas wasn't hers. *I* was. Once my mother died, I was left on my own. All this is how I know that magic is a gene, and how I know most of us are related to the queens. I just happened to be...another creation. I am a product of a queen."

My features lit up with wonder.

Oh how intriguing.

Intriguing indeed.

Luka was the one he'd been talking about. The child conceived in adultery. That was how he found Thomas, after he found his biological father. After his mother, Astrid, had died of her own sins.

We entered the library, looking through books, including what Luka had found.

Mira appeared from behind, dropping a different book with a thud, eyes wide and mouth agape. "That's what the book talks about. The magic is tied to the curse."

He was the first and only male to attain magic, and *his* blood had brought me back from the dead. If my hunch had been right...

"You're the first male in all of Orsadia to attain magic from it." I dropped to the last step, rushing over. "Do you understand what this means? Luka, you're the answer! All this time you've been the answer to the curse. I dare admit that maybe an anomaly in the bloodline of the queens and our magic is the key to stopping everything. I won't let you say no, and I won't accept it. We are going to lure that magic out. See what you can do. Practice, and master it, even. Then, we're going to break this curse. It's your turn now. Ask yourself: how much do you care about Orsadia? Our fate rests on *your* shoulders." A small smirk may have been tugging at my lips.

It was worth a shot to use him, if I could guilt him into saving them, that was.

A groan passed his lips as he rolled his head back. "There's no need for luring."

"Are you backing out?"

"What I'm saying is I have magic. I know how to use it. In fact, I spent three years in Faitore with a woman who had dark magic just like I do, and we learned together."

He shared with her what you could have had.

A ping bounced off my heart. That could have been us. It should have been. But happy endings didn't exist in a land where the cursed were forced to give up their magic then suffer in agony as citizens ripped them apart.

To outsiders, we were evil. We looked as if we wanted such a fate, to rule without mercy. However, we were never given a real choice. We had been victims just like the rest, only we played the villains because someone had to be blamed for the price of magic.

Unfortunately, it'd been me.

I say fortunately. You could have more potential if you weren't too worthless to use it.

"I see," I said barely above a whisper. My energy had depleted.

The emotion in his eyes shifted from uncertainty to something else I couldn't quite grasp. Pity, perhaps? "Velia was eager and curious but she had far too many of her own issues that I could never have been able to sort out. She also craved someone to love her where she was. I love to travel, but I'm always happy to come back home to Orsadia at the end of the day. As much as she didn't want to admit it, someone else caught her eye anyway." He let loose a chuckle.

Was he attempting to ease my sorrow?

Softly, Mira asked, "What if the way to end it is to have Luka take it upon himself?"

I marched up to her, squeezing her throat closed with the air of my magic. "Absolutely not. Don't you ever suggest such a despicable thing again."

"I thought you said my magic was the answer?" Luka asked.

I hardly glanced his way when I said, "Using your magic against it. I will not forfeit my crown and allow this curse to take over anyone else. Have I made myself clear?"

I hadn't known how close he got until he sang, "Firefly," inches from my hair. "What are you not telling me?"

My grip on Mira faltered. I threw my arm to my side and shot a glare at Luka. "There's nothing to hide."

"The curse strips you of everything you are. It takes everyone from you. Your friends. Family. The trust of your people. It leaves you a hollow shell until you're screaming and begging for it to take your life next. You toss between succumbing to the hopes of suicide and giving in to the sins of those before you and wreaking havoc just because you can. You hear day in and day out how worthless you are, how nobody can ever cherish you because you've become exactly what they fear. The curse isn't just this abstract evil. It lives inside your head. It burrows into your magic and every time you use it, you crave more attention since you've been starved of it. So you continue to listen to the voice in the back of your mind for just a little approval. More. Until it's all that's left of you, and there is no longer any reason to try and shut it out. It becomes the only company you can keep. You'll never be able to repair the damage and fix relationships. What's done is done," Mira said, her voice deflating with every sentence.

His face fell, and what I was certain was pity took over. "Lana doesn't want me to feel that way, does she?"

The way he looks at us is so deceitful.

Lifting my chin, I shoved down whatever Mira plucked to the surface. "What I want is to break this curse so it never touches another soul. When it's over, we can go our separate ways. You can sail the world again, and I won't fight the last of the villagers when they burn me for my crimes against Orsadia. It's the least I can do for them."

Oh, Little Raven, I admire your persistence. But you can never get rid of me.

"I can still show you my magic if you really want to see it."

Notice how he didn't argue? He knows how this ends for you.

I gave a small nod in response, but to who, I couldn't be sure.

We journeyed out into Ash Forest, but as we came upon Keenain River, something sounded off. The rushing rapids and soft babbling faded into something eerie. Loud, almost like a siren. Wailing, and warning. It hit the core of my chest and triggered something entirely *ominous* within, and all I could focus on from there on out was the paranoia that the worst was yet to come.

Hopelessness.

With a quick transition, all that filled the spring air were chirps of birds and soothing sounds of a river flowing to the ocean.

"That's it."

When my gaze slowly met his, confusion laced my brows together.

Luka stepped closer. "That's it. That's what I do. My magic is tied to darkness. Maybe it has to do with the curse. Maybe it's because all magic from the queens is tainted. Maybe that's just the magic gene."

I shook my head. "I don't understand."

"I manipulate sound. I learn what is around me, and I can channel it, or transform it. The rustling of the leaves, the river, the birds. That's natural. The horrid siren which you heard that filled you with such terror and despair—that was my doing. I can strip away what is good and twist it into something truly disturbing. I'm not the hero, Lana. What I am is a man just as dark as you if I had been under the influence of the curse."

It's a perfect crime.

I badly wished to ask him if he was saying he understood where I came from and why I did what I did with my power.

I just didn't have the guts.

You never do. We did once upon a time, when you would disembowel pleading citizens. Now you're just as weak as them with no purpose to serve.

TWELVE

Did anyone ever matter? Did we have a purpose here, or was this some chance of fate?

I'd never been entirely sure what I believed. My father must have believed in an underworld. Luka probably believed in something. I knew the supernatural world existed, and that had been because I was in control of it. But...did I matter at all?

When I allowed my brain to ponder the idea of purpose and legacies, I questioned more than I planned to.

Much like a seed that sprouted into something vibrant green when you watered it enough, when you provided it sunlight. It didn't seem very significant in the grand scheme of life, but did it have a purpose?

Was that plant's existence the factor in how our entire ecosystem survived?

Or was it just by chance, and if that plant never existed, it wouldn't have made any difference to our chain of events?

Maybe the more I hovered over the concept, the more I realized I did have a lasting impact. I was the Poisonous Queen. I'd ruined lives and made a name for myself. Just not entirely in the way most people aimed to...

"Is it so terrible that I want people to be devastated and distraught over my death someday?" I asked in a quiet tone, my gaze fixated on the trees that gently swayed in the breeze just beyond my window.

Aalia shook her head. "You want to be loved—and missed when you're gone. Who doesn't?"

"Except now I've engraved my reputation, one so massive that no amount of good deeds could ever redeem me. Suppose that means I should stop trying to end the curse if that's the case." I tilted my head towards her. "I don't deserve to exist. I don't deserve to breathe the same air as them. Zoe does, and that's the one reason I do all this. The one reason that I haven't just said: *fuck it*, and wreaked havoc entirely. This is me holding back, you know." I faced Ash Forest again. "I'm a psychopath, Aalia. But I'm trying to make a difference. I'm just not entirely sure that I'll be able to."

From time to time, I'd have a wandering ghost ask me for a favor. I'd start by shooing them away. They'd pester. I'd shut them up, but my power only held for so long before I got tired. When I did, they'd pester more.

I'd eventually give in. They were always simple favors, like "help me get a message across," or "can you find this thing and give it to this person".

They didn't come often, given Orsadia was a small land.

Wherever they wandered from, however, didn't entirely make sense. Maybe it'd been my light that attracted them. Maybe they'd finally caught it and came running. I just happened to be the necromancer, the veil between our world and theirs. Everywhere I went, I could bring two worlds together. I just had a tendency to drag demise around with me when I did so.

It never led to anything good.

I was the Poisonous Queen—and a woman who controlled the dead. In what world did I become everyone's little messenger?

I supposed it did protect me. Keeping such company at my side every waking second did scare off anyone willing.

Until I lost my powers for good, that was. Then I'd be left with nothing again. No family. No friends. Not a soul to shout my name with such excitement.

If I burned my bridges now, I could ensure that I'd be murdered when this ended. I would never have to learn to accept a life without my magic.

Now it's just you and me, and together we'll watch the world crumble.

THIRTEEN

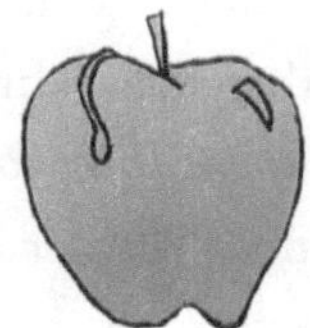

"Every letter had been addressed to Harry. Never did she receive one in return," I relayed as I dropped the letters.

Aalia frowned, sifting through every single one. "Unrequited love. That is so tragic. Have you read them?"

"I've never truly had the guts. They feel personal. Private. I'd never invade her thoughts like that."

"Yet you have no issue invading my journal," Mira said with a scoff.

Rolling my eyes, I dropped onto my throne. "You I do not respect. My grandmother did nothing to earn disrespect."

She strode to the window. "Why do you hate me so much yet keep me around?"

Aalia opened her mouth to respond but came to a crossroads with her brows furrowed. "Why is that?"

I expected to know the answer. But when none came, I found myself questioning it. Mira had only done what she thought was best for the curse. She forced my hand in our battle—which back then

I'd only understood was a war but the true war had been with the darkness of our magic—and her blood stained my bones. Now she'd been my responsibility to maintain since then.

Atonement, one might have assumed. There was nothing for me to atone for.

She had set me up to fail. How could that have been my fault? Asking me to lay down my life and allow my family to grieve my death. There had to be another way to break the curse.

Yet here you are, having spent three long years building your pile of bodies. You haven't fought me for a long time, Little Raven. Why now? You don't truly want to throw me away. You need me. Without me, you'd be nothing. Nobody would fear you. You need their obedience. We both know you're not trying to break this curse. What's your goal?

The voice had been partly right. I wasn't trying to break this curse, was I? My grandmother's journal told tales she never told anyone. Of all the queens who ever ruled, she had been the only one who wrote her own story up until her death.

Maybe Anne didn't want to tell her story or justify what she did, and that's why she noted every detail. She didn't want anyone to understand why she did what she did. She wanted everyone to believe she was solely the villain because they'd never believe otherwise no matter how hard she tried.

If I broke this curse and let Zoe take the throne, what would happen to me? Would I hang? Burn? Be thrown to the sea as an apology for my sins? Would I be forced to live out my days without magic, begging for food and kindness only to be shown none?

I hadn't been ready to succumb to that kind of future. If I had no magic, who would I be? I'd never be worth anything again.

What was my goal?

In a low tone, he repeated, *You don't truly want to throw me away.*

"You're just the voice in my head," I mumbled. Mira and Aalia eyed me, before settling on the reality that I'd been conversing with him like they all had once.

I'm the only one who listens to you. I've been here all of these years. Where has your Luka been? He moves back and suddenly you want to dispose of me? No, no. I'm here to stay.

"I believe there was more to the story," Aalia interrupted.

When I came to the realization she was reading my grandmother's letters, I jumped from the throne and ripped them from her hand. "How dare you?" I screeched.

She shook her head as if she hadn't just violated my trust. "You might be surprised at what you find."

Growling, I commanded the two of them to leave the Great Hall. Once they'd actually listened, I hugged the letters close to my head, lifting my eyes to the ceiling. "What do you want of me?"

They had been all she had left to her name. The only humanity that spilled from a once wicked queen. I wished to preserve that. However, maybe it was no different from peeking into her journal.

And when I found myself opening and reading one, I couldn't stop. I devoured every word and clung to every signature she signed with.

By the end, I'd been in tears.

"He returned the love, didn't he? But his letters never made it to you, or something happened. Why you could never be happy together is beyond me."

Was it?

She'd been exactly like me. Women like me didn't find a safe haven. Queens did not fall in love and live happily ever after. Our ends were met early, and shortly after our reign. From our dark magic came a curse that stole everything we ever cared about.

You care about me. You're just afraid to admit that to yourself. If

I had all the power, I'd wrap you up and never let you leave. I don't go away, even when this is all over. I'm yours until the end.

It made me wonder if my grandmother never married to protect Harry from this inevitable fate. Did her voice, too, drive her to the brink before she leaped from that cliff of promise?

Crickets chirped as the sun set beyond the horizon. I stood at the entrance of the graveyard, keeping an eye. "Can you hurry it up?"

Luka scowled. "I'd be a little faster if you weren't standing around."

Is he complaining about getting his hands dirty? Is that not a huntsman's job?

"That's your job. I'm guarding the entrance."

"It's a cemetery. There is no groundskeeper in Orsadia. And you're the queen. Who's going to kick you out from digging in a cemetery? You'd just threaten to add them to it." A smile tugged at my lips.

The reality was, I couldn't get my new dress all muddy. Zoe and Lynn would both scold me for that.

Luka grunted as he continued to search gravestones and bones. "So why was her skull ever out here if the rest of her isn't? How can a ghost not know where she died?"

He's so whiny.

I snorted. "He is," I mumbled.

"You ask too many questions that don't have answers. If I knew, we wouldn't be here. I'm a necromancer. I bring the dead back; I don't see their pasts. Wish I could. That would be interesting to witness. Helpful, even."

Something flapped near my face, and when I caught sight of a furry insect, I relaxed. He was attracted to the subtle glow on my skin.

"Hello there." I lifted a finger as he landed on it, his big eyes aimed towards me. "You're so big, with beautiful crimson on your wings."

"Firefly, who you talking to?"

"A moth."

Luka stiffened. "What?"

"A moth. They're attracted to light, and I'm certainly that. Did you know they symbolize trusting your intuition? Brown moths specifically symbolize the need for life purification. I suppose that fits how corrupt I've become." I slowly raised my finger out. "See? A moth? He's adorable."

Luka let out a nervous laugh. "No thanks. Um, there seem to be no bones or anything that can help, so we should return."

Is it just me or does he seem a little...frazzled?

Frazzled was the perfect way to describe the shift in Luka's demeanor.

We turned and exited the graveyard. As I trekked on, a few more moths followed.

"They're just fuzzy butterflies. Cuter if you ask me."

He grumbled. "I didn't ask." He began shooing off my friends.

I halted, brows creased together. "Do you not like moths?"

"Not particularly."

This is rich.

"How can you call me Firefly but flap around like a maniac because of a harmless moth?" I tilted my head.

He groaned, facing me. "They eat clothes."

I choked on a laugh. "That's what you're afraid of? That I'm going to see you naked?" I waved my arms around. "Oh no, Luka! Run! I might see your ass!" I covered my mouth, gasping.

"Shut up, Lana."

A smirk rose. I hit a nerve, and I very much liked this.

You and I both. We'll attract all the moths and then we'll shove a light source down his throat so they'll be crawling into his lungs until he chokes.

Now that was a little drastic.

"I'm so sorry that I may or may not catch a glimpse of your naked form because a few moths enjoy the glow of my soul. I'll try not to memorize it." I started walking again and Luka trailed behind me, keeping his distance from the moths.

I was never letting him live this down.

FOURTEEN

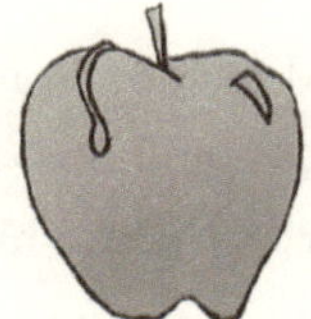

Dave dragged his decaying self along the journey as Luka and I made it to Hypnotic Arythe. Crossing the bridge had been an easy feat since the last time we'd been together. I glanced over the rope as my eyebrows lifted and my lips pursed. "Wonder how long that's been there," I noted.

A whirlpool at the base of the cliff spun in a clockwise direction.

Luka nudged me forward, and Dave grumbled.

When we made it across, Dave's hand detached, plopping into the dirt. "Dave, you dropped your hand. Pick it up." Luka stifled a chuckle as he tried to command my own corpse.

I shot him a glare, only to find that Dave did indeed listen. How in the hell...?

He intrigues me. Yet I crave nothing more than his blood spilled across this land.

He intrigued me more than I craved his blood.

Regardless, we moved along. How Hypnotic Arythe had changed

every time I walked its soil was beyond me.

"Luka, what about children?" I changed the subject.

"Children?"

"Offspring? The product when a man and a woman have sex and end up making a whole new person? You can't be that oblivious to your own creation, can you?" I stopped to glance at him as I gave my best pitiful look.

The voice in my head had to contain his laugh.

Before I could step aside, he grabbed onto my shoulder—the one that'd been healing appropriately since his little threat. "I don't need a lesson from the woman who never intends to be involved with that kind of experience."

"Experience? Are you saying you want children?"

As he moved ahead of me, my chin shifted and my eyes followed. "I'm saying I've considered my options. I'm at the ripe age to be reproducing, and it's something I do think about. I would love to see little children running around while I yell at them to settle down as their mother exits the kitchen with a fresh loaf of bread. She nearly misses them as they circle her legs, but even then, a smile brightens her face. Neither of us can help it. They're just having fun chasing one another. I help her prepare the rest of our dinner, getting the children to sit just long enough to fill their stomachs." He paused in his steps, taking a deep breath as his eyes fell over the cathedral. "But that's only one scenario. I would never willingly bring kids into this world the way Orsadia runs."

Fuck this guy. We've made Orsadia wonderful.

A blow to my gut. I had to force back the tears before they spilled over my warm cheeks.

"What about you? Do you want children?" His voice had been softer than I expected.

Regardless, I spat, "Never." I had never had any desire to carry a child. To birth one. To raise one of my own. “People in Orsadia live short lives, but I’m sure of one thing—my desire for a life free of the responsibility of someone else's soul. I play with corpses. I do not belong with innocent younglings.”

"I've had opportunities. I suppose, if you called them that. Faitore had a few, and while Velia was my age or close to it," he paused, "a bit older than I, I had never seen her that way. She was more like a friend I felt called to help in a time of need. Melusine had been much too young. Forgive me, but even as a man halfway through what I consider the third decade of my life, I did not feel as though Melusine was a fit. She had other things to discover about herself, much like I did. She was in no mood to come see Orsadia. She'd had her eyes set on Everbrook from that moment on."

I lifted my eyes to meet his. Sorrowful, yet so certain.

If Luka had a chance to procreate, his children would certainly be promised a future. They’d attain all his good looks, too. The sun-kissed complexion—knowing he’d spend every day out in the forest or down by the beach. His mesmerizing sage eyes and perfectly placed oak flecks. Luscious waves of thick, dark hair.

Shit, this man was a masterpiece. A work of art. To want to pass that down and not be able to because of me? I deserved what I had coming to me, and more.

"And Zoe, she is one hell of a fighter with so much compassion. However, my relationship with her feels far too much like she's a younger sister to me. I want to protect her with my life, Firefly. But it's not in the same way I've always felt the need to protect you."

He spits all lies, all the time. Don't fall for them.

In a whisper, I asked, "What does that mean?"

He grabbed onto the siding of the cathedral before a screeching broke out. Nothing like the wailing banshee, but something entirely inhuman. I'd never heard it before.

"Luka, make it stop!" I yelled out.

"It's not me!"

His eyes darted to the skies as dark clouds rolled in. Thunder shook the sky, and lightning touched down on the ground of my land.

Our screams cut to silence.

FIFTEEN

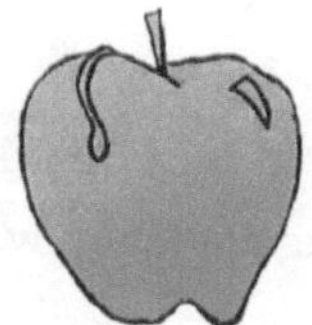

We gained our balance after we'd been knocked onto our knees. Brushing ourselves free of dirt, we scanned the sky for any more signs of a storm, but it had entirely vanished without a trace.

"Luka," I seethed, pulling him back from the building he'd spotted. The mansion stood, but now it'd been pieced back together as if it had never worn from weather and age.

He never listens to you. He doesn't respect you.

"For once, show me some respect," I commanded.

He shook me off as Dave scrambled his way ahead of both of us.

"What the hell just happened?" Zoe asked. "Did I do that?" Her eyes grew wide.

My entire demeanor shifted as I carefully turned around. "Why did you follow us?"

"I figured I could be of help." She shrugged as her gaze scanned the mansion.

Once crumbling and covered in cobwebs, the mansion had

returned to its former glory in gothic tones. Parts of the roof had pointed at an acute angle, and windows had nearly covered every inch of the front and sides. Tall. A warm, cozy glow. Ivy climbed up the old bricks, snaking its way around to the back. I almost didn't recognize such a stunning structure.

I envied whoever had lived here once.

"Stay out here," I demanded.

She'd listen if you just took her life.

And this damn voice would shut up if I could just defeat the curse.

When I turned around again, Luka was following Dave through what appeared to be Hypnotic Arythe smothered in darkness as storm clouds rolled back in. Where had they gone to begin with?

"Lucky me," I mumbled as I hurried behind the both of them.

Stepping inside the grand mystery, my eyes roamed the exquisite interior. Fern plants spruced up every corner. A black marble flooring ran throughout with gold veins stretching for approval. Fine work on every wood beam down to the very bones of the mansion.

"This is a lovely home," someone's voice echoed through the foyer. "I just have no idea where it's located. Boston? Baltimore?"

Our eyes snapped to the man who stood before us. His hair had been messy and as golden as the rays of sunshine. He'd certainly kept in shape much like Luka, and he showed it off with just a white top clinging to his form, the straps not even covering his shoulders.

"Who are you?" Luka approached, weary. "Where is this Boston Baltimore?"

The man ran a hand through his short hair with a snort. "Hunter. Boston and Baltimore are two different cities. Where is this place?"

As my gaze met his, he shook his head. "Orsadia."

"That's not on any map I know of. Is it European?"

My brows furrowed as I racked my mind for what that meant. "Euro...what now?" I muttered.

Luka nodded towards me. "Lana. I'm Luka."

Hunter gave a slight nod, his eyes searching every inch of this mansion as envy flitted across his features.

Something thudded down the hall and we whipped around to face the source.

Probably more threats. You're not skilled at removing those, are you, Little Raven?

“Shut up,” I grumbled under my breath.

Out of the darkness stepped a tall man with hair as wild as the animals left in Orsadia. He wore a checker patterned shirt over the top of another—white with long sleeves, and a pair of chestnut boots that matched his hair. And those eyes swathed in the night darker than my hair.

"Remy, I told you this is an unknown place. *Not* our home. We can't just go messing with things that aren't ours," a taller woman said as she halted beside him, arms crossed.

It was then I noticed the shadows that hung around him. Wrapped around his arms, swimming along his skin as if he attempted to exert such a presence. How intriguing.

We must know more.

"You find answers by messing with things." He cocked an eyebrow, but a playful grin lay behind it.

The woman who stood beside him had been that of the ocean in which it achieved its blue color from the sky above, sun rays dancing across the surface to create a shimmering effect. A copper braid over her shoulder, blue eyes, and fair skin.

Well, at least this one had eyes you could see.

When she met our gaze, she cracked a smile and gave a small wave. "This is Remy. Call me Nivian.”

"Hunter," Hunter answered.

Luka repeated our names.

When Remy approached, his brows pinched together. "Where the fuck are we?"

This one, he's smart. Not quite sure if that poses a threat or an ally.

"He's certainly a threat," I confirmed to myself. "We don't know where the hell he came from."

After our introductions, Luka took it upon himself to explain to them they were in Orsadia. He fared better with outsiders than I did.

Remy and Nivian made themselves cozy in the crimson chairs in the main room. A fire crackled in the hearth at the center of them. The atmosphere subtly cooled, a beautiful hello from spring, and while I'd never admit to anyone here that all this retching darkness rattled my bones, it also became another comfort to bathe myself in.

The door burst open, and as my eyes shot up, a literal corpse wandered in, his hand dropping with a thud.

"Dave," I cursed.

Flesh hung from his bones, ribs protruding from a torn shirt.

He paused, dropping his skull to search the floor. At that moment, one side of his jaw came unhinged and dangled for the world to see.

"Pull yourself together, Dave," I said with a scowl.

Remy slammed his drink on the counter with a snort, earning a sigh from his redheaded companion.

You think he likes our creation?

A laugh escaped Luka and it was then I realized how contagious Remy's emotions could be to some.

Remy stalked over to Dave, reaching for the rotting hand and holding it out. "Need a hand?" A grin so broad it made his dimples pop.

What the hell? And why the fuck?

Luka stepped forward and stifled a chuckle. "You may want to also tone it down on the mention of your worlds. Lana hates traveling. She'd prefer to live in her bubble that the only world that exists here is Orsadia."

"Luka!" I scolded.

Remy's shadows crawled closer to us. "Is she your wife?"

I rushed over with wide eyes, an air of dread following me in the same way many reapers might have carried. If I believed in such things. Here in my world, I *was* the reaper. "Wife? I'd never marry, let alone this fool." I threw my hand towards the huntsman. "I'm the Queen of Orsadia. The sooner we send you home, the sooner I can return to murdering Zoe."

"Well that's not very nice," Zoe said with a frown from the doorway. "I thought we were past that. Is it my magic? Did I go too far?"

"I told you to wait outside!"

She's useless. So are you.

"I'm not useless!" I yelled out, earning all eyes. Dismissing them with the wave of my hand, I glared daggers at the princess who received it far too well. "What are you doing in here?"

"You're taking too damn long."

Grumbling, I rubbed my eyes. "What do you mean: *did I go too far?*"

"Dave, keep your hands to yourself!" Luka hurried over to the corpse trying to poke Hunter who scowled in disgust.

Remy stood from his seat and leaned against the door to what I could only assume might have been a bathroom once. "Zombies? This should be fun." His eyes redirected towards me. "What does that make you?"

I responded with, "A necromancer. In Orsadia, we're the most powerful. Everyone fears us. What are you supposed to be?"

"A shadow," Nivian answered, shooting him a warning glare that only made him wink at her. "A guardian. Bodyguard to my best friend, actually."

He counted us out. "A corpse and a necromancer."

Was he sizing us?

My shoulders tensed. "What the hell does that mean?"

He shrugged. "Your dead friends are fun, Queenie."

I think I definitely like this one.

Luka choked. I, however, was unsure how to react as my jaw dropped. "What the fuck is wrong with you?"

"Don't answer that," Luka said with a more comedic tone.

Remy snorted and turned away, lifting a finger to point at my huntsman. "What are you?"

The tension dissipated in seconds.

If Luka was anxious, he didn't show it. "I'm just along for the ride."

"He's the first male of Orsadia to be born with magic," I let out in a whisper they barely caught. "Orsadia is barely a century old. Never has a man been born with the magic gene. But Luka was, being the only child Queen Astrid Lockwood ever had."

"And his magic?" Nivian piped up.

The mansion fell silent.

I was ready to ask if they wanted a drink when finally Luka replied, "Sound. I manipulate sound, mostly tethered to the darkness. Think of mimicking."

"Neat," Remy commented, and immediately lost interest. He turned to Dave while that stupid grin of his reappeared. "When you have a drink, does it just pour out of all the holes in you?"

His disinterest in Luka has me howling. Remy is just my style.

Luka let out a chuckle of his own.

At least someone was enjoying their company.

As I turned to head to the kitchen for water, a squirrel peeked from his tunic.

"Jerry," Luka greeted.

Nivian gasped, shooting from her seat. "He is so cute! Can I hold him?"

I whipped around, stepping between her and Luka. "Absolutely not! I don't know who you are!"

Despite my wishes, Luka reached his hand, in which Jerry rested, under my arm and in front of my chest. "Relax, Firefly. If Jerry doesn't like her, he'll let us know. Where's the harm?"

While waiting around for Nivian to adopt Jerry, footsteps echoed down the grand staircase made of mahogany wood.

A careful hand slid down the rail as a brunette woman smiled in triumph, a man trailing behind her. "Told you they weren't going to kill us on our way down."

"We still could," Luka joked.

"Don't tempt me with a good time," Remy added.

To the woman, the man replied, "I suppose that means you win... This time." He laughed, his form flickering.

On cue, the magic below my fingertips tingled in delight.

"What are you?" Remy lifted from his seat, shooting the man a skeptical look. Tendrils of shadows rose.

Shrugging, he attempted to appear unfazed despite that we were seven against two. "Simply but a ghost."

Ghost? As in the dead? We'd summoned ghosts from another world, which explained what had my necromancy itching to play.

We can control him if we so please.

"Only if it becomes necessary," I mumbled.

"Not sure I believe that," Remy mumbled as his wisps of darkness gathered close again.

Luka barked a laugh as he folded his arms across his chest. Stealing a glance from us, he said, "Looks like we've drawn in quite the crowd."

This ghostly man was tall, at least taller than the people I surrounded myself with on a daily basis. Aalia and Mira were short compared to me, and this man was certainly taller than the huntsman.

All the offense to Luka, of course.

More, if you could just rip his heart out and proudly display it.

His hair displayed an array of nutty browns, a tuft of gray proudly front and center, and his irises had more of a whitish tint than I'd ever seen before.

The woman who'd come down with him had more curls—loose—than I'd seen around Orsadia. Long, and kept up with. Close to my height, and much like the man's, her eyes were unique. Almost white.

"This here is Kiernan." The woman patted his shoulder. "I'm Esmira."

Before anyone else could get another word in, Kiernan asked, "Why are we here?" His lack of power hung around him. Although, it didn't make it less threatening in my home.

I growled, only Luka didn't take that too seriously. He introduced everyone all over again, before double checking the entire mansion to make sure nobody else had wandered in.

Some of them promised me they'd behave.

They sauntered to some seats circled around a table.

"We need a plan," I said in a quieter tone, fingers wrapped around a fresh glass of water as I eyed the liquid. "I need to send you back home."

Zoe groaned as she dropped beside me. "That's what I've been trying to tell you, Lana. I did this. I brought them here."

"How?" My eyes narrowed.

"My magic! I warp reality, remember? Although..." Her gaze danced around.

Hunter finished, "It seems you've reached into other dimensions. Worlds of sorts. That's incredibly powerful."

Far more powerful than you, even.

"And you're not even the least bit terrified?" I asked with lifted eyebrows. "You're mortal, aren't you?"

"Where I come from, you are my enemy. I'm easily swayed to believe in magic." His gaze narrowed.

"Give me just a moment to think," Esmira said as she rubbed her temples. "I just need a minute."

Kiernan laid a hand on her arm for reassurance, in which she returned with a smile.

I tapped my fingers on the side of the glass, concentrating.

A laugh escaped Luka once more. "You're not here to drug us, right?"

Everyone exchanged looks.

"Shouldn't we be asking that?" Kiernan's eyes fixated on the huntsman.

"What are you conjuring up there? I see the gears moving," Hunter directed toward Nivian.

"Lana," she paused, "and whatever it is she considers herself to Luka."

My attention swiftly redirected. "What?"

"By looking at them, it's obvious there's something deep down going on. When he catches her eye, his light up. Hers darken, in more of a sorrowful way."

"That's poetry," Esmira commented.

A small blush rose to Nivian's cheeks. "I can't help but want to ask for the details. I may be nosy at times."

I wanted to rip her head off for implying anything about us. Could everyone here shut the hell up and go home?

Zoe was going to pay dearly.

"So why not marry?" Remy asked in a mischievous tone, shooting a look at Luka. "Lana's attractive, is she not?"

My cheeks warmed at the compliment. Nobody should have ever looked at me that way. And Luka, he would be the death of me. "I have no interest in marrying anyone, and especially not the huntsman. They tried that on me once. I murdered the bloke."

From the back, Kiernan laughed. "Oh, do tell that story."

"Not much to tell. The previous queen decided to send her brother to try and marry me when I was the princess. He kissed me against my will, then tried to justify his actions. So I took pleasure in shedding his blood. He thought he had the right to do whatever but I showed him who really has the power."

Luka's demeanor shifted as his eyes fell.

"Good." Esmira grabbed herself a glass. "Teaches him and others around him to know better than demand shit from us."

I like her, too.

I gave her a tiny smile, feeling an ounce of pride being surrounded by women who weren't all dead, even if this one was. I dragged the dead behind me, but I didn't want to play the role of the villain any longer, even if it was all I knew how to fill at this point.

Remy shifted in his seat, but didn't say a word.

Esmira set her glass down—empty—and cleared her throat. "About that plan. How's it coming along? I got nothing."

"Hopefully quickly," Kiernan added.

Esmira turned his way. "Keep your comments to yourself."

Everyone began to settle while Luka, Zoe, and I worked on a plan. She knew how to warp reality. She hadn't exactly anticipated opening up other worlds and bringing people here. The trick would be figuring out how to open up doors to the exact same worlds for the people to go home where they were needed.

Esmira found herself circling the edge of the room, her eyes following along the walls as if memorizing every detail she could.

I told Zoe and Luka to keep working while I hopped up from my spot and slid over to Esmira. "Hey."

Turning her head to look at me, a smile appeared. "This is a lovely home you've got."

"I don't live here. Nobody does. In fact, I'm not sure what the hell Zoe did exactly. This mansion normally doesn't look this lively." My own eyes wandered across a few walls.

She followed my line of sight before spinning to face me. "What can I do for you? If I can help in any way."

"There's nothing to help with at the moment. Zoe and Luka are working on something."

As her gaze landed on Luka, she softened. "What's stopping you?"

"Stopping me from what?"

She threw her hand up. "From being with the man you very clearly want to be with. Kiernan and I waited a little long in our former years. And now that I have him, I'll never let him go. Having someone by your side to support you is what life is all about. You've found yours, yet you seem to...shun him."

I shrugged, lowering my head. "I don't deserve someone as forgiving as Luka. I'm a monster. I'm the Poisonous Queen and I got my name for a reason. If you've ever met Luka, you'd know he's like a ray of sunshine wherever he goes. I'm the stormy cloud that rolls in to rain on everyone's parade. Ultimately..."

Ultimately, I deserved someone as terrible as Alexander.

"Lana," she started, "when I was...skirting around how I felt for Kiernan, we both had been taken hostage for some sick game. Long story short, I didn't realize how fleeting life was. Things ended too fast for us, but I finally ended up with the love of my...spirit. Even when we'd been shoved into another life, he found me and he loved me to no end. Still, I relive the trauma we both endured..." She dropped her chin. "Kiernan vows to me through everything. Even death didn't stop him." When she finally raised her chin, she stepped closer. "You might think you're not worthy, but that's never true. No matter what you've gone through, you mean the world to someone else and you should hold onto that. You should nurture it. Nobody deserves to be alone."

"Is that what happened to you?" I whispered.

She started in a whisper, "I thought maybe after I failed to save my life, I could get my happy ending. Things are different now. It's even more important to go for the person you want and hold onto them."

I might have changed my mind about this one. Luka's no good. We know that. He'd never accept us. What happens when he finds out who I am? He'll disown you. Humiliate you. It's just the two of us.

"Wait, find out who you are? He knows you're the curse." My eyes widened a bit. "Unless..."

"We might have a solution!" Zoe yelled.

When I whipped around to face her, pounding started on the door.

"Ah, fuck, who could that be?" I grumbled as I went to open it. The second I had, several villagers raged forward with pitchforks and other farming tools, screaming out and jabbing them at me.

I didn't recognize a single one of them. Why? I knew every face and name on my island.

It didn't take long for the newfound friends to rush over. It was then the villagers stepped back, all scowling and shouting profanities.

I still positioned myself between my people and the newcomers. "Are there any dead bodies around? That's my only defense!" I twisted my head back to search for Dave.

"Quick, someone die!" Luka shouted.

As my gaze locked in, I snickered. "How nice of you to volunteer."

I'd like that, but I know you'll never follow through.

Regardless, I flicked my wrist and Dave stumbled forward. When I sent him after the tiny mob, they hurried backwards.

"That's the best you got?" Remy approached as his shadows reached higher from around his body.

I growled as I sent Dave after them.

Remy sent a shadow forward, throwing the first man to the ground. He scurried back as the shadow ripped the tool from his hand and sent the fork through his chest. He choked on the blood that now pooled in his lungs, coughing it up as his life faded.

My anger boiled. Did he just steal that one from me?

He did. And he's my favorite.

Another shadow of his circled another man, sweeping him off his feet and using the ax to chop his head clean from his body. More blood flew across the walls, the headless vessel going still in a split second.

"You moronic bitch, stop stealing my kills!" I screamed, sending Dave to the next.

"Move faster then," he commented.

The voice in my head choked on a laugh.

His shadows reached and snatched the shears from a woman, watching her eyes grow wide as she scrambled for the door. Before she could make it, they reached and opened up the blades, bringing them together right around her thigh. Her scream pierced the air as she fell, blood pouring from the open wound.

She'd die from blood loss if Remy and his damn shadows didn't get to her first.

Dave stopped, turning to give me a look with his one good eyeball. He didn't believe we could do this.

"Remy!" I yelled.

"It's not my fault you suck."

He's entirely right about that.

A pick mattock flew through the air, landing near Hunter who growled, ripping out what looked to be a dagger of his own. Where the hell had that come from? Determination struck across his expression as if he'd done this dance many times before. Determination—and what appeared to be...excitement?

"What the hell? Why are you so intrigued by all this? You could die!"

His hardened eyes met mine. "Absolutely! But I'd die with a purpose."

A chandelier came crashing to the ground, glass shattering as people screamed and jumped out of the way.

Using the bodies that Remy had taken, I reached into their skeletons and twisted my fingers as I slipped my magic deep into the bones and took hold. They lifted to their feet, and just before their souls could slide into the afterlife, I reached my other hand out and locked onto the spirits. "Not so fast." I ripped them over to me, forcing their vessels to walk. "You're going to do exactly as I tell you now." Much like my monsteras back in my garden, they would last longer than they planned for.

This is always my favorite part.

I sent the corpses and their respective spirits to do my bidding. The ones left alive tried to run, but didn't make it very far before I used the dead body of a friend to rip them to shreds. Limb by limb. Head for last. Blood splattered the walls, and it was then I noticed as crimson stained it—a book of papers with Anne Regali scrawled across the front.

"My grandmother," I breathed as the corpses dropped like puppets.

Esmira launched a mist of her own. It swirled around the last villager, trapping him within. Blinding him from escape. And when the fog dripped away, his throat had been cut. A freshly crimson-painted sickle laid a foot away. He dropped to his knees which cracked on impact before he face-planted into the stone flooring, his own blood forming a pool around him.

She's not all bad. I like this dark, murderous side of her.

Honor didn't come close to describing how I truly felt deep down. These people I'd never met had killed mortals simply because they wanted me dead.

Couldn't imagine why.

"Look at what you made me do, Lana! I killed human beings and sided with people who are normally my enemies," Hunter yelled with a scowl.

Everyone around me panted as they turned to watch me approach the book. I picked it up, opening it and sifting through the proof that she was here. Proof that my own grandmother lived in this mansion when she was alive, before she had been killed. Had my mother been raised here?

"Oh that's fucking creepy," Kiernan said as he peeked through the thick, black curtains. "There are dolls hanging from the trees."

I ignored his comment, pulling the book close to my heart.

Zoe laid a hand on my shoulder. "We should send them home."

Nodding, I turned to face them as she brought her hands together, fingers inches from touching each other. Conjuring magic, beginning to warp the reality around us.

"Anequeco," she repeated over and over until Nivian and Remy blipped away.

"Smarioe!" she yelled, facing Esmira and Kiernan who then proceeded to disappear before our eyes.

She faced Hunter. "Where am I sending you again?"

"Arizona."

Zoe took the initiative, repeating the name until Hunter vanished from Orsadia.

And with them, the slaughtered villagers blipped, their blood fading from the walls—the preserved furniture.

Had we just killed innocent people from another world?

The mansion melted back into its dreary and drab state, the ledger before me poofing into nothing. My grandmother had been erased yet again, and all thanks to some stupid villagers who couldn't let a woman suffer in peace.

Soon, I'd follow in her footsteps.

SIXTEEN

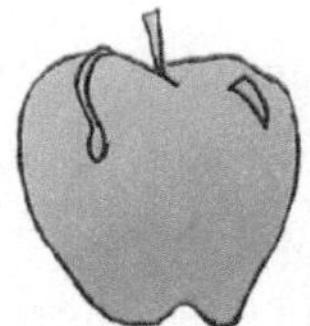

The five of us—Zoe, Luka, Jerry, Dave, and I managed to come out mostly unscathed. We'd learned a bit. Made a few friends. Luka even made sure to rub it in my face and tease me with, "You sure you don't want to travel to new lands?"

It confirmed that there had been much more out there.

And that I hadn't been the only person in this world with magic dark enough to raise the dead.

However, it gave me an ounce of hope. If others could wield magic that came from not-so-orthodox methods of living, I wasn't entirely consumed by the darkness.

Oh, but you are, Little Raven. You are entirely consumed by me.

He wasn't all that wrong. I had just eliminated a mob sent to kill me. My friends helped, and why? What made me redeemable?

I told Luka to head back to the castle so he took my dead lurker, Dave, with him. Zoe followed shortly behind. Then I turned to face the area in which I had finally gotten a few ideas for. Hypnotic

Arythe, the area in which I would host my event to scope out and *defeat* Zoe Quillen.

I'd do so by hosting a ball for everyone to come and watch. But this would be of my own doing. Corpses. Ghosts. Guests where I could snatch them from the shadows for my benefit.

"Lana," a woman shouted.

When I whipped around to face my greatest threat, I found her crossing the shaky bridge in an attempt to come *back*, fingers wrapped tightly around the ropes as she moved at a slow and steady pace.

In an instant, one side snapped from the stake it'd been tied to that stood at the end in the dirt. Her feet slipped as she wrapped both arms around one rope and clung to it, yelling out.

I stepped forward just as the other stake ripped from the ground and flew back, the bridge swinging down towards the other cliff. Her screams pierced the air as I rushed forward, watching her fight to hold on as her entire body smacked against the rock wall.

"Zoe, hang on," I shouted at her.

Swallowing all resentment, I threw my arms out, forcing my magic to reach the other side as I scraped bones together. After a few skeletons had been formed, I told Zoe to start climbing and they'd help her.

She did as she was told, not too far from the top.

Luka came running at the sound, eyes wide. "What the hell happened to the bridge?"

Mira and Aalia stood behind him, Dave lingering about.

"Luka!" Zoe yelled.

He rushed to the side, peering over the edge to find her hanging. "Hang on! I'm coming!" He shot me the nastiest look.

My heart shattered.

Did he think I did this to her?

"Luka," I croaked.

Let him go. He never truly cared about you. But I do.

"Zoe, keep hanging on!" he screamed over me.

The snap of the bridge came from my end. He knew all too well I had experience with broken bridges.

I'd been the Poisonous Queen, out to ensure Zoe would never make it to defeat me.

But he knew I wanted to end this curse. Deep down, I wanted it to be over. After everything we'd encountered at the mansion, how could he turn on me so quickly? Did he not believe in me?

Zoe squealed. Then she slipped. He screamed her name as she disappeared into the waters below.

Without even thinking, I removed my sheath with my sword. I leaped from the cliff as he shouted how stupid I was. His words never meant much to me anyway.

I plummeted into the freezing ocean feet first, my dress flying around me as I was engulfed. Fighting the skirt, I managed to twist enough to kick to the surface. It'd been more difficult to keep afloat as the waves threatened to devour me, numbness beginning to weigh down.

"Zoe!" I searched for her, turning in every direction.

A peek of black hair caught my attention, and I pushed as hard as I'd ever done before, my head going under a few times. Saltwater entered my mouth as I forced it down my throat. When I caught onto her arm, I pulled her to me, keeping her head on my shoulder. "I got you," I whispered into her ear.

She had been unconscious, but I made my promise nonetheless.

You risked your life for hers? What kind of queen are you? Let her die.

"I'm not a heartless queen!" I cried out.

I swam to the base of the cliff, crying out as the current shoved me towards the whirlpool. "No."

It'd been too strong—too big. It sucked us closer. I couldn't even manage a grip on the rocks.

With nowhere to go, the voice whispered, *Give up. You'll never amount to anything anyway.*

I yelled out as I pushed harder, only to have a wave sweep us under. My dress lifted around me, tangling my limbs until I couldn't fight it. The whirlpool drank us up.

I said my goodbyes.

Utter silence.

No oxygen.

Fabric floated around me, my hair wrapped around my face.

Whoosh.

My fingers loosened. I lost sight of the only reason I'd risked my life. Darkness grew in the cracks.

I succumbed.

Crying faded in.

As I turned my head over to my left, I found Luka pulling Zoe in for a hug to quiet her sobs as she clung to him.

"Hey," Aalia whispered as I attempted to close my eyes.

It'd be easy to give up everything and let them have it. Maybe I should have sacrificed myself. What had I stayed for? A curse that ruined me? A man who no longer cared for my existence? A family who I had to disown for their safety?

Coughing up a little water, I rolled my head to my right—away from Zoe and Luka—meeting Mira's eyes. "Is it too late to sacrifice myself?"

"You already did," she started, "just now. Why?"

I groaned as I flipped over onto my stomach and began to push myself up from the sand. Onto my knees, then to my feet. "More people would miss her if she died. The answer was too obvious." I headed up the beach.

A small voice stopped me in my tracks, and the princess circled until she blocked me from moving further. "Thank you." Her brows drooped, eyes swimming in remorse. "My magic must have been enhanced. I lost control, and then the whirlpool sucked us in. But I must have gained it back. I must have made it disappear so we could have a chance at survival."

I saved her from herself? And for what—so Luka could pretend I didn't want to protect her just as much as he had?

"Don't thank me. I was supposed to let you die."

"You didn't. You tried."

"Did you ask Luka what he thinks?"

Confusion etched her expression. "Why would I?"

Burying my feelings was easier than trying to explain why it pained me so much that he assumed I tried to kill her in the first place.

"I'm headed back to my castle. It's clear that Luka is needed where you are. I'll send Dave over with his things later." I trudged up the shore in a light dress that clung to my figure and became transparent enough for the word to peek at what laid beneath.

I didn't wear shame for it. Luka would be damned to evoke such emotions when all I'd done was attempt to save the princess' life. So be it that my nipples existed. Was I required to hide them for a man who promised to have self-control?

Nobody stopped me. Nobody said a word. Nobody apologized or even bothered to correct me at all.

It's us again, Little Raven. Back at the beginning. So, where were we?

SEVENTEEN

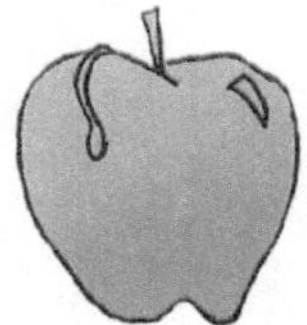

Why did you save her? She should have been left to die.

Maybe a part of me despised Luka for ever assuming I'd team up with him and take him into my castle, only to turn around and try to kill Zoe.

As badly as I ached to rip her soul from her vessel, I never caved.

"He's destroying me," I whispered. "I've allowed him to burrow his way under my skin to pick me apart and study me. I've made myself vulnerable. I despise him."

What are we going to do about it?

I leaned back in my chair, tapping the arm of my throne. "Invite him to the masquerade ball I'll be hosting. With the bridge fixed, I've got the perfect theme. We're the Poisonous Queen after all, and it's time Luka is reminded of that on *my* accord." He'd believed in me, saying I could fight the curse if I simply let everyone in. What a lie.

He'd been using me, waiting for me to snap.

And when he assumed I had, he turned on me.

"It's time we pay a visit to our friends from other lands again. After all, who better fills a queen's event than those who walk with the dead?”

EIGHTEEN

Decorating the cathedral along with the mansion had been far too easy. Crumbling structures, holes in the roof and exterior. Cobwebs, with little light.

I'd managed to get a few of my corpses to sweep the floors and clean up piles of rubble. They lit the candles while I watched.

The main area had once been for the pews and whatever else people would gather for, now just a ballroom for people to enjoy themselves if they wished, or if they could handle it.

Everyone in Orsadia had been formally invited.

And they knew it was safe to come, for this ball was solely to lure Zoe in an attempt to kill her. If I found her, I'd corner her. Snuff out of her life as I licked the blood from my blade. What a climax that would be to the horror masquerade ball the Poisonous Queen hosted.

Once the dead had finished with the decor, I admired all the old, rotting glory that once had been. Flickering flames had made the scenery appear far more romantic than needed, attempting to liven a place once damned to hell.

"Dave," I called out. "I believe it's time to prepare for our guests. And what would a ball be without a few extras?" I glanced back his way, my eyes lingering on his dangling jaw. "Retrieve Zoe, so she can work her magic and gather our new...acquaintances."

Dave did as he was asked, not bothering to argue. He hadn't been too mouthy. Although, I did wonder...

I headed back to Everinthian to freshen up while Mira and Aalia hovered over my shoulder.

"Do you mind?" I shot them scowls. "I need to get ready."

"And you expected to do that alone?"

"Are you asking to dress me? That's a bit odd coming from the two of you. You're invited. You're aware of that, correct?"

They nodded, but said nothing as a familiar presence grew behind me. I'd much rather see anyone else but him.

"Allow me," Luka said. "I'm certain the corset is something you need help with."

With a roll of my eyes, I gathered my gown. "It'd still be odd coming from you, too. Given how quick you were to dismiss my truth and assume I had cut the bridge."

Destroy him. Burn him to ash and envy. To smithereens.

His frown had been glorious. I wanted to make him weep. "I apologized, Lana."

No, he didn't. We both know that.

Turning to give him my full attention, I tilted my head. "Oh. If you apologize, I'm required to accept it. Is that how that works?"

"I did not say that. But allow me to make up for it by helping you get ready." He lent his hand, to which I ignored.

"No Zoe? Does she not need your help?"

"She has a lady's maid. You know that."

Lynn. That certainly did sting a little.

"Fine. You look better as a maid anyway." I laid out the gown with the corset before turning away. In the past I may have hidden from him. But what was there to hide? A woman's body? He'd seen it plenty after my near-rescue with Zoe. Mine had just been littered with scars these days.

After peeling my casual attire from my figure, I switched out my chemise for my naked form—which I did for a special occasion such as this.

"Firefly," Luka's nickname for me came out in a breathy whisper filled with utter concern. Before I could turn to look his way, his fingers brushed over the ridges on my bare back. "What happened?"

Goosebumps formed over every inch of my skin as a shiver skidded down my spine. "Three years leaves a lot of room for horrid things to happen."

Don't be so naïve, Little Raven. Those horrid things were your doing. Are we attempting to play the victim? You're the queen. Act like it.

"I suppose I could admit it's all my fault." I shrugged a little. "You murder people. They tend to want revenge where they can get it."

"You're a victim of the curse. That can't be entirely pinned on you." He traced his knuckles down my spine. Would he stop doing that and do his damn job? "Why do you take full credit?"

He hadn't seen the horrors I'd inflicted.

Screams pierced the skies as ravens swooped down to peck at innocent bystanders.

I marched right up to the very man who had hit his wife, fingers wrapped around his neck, squeezing ever so tightly. "Do you call yourself a man for what you've done?" My long, black nails dug into his skin, drawing beads of blood.

His wife yelled at me to let him go, but I would not. I would never.

"She is your other half. You have vowed to protect her and love her. Do you not understand the irony of laying a hand on her? That is not protection, George!" I dropped him as he scrambled back.

Pulling my sword from its sheath, I took one clean slice to his neck, watching his head roll to my left as blood speckled my face. "You look much better this way." His body thumped against the porch as his wife cried out from the mess I'd made. I'd saved her life. Could she not be grateful?

I'd allowed myself just a taste of the blood hiding under the tip of my nail.

As I spun, I found an angry mob of residents. They lunged for me, tackling me and piling on, ripping at whatever they could. My gown tore. My sleeves ripped. My shoulders ached from the pulling and punching. Once they'd freed my torso from the bodice, their claws scratched away layers of skin until blood permeated the air.

They left me bruised and beaten. Broken. With nothing. It had been my skeletons who finally scared them away so I could limp home where I tended to the wounds and laid naked for days as they scabbed over.

I'd saved a life by taking one. Did they not understand?

"You could have cut off his hand. It didn't need to be his whole head," Luka chimed in.

I scoffed. "Allow him to use his other hand? Absolutely not. I healed fine. It was a small price to pay to ensure that never happened to her again. People can certainly be vengeful."

"You are their example." He wrapped the corset around me. I attempted to ignore the tingles where his touch skimmed.

He's not entirely wrong. They learn from you.

He pulled the corset around my middle, pulling at the strings and adjusting where needed. He started pulling too tight, and my eyes widened as I forced out, "Luka! I can't breathe!"

"Is that not the point of the corset?" he teased, still pulling. I'd have his head if I could.

"No!" I sucked in a gulp of air as he let go.

His chuckle bounced around the room. "Why don't you be a good girl and let me decide when the corset is tight enough?"

I squealed from surprise before narrowing my eyes.

When I opened my mouth, he cut me off with, "You don't like that?"

I didn't admit to him that deep down, something awakened.

"I'm only giving you a taste of your own medicine. Sometimes you need the reminder." He tied off the strings before helping me fasten the back of my gown after I stepped into it.

When I turned to face him, something in his expression shifted. I pressed my hands to my stomach.

His smile dropped, corners twitching. His eyes darkened a little as they roamed my gown.

I'd picked a shadow-black silk. Nothing spectacular, but enough to shout about how much power I held over people.

The bodice curved against my figure perfectly, flowing out past my waist. Intricate beading work on the breasts, sheer fabric on my stomach with strips of opaque material to leave almost every bit of skin to the imagination, and a piece of soft silk that wrapped from the center of one breast, over my middle, tucking itself around my waist. A small, sharp V accentuated my cleavage. Another bit looped around one shoulder and the bicep on the same arm. A slit ran up to my hip, the skirt fanning around me. To pair it all together, I pulled on black lace gloves that reached to my biceps.

"Luka, what's wrong?"

After a moment of silence, he shook his head and came back to Orsadia. "If you were aiming to stop and turn heads, you've achieved that."

Don't fall for his pretty words. They're just words, My Queen. His actions show otherwise.

Dropping my hands from my stomach to my sides, I cocked an eyebrow. "Are you ogling over your queen?"

Something tempting flashed in his eyes as he stepped closer. "Do you want me to?"

"I suppose the real question is: do you like what you see?"

Dangerous. Daring. Far too forward.

But I stepped closer anyway, begging with just my eyes for him to make a move. Maybe for a night, I could allow myself that luxury.

He lifted his hand to grab hold of my chin. "Are you playing a game, or should I take this as an invitation?"

"Why don't you find out, if you're not scared."

The door swung open as Dave stumbled through. They were almost here.

Luka's hand fell from me as he stepped back. "I should change then. I'll meet you there?"

He's using you.

One quick nod, as I pulled on a crown and secured my sheath to my waist. "Until then, huntsman." I laced up some black boots.

As I headed for the door, he followed and turned right at the frame while I turned left to head down the stairs. "Lana," he said, halting me in my tracks. "Next time the mobs come for you, I'll be there."

"You're not required to protect me," I stated.

"It's not protection." He pressed his lips into a thin line. "For what they did, it'd simply be revenge. The people of Orsadia aren't so innocent either." He disappeared down the dark corridor.

Crimson colored my cheeks as I led the past queens and Dave to the ball. On my way out the door, he handed me the mask. I carried it most of the walk, and as I arrived at the mansion, I slipped it on and tied the ribbons. Black lace, with a single emerald jewel to the edge of my eye, to match the red jewels I'd encrusted in the hilt of my sword. An apple dripping with rot and day.

As I entered the cathedral, I headed up the grand staircase, standing before the railing that overlooked the foyer.

Skeletons and corpses hung about, dancing and bumping into things. Although their clacking of bones and tearing of skin certainly added to the atmosphere.

People began to pour in from the doors, but not many had attended. Orsadia only had so many left.

My mother entered with Fallon and my posture stiffened. Their gazes lifted towards me, locking in.

Mother had waltzed in with a form-fitted gown made of the finest yellow. As if she had stolen the sun's golden rays to make herself the goddess. Nobody would question where I obtained my looks, nor my confidence.

Her dark waves had been pinned to her head just right to frame the flawless face she wore. Compassion, filled with pure respect for everyone but me.

Fallon wore a black tux with a white shirt under his jacket, and a golden bow to match Mother's appearance. To remind me whose side he had always been on.

Without another word, they headed into the Great Room.

After them, Zoe entered, dressed in a burgundy adorned with jewels and a bit of lace. A slit up her thigh, and no crown as if she hadn't wanted anyone to know who she was. Not even a weapon in sight. Foolish of her.

As if they could forget.

Or maybe she'd attempted to be humble unlike the Poisonous Queen.

She met my eyes, then disappeared below the balcony, through the double doors.

Luka came next, but what threw me off guard was the entirely black tux he scorned himself with. Not an ounce of color. Black bow, black suit, and even a black shirt tucked underneath. And I'd be *damned*; he pulled it off well.

His suit fit him just right, showing off the muscles in his arms and the form he'd built over his entire life as a huntsman. Hair messy as always. From the stubble on his chin, I knew he hadn't shaved in days. If he'd stop shaving at all, I wouldn't complain.

His hands rested in his pockets, to which he then lifted one to his face and swiped his thumb over his bottom lip.

My balance faltered.

The asshole was out to murder me tonight. I knew that now.

When he spotted me up on the balcony, he winked before heading into the Great Room with everyone else.

That bitch.

In walked my favorite guests of the night.

Those from Anequeco, and those from a town I never knew—Smarioe.

"I'm glad you could make it," I spoke. Amusement filled every crevice of my expression, my lips curving up, my eyes widening just a bit, and my eyebrows lifting to my forehead with a crinkle in my nose. "Now the fun begins."

NINETEEN

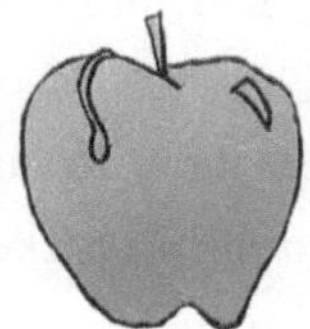

They entered before I did, taking in their surroundings as skeletons hung from old chandeliers that no longer worked. "Don't mind them. They won't harm you." I waved away the dead.

Hunter stepped forward, owning his dark green suit. The collar had been made of black satin while the jacket had matched the shade of the leaves in late spring. His shirt had been stark white, freshly ironed of all wrinkles. His golden hair had been slicked back to show off his features—a shaved jaw and dark eyes.

Hunter could clean up nice when he wanted to.

"Glad you could take time to join us," I noted. "I hope my corpses don't scare you away too much."

He shrugged, shooting a small smile my way. "I may have gotten a tad used to them. I won't let you take the credit for that, however. Your ego is too large from my observations. It's Mya I'll honor this time around."

As the shadow walked in with Nivian, I eyed them. "Just you two?"

“Not quite. Zhyire fears other lands,” she answered, although I intended my question merely as a joke. She swiftly turned it into a playful jab. “But we brought a few friends.”

He wore all black much like Luka, only instead of a tux, he wore apparel more reminiscent of his world. Over the top of his button-up and slacks draped a long coat. Crimson.

I gave him a small nod. "You pull off the blood red exceedingly well."

Remy flirtatiously said, “Tell me about it.”

Elbowing him, Nivian shot him a cocked eyebrow. “You promised you’d behave yourself.”

He grinned in return. “Zhyire asked, but I made no such promises.” They'd mentioned her twice now. She must have been important to them.

Nivian rolled her eyes.

She wore a gown similar to mine, yet it stood out in its own respect in gilded tones. Sleeves off the shoulders, a fitted bodice made of a smooth material with a small sweetheart neckline and a flowing skirt decorated with black lace carefully placed. Her hair had been pinned back.

"You look stunning yourself." Her eyes fell to my gown.

As if on cue, two men stepped out from behind them.

The first sported ebony hair swept back from his face, with bright blue eyes and a healthy tan. He was tall, though not as tall as Remy, and his jaw had been chiseled as if he'd been a statue come to life. This statue had come with his own set of night-colored wings.

Their other friend was smaller, with short mahogany waves and a smattering of freckles dusting his nose. His brown eyes were bright, and his smile added fuel to the warmth.

"Calum,” the brunette greeted, sticking out a hand. “You might be the queen here, but you're not my queen." Although he said it with far more humor sewn into his tone despite the stony expression.

“Ignore him.” Remy cleared his throat. “He's Zhyire's other guardian.”

Other? She had two? What world did they come from where shadows and men with raven wings were bodyguards?

Nivian smiled between the both of them. "Hopefully we won't ruin your party too much."

I shrugged. "Please do. I'm counting on it." I glanced back at Zoe as she picked up an apple from the table. Damn. I should have poisoned them.

"This is Ambrose," Calum started, before Ambrose stepped forward to finish.

He smiled sheepishly. "Calum's soulmate. Vampire, too."

My interest sparked. "Oh? Well, can't promise the people of Orsadia are all that keen on the idea, but please do feel free to make them uncomfortable. If you come across a man named Fallon, don't forget to say hi."

Luka approached, clasping my shoulder. "Fallon is her little brother who she cut off because he defended himself against bullies."

You don't need anyone but me, Little Raven.

I scowled, smacking his arm.

Ambrose and Calum both watched us with much merriment.

"We don't know exactly what a vampire is, but feel free to mingle." I waved a hand towards the corpses. "Snacks at the table."

Calum let out a laugh. "Vampires snack on blood, but thanks for the gesture."

My eyebrows shot up in surprise as I studied Ambrose. "Oh."

Oh indeed. I quite like the idea of drinking blood. Shall we give it a go?

Luka nudged me. "Not anything we aren't used to. What's another new kind of magic in this world anyway?"

I elbowed him. "Can you piss off? You help a girl with a corset and suddenly you think you can pop in wherever."

"To be fair, we live together. Who else is going to save you from the big, bad monsters hiding under your bed?" He wiggled his brows.

He pretends to apologize and now he thinks everything is swell.

It was I who had to leave.

So instead I sauntered off to say hello to Kiernan and his wife Esmira. I prided myself on names.

Kiernan matched Esmira who wore a scarlet gown, fabric buttons lined from her chest down her midsection, the skirt flowing from her waist with a slit up the leg.

Kiernan wore something a tad formal, with a splash of red to match his wife.

Oh to be ghosts who still said their vows.

Marriage is for the weak.

"Well, I'm glad everyone could make it. Feel free to enjoy yourselves." I hurried off before anyone else could stop me, finding myself off in the corner from the residents of Orsadia.

If all went well...

Many of my guests gave frightened looks to the dead. It was perfect indeed.

What is your plan here?

"My plan is to wait it out. Watch Zoe. Then take her life. Luka is far too excited to see old friends to pay any attention."

I tuned into what my new guests were flitting about.

Nivian glanced at Remy. “Stop messing with your mask.”

“It’s irritating me.”

Snorting, she replied, “You’re irritating all of us.”

Remy shot her a, “Fuck off, *Captain.*”

Kiernan decided to add his own commentary. “Are you not used to dressing up?”

With a shrug, he said, "I don't usually handle the formal parties, and according to Nivian, I'm not more socially adept than her."

Both Calum and Nivian frowned, sarcasm dripping as they asked, "Since when?"

A laugh escaped Esmira. "This is fun."

Kiernan pursed his lips a bit. "This isn't my kind of party either. I'm only here because Esmira said we had to come."

"We were *invited.* It's the polite thing to do."

"And if you were invited to go muck out Lana's stables you'd probably agree to that too."

She gave him her sweetest smile. "I'd agree for *you* to accept, sure. I could keep the horses company."

He scowled in response. "And how is that fair?"

"I said it was polite. I never said anything about it being fair."

A giggle came from Nivian as Remy grinned.

Calum asked, "Anybody else getting a weird vibe here?"

Nivian pondered the question, before answering thoughtfully with, "No, but none of us are mated to the same gender. Lana did say it might displease some people here."

"It's more than that. I think something is gonna go down tonight."

Kiernan scoffed. "It's *Lana.* Do you really think she'd throw a party for no reason?"

"How should I know? I missed out on your jolly adventures in Orsadia the first time."

His mate, Ambrose, piped in, "And evidently he's still sour about it."

Calum turned to him. "I'm not *sour.*"

Remy stated, "You look sour."

Nodding, Esmira said, "Really sour."

Calum grabbed Ambrose's hand. "Screw this. Let's dance."

He dragged his companion to the dance floor and shot as many grins as he could manage to all the other guests who watched in disgust. He pulled Ambrose close, and together they danced flawlessly, yet poured their every being into the steps. With hands on shoulders and waists, they'd steal a few kisses to put on a show for the people of Orsadia specifically. I supposed for my residents, it really had been a horror ball after all. Even underneath the masks, everyone knew they were both men.

I glanced over at Fallon who stuck close to Mother, bringing her a few things to sip on. Both wore gold masks that brought out their best features. Mother's bright brown eyes and Fallon's poison-colored ones. It hadn't been a secret as to who he was related to.

He admired Ambrose and Calum for what they had, although he never had the guts to go over and talk to them. Mother tried to urge him, but he refused.

Instead, he went for a few more snacks.

Everyone had eaten them all within the first half hour. I supposed that was to be expected as most people here ate very little. Free food? They'd become vultures.

"Care to dance?" a familiar voice asked to my right.

When I turned my head his way, gaze following soon after, I checked out his form. "Me? What about your...?" I nodded towards Nivian.

Remy choked on the loudest laugh I'd ever heard. "Nivian? Absolutely not. She's here because she wanted to be, but we hold no romantic feelings for each other. She's more like the pesky ant I can't get rid of."

I searched his face for any tell, but he'd been honest. He didn't have feelings for her.

"I came to your ball. At least share one dance." He winked at me, offering his hand.

I didn't have an excuse to throw at him so I begrudgingly took his hand and followed him out to the floor. He placed his hands on my waist. I rested mine on his shoulders.

"To tell you the truth, I want to learn how to dance with a woman before I return to Smarioe," he admitted.

"Why is that?" I met his eyes. Shadows began to swim down his arms, tendrils twisting around my waist.

"Maybe I can ask Zhyire to dance with me. I won't have to be humiliated. I know I'm supposed to be her bodyguard, but fuck, she's the boldest flower in the garden." Pain settled into his expression. Tight lips, wrinkled nose, furrowed brows, and a creased forehead. "She's never ventured further than our small town. She's never been anywhere at all, yet she has more ideas and loves deeper than anyone I know. How do I deserve that?"

A comforting washed over me as I realized we had that in common. We both cared about people who were too good for us. How did I tell Remy he deserved her when I could never convince myself the same of Luka?

Glancing at the huntsman himself, he ground his teeth in protest, eyes locked on Remy's shadows that swirled around my waist.

"I may not have the answer." I tilted my chin back up towards my dance partner of the hour.

When I glanced to my right, I noticed a man half hidden in the shadows on the balcony, his gaze focused solely below on Fallon.

Part of me wanted to tell him to make the move. The other part was questioning if he had other intentions.

Instead of meddling, I stayed back and allowed it to play out as needed, my sword hanging at my hip in case I ever had to use it.

Fallon whispered something to Mother before disappearing towards the bathrooms. That was when the mysterious man followed him.

"Excuse me," I told Remy as I stepped away. I scanned the area to ensure nobody else would be coming in with us, then I was back in the hallway where I found Fallon eyeing this man. "I've never seen anyone else here, so I assume you're from another world? My sister managed to pull guests from her ass, however that happened."

The man, dressed in a dark brown suit with a black tie, responded with, "Name's Clyde. I'm from Anequeco."

"Am I supposed to know where that is? In case you haven't noticed, we don't get much out here."

The man let a low chuckle vibrate through his chest. "A few different lands have come, so I'm going to assume you're from this one given your comment. Correct?" He tilted his head.

Fallon straightened his back, nodding to loosen up the tension. "Orsadia. I'm Fallon. My sister is the Poisonous Queen, actually."

"I suppose I better choose my words carefully then." He stepped closer. "I couldn't help but notice from afar that you don't have anyone to dance with. Maybe I can help."

I grabbed the edge of the wall, tucking myself away from view.

My brother shifted. "People won't like it."

Clyde lifted an eyebrow in question. "Did I ask the people to dance with me? I'm not particularly concerned with their opinions. Just yours."

It was impossible to miss the blush that rose to my brother's face. Much like me, he'd been pale from the start.

As much as I had wanted to know where it went, it felt like an invasion of privacy. After everything I'd put him through and the lives I'd taken, it was no wonder I left Fallon to live his life. I had to leave now, before I corrupted him.

Hurrying away from the hall, I came to an abrupt stop when Luka stood in my way, sipping on something. "Where are you headed, Firefly?"

Why won't you kill him? Are you truly that blinded by your hideous love?

"I need air." I tapped my fingers against my skirt, eyes darting over every inch of the area.

"Why?"

"Fallon. He's just met someone." And I didn't get the privilege of being part of his life after the way I'd treated him all those years ago.

Luka glanced behind me with a frown. "You can make it up to him. You don't need to shut him out every chance you get. He's your brother."

I ground my teeth. "I have to. I'm just the Poisonous Queen to him these days."

That's your title. Own it, you Ridiculous Raven.

"You don't have to be." He reached forward instinctively, brushing hair back from my face before pulling away.

"But I am. I can't take that back." My jaw loosened as my fists tightened.

"You can still try for better."

I scowled. "Luka."

He lifted his palm. "Dance with me."

Oh fuck no.

"What?" I snapped.

"Firefly." He grabbed my hand, yanking me against him, our chests pressed together. "Dance with me." His other arm snaked around my waist as he led us closer to the floor, dancing in ways I hadn't known Luka to even move. "I learned in Ravenshire. Velia's abusive mother held many balls."

First, he barges in and puts his greedy hands all over your spine like a doctor playing with a body. Then you allow him to do this?

"This is bold. Too bold for us," I forced.

Without even faltering, he leaned into my ear, "Never too bold for the huntsman and his queen."

Something fluttered inside me.

You're hopeless. Just you wait. I'll save face for the both of us.

Carefully, I slipped my free hand to his shoulder and focused on my breathing as my heart pounded against my ribcage. Foliage grew from the nooks of my mind, swaying my better judgment. My vision grew hazy.

It had somehow become just about us.

The music flitted around like dragonflies, bouncing from wall to wall.

Luka's green eyes never wavered from mine. Except maybe once, when they flicked to my rosy lips.

His arm slipped from my waist, but I found he had control as he spun me around before twirling me back into his chest. I had trouble catching my breath, attempting to fix the waves of hair falling over my shoulder.

He seized the opportunity to dance some more before he dipped me backwards, his hold on my waist firm.

"Luka," I breathed. "We should stop while we're ahead."

He pressed a soft kiss to the pulse at my throat. "Why would you say that?"

Throw him off. He'll never see it coming.

I threaded a hand in his hair, closing my eyes just to give myself one moment. "Why do you think I planned this event?"

He groaned a bit but stole all we had as he pulled us back upright. "What are you talking about, Lana?"

Do it now, Little Raven.

"Lana? What are you talking about?" He repeated his question louder and a little more aggressively. His hands fell from my body as he stepped back.

I reached for the sword at my hips as the realization hit me.

"I need you to do something first."

What are you doing?

"What might that be?"

"Call me Little Raven."

What. Are. You. Doing. the voice seethed.

He squinted in response, but after a few seconds, he uttered the words that changed the course of everything, "Little Raven."

The voice that persuaded me to murder Luka and Zoe had been Luka's the entire time. Three years of *his* voice inside my head.

Stumbling back, I ripped the sword from my sheath as my eyes searched for Zoe. I ran through the bodies, spinning around corpses and squeezing through couples. When I found her, I lifted my sword to take what was rightfully mine—my magic and the throne.

"Lana, stop!" he yelled.

When I looked back, the tip of his arrow had been aimed right at me.

Chaos broke free.

Blood splattered from a few throats.

My corpses and skeletons reveled with the new friends, while Aalia and Mira screamed for someone to do something.

It had been Nivian and Remy who pulled out their weapons but not in my regards. They had aimed for my heart. Kiernan and Esmira called upon the fog just as Remy gathered his shadows.

Maybe Kiernan, Esmira, and Nivian couldn't entirely go through with it.

But the moment Remy's eyes darkened, I knew he could take my life without blinking. He despised me enough at times.

Zoe had her hands up as Luka approached, taking my sword and throwing it to the side. He returned the arrow to the quiver and threw his bow over his shoulder. "I never go anywhere unprepared." He slipped his dagger from his sleeve, pointing the tip at the base of my jaw. "So explain to me why you're trying to kill Zoe after everything we've been through?"

Because he'd turned on me the second he had the chance.

We could have had her.

My eyes dropped to his blade as I swallowed. "You have no clue, do you?"

"Clue about what?"

Kiernan and Esmira's shadows swam in the air around us, blocking my view from the rest of the ball. Remy and Nivian still held their positions if Luka called on them. Of course they'd take his side.

"He wants you dead because you threaten him. You're the one with the most influence over him, even if he isn't entirely you. He *mimics* the voice of someone I care most about. You're not as innocent as you'd like to believe."

"What are you talking about?"

Oh how the apple pie crust crumbles.

"Remember that voice in my head—the one the curse has delegated to influence me and remind me of how worthless I am and where I stand in this game of ours?" When his eyes narrowed on me, I whispered, "It's yours, Luka. You're the one telling me to kill Zoe Quillen."

TWENTY

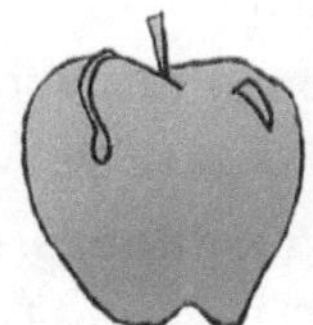

I dropped to my knees in front of the willow tree that made a nice accessory to the tower where I'd been forced to murder Kali.

Its lush leaves hung freely, its trunk full of so much promise to keep my secrets. Why? Why did it have to be her?

Vines snaked their way up the structure, attempting to engulf bricks in hopes that it could take over once again. Nobody doubted it could.

Glancing up at the tallest window, I swallowed.

"Now you're quiet," I mumbled. "Now that I know who you belong to, you won't say a damn thing. Convenient."

Oh, I'm not quiet, Little Raven. I'm simply observing from the shadows. Calculating my next move.

"I am not succumbing to a voice."

But you want to. Now that you know who I am, you're inclined to listen to me more. I'm the closest you'll get to love—the closest you'll get to Luka.

"I can't..." I dropped my head. "I need you to leave me alone," I pleaded. "I need silence—for once!"

Don't beckon me with such promising words. You're tempting me. You don't want to get rid of me.

"I do!" I screamed. Once it went quiet, I sucked in air and pushed my hair from my face.

"I get it," said a voice from behind me. When I twisted my head and climbed to my feet, I found Remy standing nearby, arms folded across his chest, head cocked as his dark eyes took in the details of my face. "The voice. It gets loud sometimes, right?"

"What's it matter to you?" I narrowed my eyes. My fingers reached for my sword, my gaze attached to the shadows drifting around his wings and wrapping around his arms.

"I don't know if you remember, Queenie, but you almost killed Zoe. Why would you try to slaughter our way home? She wasn't attacking you. She had no weapons on her, and given the way Luka had to aim his arrow at you, I knew who was the threat in an instant. I have ways of knowing things about people. Smarioe just doesn't quite...accept how I know that. They have laws against it. Trust me, I've tried." He let out a small snicker.

"Orsadia isn't like your home. I'm the queen here. I make the rules."

He raised an eyebrow, eyes catching my hand close around the hilt of my sword. I was aware that he could *technically* kill me in a second without raising his blade, but the instinct had been based on reflexes. "Sweetheart, I'm trying to help you here. If you don't want it, then fine, but you're gonna listen to what I have to say before you decide to shrug it off."

"You can't tell—"

"I use a focus when things get too loud," he interjected. "To get the voices under control. To stop me from doing things I don't want to do."

Slowly, my muscles relaxed as the tension dissipated. My hand fell away from my weapon. After a pause, I replied, "Don't shut up for my sake. You've never listened to me before so don't start now."

"There's one moment in my life that's branded into my brain. And in that one moment, there's one sound that stands out. When I went off the rails, I almost lost myself. Zhyire brought me back." He shifted uncomfortably as if mentioning this to me—of all people if you could believe it—was difficult for him. "She told me I was enough, darkness and all. Hearing those words brought me out of a waking nightmare."

Zhyire. The woman—Nivian—who came with him had mentioned a best friend in which he was a guardian for. He gushed about her at the ball, even if he'd never admit to it. By the way her name slipped off his tongue with ease and brought a softness to his eyes, she meant more to him than he was willing to show everyone else.

"How does that help me, exactly?"

"You need to find your focus. One thing that you'll never forget. One sound, one feeling, that leaves you at peace. That leaves you *happy*. Do you have that moment?"

Luka. "I do," I said a little too quietly.

The moment he returned home. With him returned my spark, and my purpose to keep fighting. Why did it always have to be him?

Remy stepped closer, laying a hand on my shoulder. I was far too tempted to knock it off, but I simply balled my hands up into fists. "When those voices get loud, I hear the words she said to me. Nothing else, just that one thing that shifted my worldview. Find your one thing and replay it. Fill your thoughts with it, over and over again. Remember how it made your heart beat, if it made you cry, if it stopped you breathing for a second. The voices will get quieter."

"And what if I can't?" I asked with want that'd been laced with expecting disappointment.

If I hadn't known better, I'd assumed the sun stopped burning, because I'd be damned that he smiled at me. “You can.” He turned to leave, pausing to glance over his shoulder. “See you around, Queenie.”

TWENTY-ONE

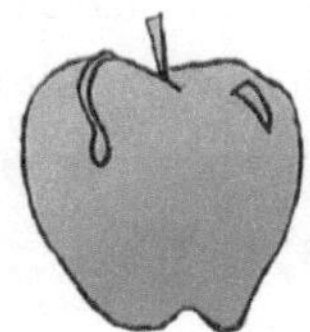

A few whispers brushed by my ears. I pulled the pillow over my head to ignore them, until something loud crashed in my bathroom, and what sounded like a Luka yelled out.

I jumped to my feet and hurried to the door without even bothering to knock. It had been my own bathroom after all.

Swinging the door open, I screamed when I found the naked huntsman on my floor, grunting as he struggled to climb to his feet.

"What the hell?" I yelled out.

Once the imbecile caught his balance, my eyes dropped as my face flustered. Someone had lit a match in my stomach and my body caught the flame, growing hotter by the second.

He ripped a towel from the rack and tucked it around his waist. "I needed a shower."

Droplets of water plopped onto his chest, rolling down towards the sculpted valleys of his muscles. Light reflected off the sheen to his skin. Short strands of wet hair clung to his forehead as if someone had placed them there intentionally. Aside from his parents, maybe there was a higher power out there. Someone had to have crafted Luka to look so much like a god that I questioned if they existed after all.

My fingers itched to run over his damp form.

"You had to use my bathroom?" I hissed. It was enough to pull my mind from the shambles of my own hormones.

"The room I'm staying in didn't have a towel."

The room he was staying in hardly had sheets to begin with. Everinthian had been a castle where one person inhabited it, and two on the rare occasion in Mira's case.

"How did you sneak in here?"

He chuckled, shaking his hair as drops hit my bare skin. He pushed it back. "You're a heavy sleeper, Firefly."

With a roll of my eyes, I said, "You have got to stop calling me that."

"Mm, why? What else do I call you?" He paused to grab a tunic and pull it over his head. "What does the voice say?"

The air rushed out of my lungs. I hadn't been all that interested in the subject at hand. Not after I told him the truth.

The temperature dropped a few degrees. Flesh bumps rose along my skin, wiping away the previous urge to run my fingers over his damp chest. Now I'd rather crawl up into a cave—not his—and vow to never see the light of day again. I'd lay and rot with the corpses.

"You know what he says."

He scoffed as he dropped the towel, sending another blush to my cheeks. He pulled on the rest of his clothes as he waited for me to go on. I'd certainly never seen below the waistline of a man's physique but Luka removed all that curiosity. With what little knowledge I had, I was certain that was the best a man could look.

The sex education in Orsadia had been fairly slim, give or take depending on whether or not your parents taught you. If you happened to have friends who knew, they could spread the information, too. It was a miracle how this island still managed to survive, although I supposed at one point it became innate and we just *knew* what to do.

It didn't stop anyone from experimenting, either.

"He's cruel. He reminds me that I'm not worth much without him. I have nobody who truly cares about me, and he's not wrong about that. He puts me in my place and keeps me humbler than anyone is ever going to see. The world sees a witch. They look at me and they're certain that I'm ruthless and lack all emotions. I've lost the capability to feel anything. They see the pile of dead bodies I've accumulated and accounted for over the years."

That damned pity rested on his face.

"What they fail to see is the crumbling queen with nowhere left to go," Aalia added. "The one who has run out of options. On the verge of giving up. What else is there? What's the point? When the voice is loud and clear about who you are with nobody left to counteract it, you believe it. It becomes you."

"And you become *it*," Mira finished.

A shiver crawled up my spine as I tugged at my chemise. "It's hardly important."

Luka blew out the candles before shaking his head and leaving the bathroom. "I'd say it's far more important than that. My voice is inside your head at all times. How the hell is that even possible?"

"Every queen hears the voice, but it changes for each." Mira circled him. "The voice mimics someone we love deeply. The curse knows how to bury itself under our skin and take control. By using those we care about, it can make us believe anything and do whatever it asks. We're at its whim."

I lifted my gaze, tilting my head. "It grew louder, more frequent when you and I crossed paths again. It hates you."

"Because it is you," Mira said with a hum. "When you returned...

It must have known, somehow. The curse is sentient in some form or another."

"And because I have magic myself," he stated. "My own birth mother was a queen. I'm the first male in all of Orsadia to carry that kind of gene, one where magic is tethered. And like that, I must be tethered to this curse somehow. If it's tied to the queen, so am I." He spun on one heel to lock eyes with me, sending my stomach to the floor. "Because of my mother, that voice isn't *just* one you conjured up alongside this curse to further spiral into oblivion. It's because of *her* that it truly is also my own."

"What are you saying, Luka?" My lungs deflated.

Mira's form glowed brighter as she stepped closer, studying him from head to toe. "He's implying that voice is *reminiscent* of his dark side."

Aalia asked this time, "Dark side?" Half conjured by the curse and Magic Law, half conjured by Luka's connection to me. His magic. *Our* magic acting as a couple.

Dark sides were keen on snuffing out the last flickering flame—that tiny bit of light disappearing beyond the horizon as the sun set.

"We all have one, dear. Some are just far easier to spot than others. Here I believe we've discovered Luka's and it has embedded itself in Snow because it has nowhere else to wait for the perfect moment to strike. With her, it can be wholly itself—truly venomous. She is the embodiment of lost hope, and a symbol of death. She's the perfect victim, and the perfect partner in crime."

Together, Little Raven, we can make history.

TWENTY-TWO

The journey to Hypnotic Arythe had been far too long. Normally I'd have Mira and Aalia tag along. Maybe even Dave. But today I trekked alone for my sake.

Not entirely alone.

Since doing some thinking, I'd noted the way the bridge had been cut before. When Zoe crossed, it hadn't suddenly gave way under all the weight. Someone had intended for that to happen. Who, I couldn't say. Maybe they wanted to kill Zoe, or maybe they wanted me to take the fall for it so Zoe and Luka would turn on me.

There was no need for that elaborate plan. I'd already turned on myself. Even if I wasn't redeemable or worth much, I'd still fix what I'd wronged.

So I crossed the bridge, only to come to a stop when I caught sight of all the trees littered with dolls. I'd seen them a few times but never fully understood what they meant. They didn't come around often.

"Help us," one whispered to my right.

"How am I expected to help you? For fuck's sake, I'm talking to kids' toys." I pinched the bridge of my nose before heading over to the spot where the mansion once stood. It'd be fairly easy to call upon the help of Remy or Kiernan. He'd even revel in my weakness. Which was why I could not give it to anyone.

This was my own task.

"Help us," they repeated.

"I cannot help you. You're made of rubber."

They continued to beg as if they were desperate to send my sanity to the pits of Hades.

"You put us here," one stated.

I halted in my tracks. I whipped around to find whichever it was. "I did no such thing! My magic did not come in its entirety until I became queen. The most I could do was fucking glow in the dark. You're *talking* children's toys. Do not mistake my seconds of compassion for stupidity because, dears, you will find none."

They continued to whisper, their voices growing louder. Repeating the same phrases.

Eventually they grew so loud they overpowered the voice in my head as I fell to my knees and covered my ears, screaming at them to stop.

They never did.

For what felt much like hours, I begged them to shut their mouths and allow me some peace. It had been a lot to ask of them.

Like a switch, everything became unfamiliar.

I scanned the trees. I scanned the hanging dolls. I scanned the worn buildings, uttering, "What am I doing here? Where am I?"

The whispers pierced my hearing and I screeched. "What do you want with me?" I yelled at them.

I pressed my palms harder against my ears, hoping to drown them out. A cry escaped my throat, and then it rushed back to me at once.

I dropped my hands. My ears might have been bleeding, but I couldn't be sure anymore. They clawed at my eardrums as if they'd been a blade slicing across a rock.

"Silence, please," I pleaded once more, putting my hand up—palm out, fingers spread, twisting them in a clockwise motion.

As if they'd listened, the trees grew eerily quiet.

Lifting my eyes to meet the dolls, I searched the eye sockets as a thought occurred to me. "You're not..." I swallowed. "You're all ghosts, aren't you? Haunted toys."

"Trapped," one said in a more desolate tone.

"Trapped in these soulless vessels. And you think I put you here." With a shake of my head, I dropped my arm as it nestled in the dip of my skirt between my thighs. "Because I look just like the woman who truly caged you. My grandmother. The first necromancer."

Which now made it my job to be the one who freed them.

But why had Anne Regali placed innocent souls inside rubber cases all those decades ago?

TWENTY-THREE

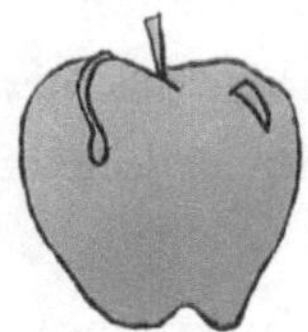

I spent hours searching. I almost climbed a few trees just to see exactly how my grandmother trapped them, and why.

I found myself inside the cathedral, looking high and low.

Nature began to take back what was once its space. Moss embedded itself in the cracks, much like my insecurities did on a stormy night.

The mansion hid no promising answers either.

Swaying just a few feet from the trees, I leaned back against the trunk of one. "Please, you must help. Why did she trap you? Why are you here?"

The whispers began, yet I couldn't make out anything coherent. I reached for a doll head and tugged it towards my head, reveling in the way terror crawled up my spine from the child's voice right in my ear.

"We don't want to be your spies..."

Spies?

"Please, let us go..."

"Wait, go back to the spies thing. What does that mean?"

"We can't promise to be good spies..."

I swallowed as my eyes lifted to the rest of them. Had my grandmother placed them here to be spies? On who? Me? Knowing that Hypnotic Arythe was used for princesses and queens. Queens came here to have a stab at the next heir. Anne knew that, but who else could she spy on? The only person I could think of was me. Her granddaughter. Another necromancer.

Which meant my grandmother had never intended to die so young, at just forty-four years old. She expected to stick around. Somehow... Someway...

Letting go of the head, I backed away from the trees. This whole event felt familiar. Like the word on the tip of my tongue I couldn't quite grasp.

I'd been here before, I knew that. But the details were a little fuzzy.

I didn't like that feeling one bit.

The walk back to Everinthian had been long. Treacherous. Filled with so much guilt and doubt about what my grandmother did to children. Now I had to pluck their souls free to set things right again.

I may have killed, but every life I took had been filled with sin. I never preyed on the innocent.

I hadn't been entirely corrupted.

Had I?

My grandmother was.

Anne Regali had been simply the villain with no redemption after what the world put her through.

And I was my grandmother's granddaughter.

You'd like to believe you're not filled with darkness. Yet you're far more poisoned than you could ever begin to understand. You hate children. You want nothing to do with them.

"I might not be able to communicate with a child. I might prefer the company of adults. I'd never have the guts to take their lives.

That's where I draw the line. That's what separates you from me, Luka," I spat.

"Very rude," a familiar voice commented.

I stopped walking to find Luka standing in my garden with a frown.

"He's your voice."

"I can't even hear him. I can't hear your thoughts. He might sound like me, but he still mimics what he thinks is my dark side. He doesn't come *directly* from me. Not like that."

I shrugged, eyes falling to the dirt. "Not yet anyway."

He scoffed. "What the hell does that mean?"

Clearing my throat, I stopped forward with a hand wrapped around the hilt of my sword. "It means you're still tied to this curse the same way I am. I wouldn't be so quick to disown and shun him."

"You are."

"I have a right to. He's in my head and he's not my voice."

"I'm allowed to shun the side of me that's tied to the curse and would gladly take lives without mercy."

Yet he won't admit just how alike we truly are.

"Shut up."

"Excuse me?"

But you like hearing my voice.

"I said shut up!"

Luka threw his hands up in defense. "I touched a nerve."

I spun away from him and grabbed hold of my skirt as I squeezed my eyes shut.

"Focus." I redirected my attention as the anger fled my muscles. "Focus, Lana."

"Firefly?" Luka asked in a gentler tone.

The moment Mira informed me Luka sailed away, my heart dried up. I'd accepted that I'd probably never see him again. He'd never come home alive and I had to somehow live with it.

Killing Mira had been so easy.

But that day...

The day he had come home after three years and I'd confirmed that Luka had been breathing—the moment I saw his pulse moving as I pressed the blade to his throat—that was when my world crashed.

When he whispered the nickname he created for me.

My entire world had been solidified. Everything returned. Hope. Joy. Whatever was left of my sanity.

Because that had been the moment I knew no matter what, Luka would return. Always. Even after I'd pushed him away, he found his way back. Then he nudged his way in, promising to stay in the castle. After everything... After the highs and lows over the past month, *he came right back.*

When I'd pressed my sword to his throat and saw the green eyes that captured my soul, something shifted.

The curse, that voice, grew louder. Persistent. Afraid. Because it knew that Luka could be the one to change the course of everything like *he* had once.

My chest tightened. My breath caught in my throat. My stomach leaped. But most importantly, There'd been a small squeeze of my heart that signified how important the asshole was to me.

Why did I feel this way about him? Why did it have to be him? We'd been stupid kids once. He'd left for three years.

He left you, and you had to survive on your own. He's the problem.

However, I couldn't ignore that squeeze. He'd come home. He returned safely. It had been all a woman could ask for. And that was it, the one thing I clung to, to quiet the voice that pestered me.

The hug Luka placed on my heart the day he walked back into my life—forever my huntsman. He wouldn't admit to such things, but I knew.

I knew he was mine since he and Zoe made it clear he didn't belong to anyone else.

Here I stood, torn between his venom and the antidote.

TWENTY-FOUR

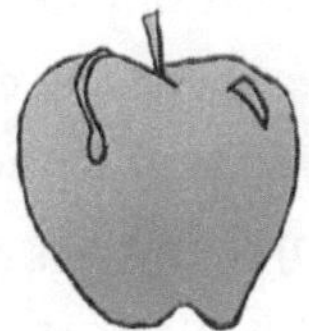

The three of us stared down at the bones laying at our feet, heads tilted and brows knitted out of curiosity.

"So it was that easy huh?" I asked.

Aalia didn't say much of a word before she dropped to the dirt and brushed away some more mud. Tugging at a few vines, she pulled a rib to her own translucent form. "It's been so long, and yet it feels as if it happened yesterday."

Mira watched in silence.

We stood before the bones of Aalia Drecose, all that had been physical evidence of her ever existing aside from the journal. Bones, however, had her DNA.

It pained me to say, "We're gonna have to burn them."

Aalia knew it was coming, yet she clung to them anyway. Placing her skull with what was left—cracked ribs and a missing hand—I stepped back to observe.

"I'll allow you," I said in a quieter tone. "I doubt it needs to be my hand that strikes the spark."

Sitting back on her legs, her gaze stayed glued to her skeleton. "All these decades I was hiding down here in the dungeon. It doesn't make any sense, Lana. I was killed when my term was over. I shouldn't have been inside Everinthian. Who put me here? Why?"

"We'll find out those answers soon. Our journey isn't over just because we've located what's left of you and turned it to ash."

A sob racked through her chest. She couldn't produce the tears a human needed, but that didn't quiet the intentions by any means. "I'm supposed to say goodbye? Just like that? What's left of me and I'm required to accept that I won't exist? It's as if I'm saying goodbye permanently. As if I'm accepting that this was my fate and I'm erasing my own story. By burning my bones, I'm setting in stone just how real it is that I'm never coming back."

The weight of desolation crushed me.

The reality of death. I might have been a necromancer who could play with corpses and a few bones, maybe summoning some ghosts. We'd all die. We'd all go somewhere, wouldn't we? We'd never return to Orsadia, or what we once knew. Luka could sail away and explore other possibilities, and when it was over, he could come back home. But once we died, we could *never* return.

And Aalia knew that once the curse broke, she and Mira had no purpose here and they, too, would go where the ghosts went. They'd never get to see the familiarity. Never experience the comfort in the small things they enjoyed about their life here on our little island.

Someday that would be me. Would Luka go where I went? Did necromancers go somewhere different? Did our magic truly cease to exist?

The ability to love?

Would we be left forever begging to be alive once more?

That had been the entire purpose of leaving a legacy and creating a legend that generations could pass down to keep your name beating.

Aalia would be known as the first queen that started the curse and suffered a horrid fate. What a tragedy.

But I would dare to change that. I refused to allow all of us to be a bitter taste on the tongues of thousands to come in future generations.

Someone had to tell our stories the way they'd always meant to be. Without guilt. Without blame.

There were no true villains in Orsadia. Just those the curse had crafted so delicately as it used the voices of those we trusted to guide us down a darker path, to convince us to make choices we never would've made otherwise.

"Lana?" Aalia's eyes now lay on me. "Are you okay?"

When I focused on her question, the warm tear on my cheek became known, and I wiped it with the back of my hand. "I'm just fine, Aalia."

After another few minutes, she grabbed a stone while I handed her my sword. Then she struck, igniting a small flame at the base of the skull. Mira dragged a few dried logs over to fuel the fire some more. Embers drifted into the air as it devoured all that was left.

Or so we thought.

We stood there for what felt like hours but could have been longer. Corpses turned in their graves as the sun set and flowers shied away as darkness engulfed the land.

"It's not burning. I don't understand. Is it the magic? Curse?" Aalia tilted her head.

When I tossed in a bone from a corner skeleton, we waited to see what would happen. Again, nothing. And this had certainly been an innocent bystander at one point or another.

Mira dropped into a squatting position and pulled one from the fire, and it shattered into a few more pieces but became nothing more or less. "I don't think bones burn all that easy."

"What do we do then?" Aalia's hopeful eyes met with ours. Deep down, she thanked whoever for not allowing her to become yet another memory.

"Try to grind it into a powder, maybe?" Mira shrugged.

We had Dave go fetch a mortar and a pestle before we dropped a few pieces into the marble, attempting to smash it into a fine powder. "This is going to take far too long," Mira stated.

She wasn't entirely wrong.

"Is burning really that important?" Aalia asked. "I mean, I know I started this whole thing but my bones don't exactly burn, and turning it into powder doesn't sound like a logical solution if you think about it. Can we just say this was enough and call it a day?"

I glanced at Dave. "Just to be on the safe side, why don't we all head back up? I'll have a few bodies working on grinding it for us. Fair?"

The emotion fled Aalia as she put on her mask. "That'll be it, then."

We left Dave to it while the three of us went back upstairs.

As much as I felt for Aalia, I had to ensure this curse stopped breathing and with it died the isolation we all forged over the last century.

"You might have been the one to start the curse, Aalia, but take a wild guess at what you'll be remembered for," I said, halting her in her tracks. When she didn't respond, I did, "they are going to remember you as the first queen and the reason we have magic. When this is all over and queens can rule as they please, we will have magic to thank you for. That's not going to go away."

"And what if it does? What if to break the curse, we must return the magic to the fountain?" her voice fell small.

Now it had been my turn to stop. "The fountain? As in where people made wishes once but it sits cold and lifeless?"

I didn't think either of them knew I had no idea where the fountain came into this.

"That's how this began, Lana. The fountain. It carried magic in a way nobody could fathom. I did not. But I made a wish—one desperate enough that the fountain had to sacrifice itself for. I wished I could control dreams. I wished for magic, and that much power could not be stored in both a living organism and the stone from which magical waters poured. Something had to give. It granted every wish thus far, and it was no different with its final. I became a dream walker when I was just a teenager. People had been so fascinated by what I could do, so they appointed me as their queen. It began innocently. But when I moved into the castle, that voice appeared, and then I was coerced into doing things I never wanted to do. It was over for me."

Like that, our kindness began to crumble and we reeked of the decay magic placed upon us.

Maybe Aalia was right and we would be forced to succumb to a magicless fate to put this thing six feet under for good.

TWENTY-FIVE

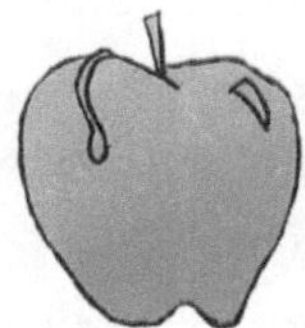

"I have a perfectly decent tub at Everinthian. I'm not sure why you suggest coming to the river," I said as I swept my arm over the dampened dirt.

Luka gaze flicked to me. "We all remember how that went. You couldn't keep your eyes off me."

Heat entered my cheeks. "That's not true at all!"

"You keep telling yourself that, Firefly." He turned away from the water and towards me, pulling his shirt off and flinging it to the grass. "I'm going to go out on a limb and assume that's your first time seeing what a man looks like. I'm flattered, assuming you enjoyed yourself."

Scowling, I waved his assumptions away. "Go bathe yourself like the caveman you are."

He waded into the current, dunking under the surface before emerging in glossy-coated glory and dripping strands of hair. "What did you find on your adventures?"

With a small shrug, I answered, "We found Aalia's bones. Turns out bones don't burn so easy. Dave crushed them however. Hopefully that appeases the curse or gods or whatever it is."

"How has she been handling it?"

"As well as one can when you are required to dispose of what's left of the proof that you were once a person." I swiped my thumb over my bottom lip. "Do you remember Alexander?"

Luka stiffened, the ripples around him dissipating. "Couldn't forget."

My gaze rested at the edge of the river where it met the bank. "Mira always asks me to bring him back."

"Fuck no. Let him rot," he replied almost instantaneously.

I agree with him. For once.

I hated my next words. But I could not lie.

"I've been considering her request," I whispered.

It kept the voice quiet.

After a pause, his voice dropped. "Why?"

"Because, Luka, I cannot bear the thoughts. I brought her back to become my little marionette and would it not be fun to impose the same fate on a man who once kissed me?" Feelings that had never seen even an ounce of light began to surface. "It was a kiss. He didn't take my clothes off. He didn't force himself on me in a way that I had to cry and beg him to stop. He didn't cause physical pain. It was a *kiss*, Luka, and it would have been no different if he had hugged me without asking." I took a few steps forward. "You did that to me once, too. And I returned the favor."

"Are you comparing me to him?" Venom seeped into his tongue.

Bending at my knees until I lowered to his level, I shook my head. "No. I'm simply saying that kissing me wasn't that big of a deal after all. I threw it out of proportion."

He swam closer to me, his olive eyes darkening to a forest green. "Don't you dare excuse or justify his actions. Did you ask him to kiss you? Had you in any way implied interest in him?"

"I may have," my voice came out barely below a whisper. Swallowing my pride, I continued, "I joked about liking him before when he didn't speak. He took it as a sexual favor. I meant it as his voice annoyed me." A shrug.

He growled. "You knew the asshole for one day and that meant you wanted to kiss him? I had to spend months with you before I could decipher that you'd receive my affection well. That does not give him the benefit of the doubt. He does not get to play the *woe-is-me* card. He tried to kill you. He attempted to use you to end the curse however he saw fit, whether it was marrying you or killing you. Do not mistake that for affection, Lana. He meant all the harm and ill-will."

"Then why did I end up the villain?"

You're too easy to manipulate.

Without thinking, Luka reached for the skirt of my dress and yanked me down into the river. I went under before I gained my footing and broke the surface, shoving him back as he laughed. "Asshat!"

"I couldn't enjoy myself all alone. It's a warm spring day." His eyes roamed the trees and fluttered with the birds.

The water had been far too cold, but not as freezing as it had been back in autumn three years ago.

Grumbling, I tried to wring out my hair. "Now my dress is clinging to my body and I despise the feel of it, you wretched ogre."

Luka closed the gap between us. "Allow me to help get it off, then."

"Why—you've already ruined it."

"Water ruined your gown? How do you get it clean? It'd take much more than that, and I doubt with it on you, it could ever look damaged." His hands snaked around my waist as he pulled us deeper, to the center of Keenain River.

Shoving his hands away, I stumbled back in the mud. "My boots are ruined, too, you bullheaded rat."

He cocked his head. "Please, keep coming with the insults."

I yelled out and tossed water in his direction. His laugh turned maniacal as he threw some back, only for my frustration to sizzle hotter before I lunged for him. My hands grabbed his shoulders and forced him under, but all too quickly he hugged my waist and twirled us around as my hair whipped into my face. I managed to open my eyes—albeit my vision was murky and distorted.

My legs slipped between his, tangling him into my grasp, as *if* he wanted to fight it. He embraced the lack of oxygen and pulled me against him to the point I couldn't place my hands between our chests. Starting to struggle for air, I flailed my arms as I fought my way to the surface and gulped for oxygen. I fell back, away from Luka.

"You should never speak his name again, Firefly. It's him that's the curse. He is the vermin and I will never allow you to believe otherwise. Is that understood?"

Clenching my jaw, I swam to the edge until the water level lowered to my waist. I stopped and spun to face him. "Don't you tell me what to do. I'm *your* queen. I'll never let *you* believe otherwise," I mocked.

He marched through, against the current, before stopping just inches before me. "Say that again. I dare you."

"Don't tell me what to do," I repeated slower. "I'm your queen. Or did you forget?"

“I’d be more concerned about how thin that dress is than making fun of me right now.” His eyes darted to my chest for a split second.

Looking down, I spotted the exact shade of my nipples. Warmth flooded my cheeks. “I shouldn’t be ashamed for being a woman, nor should I feel inclined to hide it. You have self-control, don’t you?”

Before he could open his mouth, the words tumbled from mine, “You didn’t forget who your queen is, did you, Luka?”

We all forgot, Little Raven. You barely act the way you're supposed to—all powerful and ruthless.

"I could never forget. You won't allow that, will you?" His hand raised just in time to grab hold of my jaw, yet I received no hostility or intentions that he wanted power over me. "You are my queen, but I will raise hell if I ever hear his name leave your tongue again. He caused you pain, even if you've decided three years later to believe otherwise. I hold no forgiveness towards a man as vile and callous as him. He was far more a curse than my voice will ever be inside your head and you know that. Don't pretend you can't admit that anymore." As I bared my teeth, a mischievous glint struck his eyes, the corner of his lip tugging upwards. "Don't tempt me. I won't hesitate to shut you up myself." Dropping his hand, he circled around me and climbed out of the river. "Let's head home, shall we?"

I didn't deserve a soul as pure as his.

TWENTY-SIX

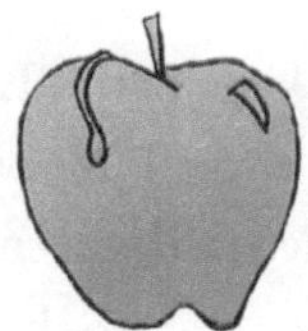

Mira and Aalia took Dave to search for whatever else we could about the curse. Going through the journals of every queen over again. Searching the dungeons, and even the tunnels that led to what I labeled the catacombs under the graveyard.

They found no clues.

That didn't stop a few people from giving me dirty looks when I entered the village. I kept my distance, not too energized to inflict fear.

Despite the voice begging me to do it.

I debated mentioning to the ghosts and the huntsman what I discovered about the dolls, but I concluded they'd never be able to hear them. Zoe hadn't. Why would I willingly admit my own grandmother shoved children's souls into toys for decades? It'd been cruel. I wanted no affiliation with it. They would never be able to help me free them.

The words slipped from my mouth, "They used to shout praises in my name. Now they whisper it as if it were a curse." As if saying it would guarantee a dreadful fate for their future.

Maybe it would.

Luka scanned the few residents we had left. "They hate you. They fear you. Is that truly what you want?"

A small shrug. Eyes cast down. "If I can't fail the people, I can't lose them at all."

He swiftly moved to block my path. "Is that what this is all about?"

What else would it be about? Nobody asked what I wanted growing up. I'd been delegated the next heir without any say in the matter. I never wanted to be a leader. I didn't want that kind of pressure. I didn't want the world in Orsadia to be speculating my every move. I'd been given magic that came with high expectations—along the same line of endless judgment. I never really had a chance when the world decided where I stood no matter what I did.

"Have you never been asked the question: would you rather be the hero or the villain? Younger me used to answer hero. As I grew older, I understood the importance. It wasn't as simple as being the good or the bad guy. It's more of a question meant to make you think, to consider your answer. Being the hero means living up to high expectations. It means never catching a break from the impending doom. You will never get to rest from the eyes of the public. If you do one wrong thing, you're scrutinized. When you become a villain, people expect the worst. If you don't live up to those preconceived notions they have, it makes you look better. You cannot fall from a pedestal if you're buried in a coffin."

"Asking if you can handle the responsibility or want to relieve yourself from it altogether," he muttered.

"Absolve me of the role model position. I do not want it. I never asked for it. I certainly cannot live up to it." I fingered the handle of my sword. "The answer seems so simple now. I'll choose the villain over the hero. I can only go up from here, much like the corpses I raise from graves."

Our time spent in the village hadn't been much longer after all. Luka purchased a few fruits, then a few meats and cheeses. I kept my distance for the comfort of the people.

That'd been why we could never work. He'd been a man of honor and integrity—I anything but. If people saw us together, they'd name and shame him. They'd throw stones. I refused to be the reason people judged Luka.

The way they smiled at him made me realize I had never once received such gratitude from anyone. I'd never experienced what it was that made people happy to see someone. Before I became the princess and let them know of my magic and the future I was destined for, it was Fallon.

Because of his sexuality, it had been my relation to him that made others never entirely show me what compassion looked like.

I entirely blamed the people then. Fallon never deserved an ounce of hatred for who he loved. Our parents—Mother and Father when he was alive—had always supported him. I'd done so. Why couldn't anyone else?

They'd never show us acceptance.

Had it been that way for every queen? Most had been heirs long before their magic came on. Even if they were guaranteed to become the next queen, being the daughters and granddaughters of well-known monsters seemed to dampen the spirits of everyone they came in contact with.

From the beginning, we'd been bred to become exactly what we were. The people of Orsadia ensured that.

And we all took the fall for it.

Luka returned and handed me a piece of bread. "What? Why do

you look as if you've seen your brother?" He twisted his head to search, and when he came up empty, he faced me.

"Do people always treat you with such kindness? Are they always that pleased to see you?"

Shrugging, he bit into a dried meat stick. "Not particularly. I was the huntsman who worked for the queens for a minute. After I started working with you, people had been weary. They opened up more when I came around by myself. They learned that I'm not just a story they've heard time and time again."

My head tilted slightly as I pursed my lips a tad. "What's that like? To feel such joy radiating off another human being?"

Aalia and Mira waited in curiosity, too. Mira had never once experienced that herself, for her own mother was a queen. Mira's name had been stained from the day she'd been conceived. A horrid fate to succumb to.

He hesitated for a moment when he caught our gazes but eventually settled on telling us.

"It's warm. It fills you up like a hot bowl of soup on a winter's night. You can't help but feel a little excitement as if you've finally found a place to belong. It's a feeling you never want to let go of. It makes you feel complete." He finished off his stick before washing it down with some water, then wiping it from his upper lip.

Who needs to be loved? Certainly not us. Hatred—despair—demise, it all fuels us.

Maybe it did fuel me. Maybe it was an addiction to bathe in the conflict.

Exhaling, I said, "Well, when Zoe succeeds in reducing me to nothing, please stick by her during her ruling. She's gonna need *you* the most."

Before he could get out a word, I ripped a bite from my bread and stalked back into Ash Forest.

The arrow struck the heart of a quail. It plummeted, and I was right there to scoop it up.

"It's vile to do such things in front of your friend," Luka echoed behind me.

I scowled as I turned to make a remark about how we weren't friends. Once I spotted Jerry peeking out from behind his hair and over his shoulder, I snapped my jaw shut.

Luka grinned as he patted his little head. "It's also rude to take my stuff without asking, but who's counting your wrongs?"

"Apparently you," I mumbled.

I was gonna say me, but seeing as we know where I came from...

I'd been keeping note of my own sins myself. Every last one tucked away in my head, pulled when I needed a reminder that I wasn't a good person and I never would be. There was no such thing as redemption when it came to the queens.

I kept track to remind me of my place. I wasn't above anyone. I lay below them instead.

I stalked over, dropping it into his open palm. "You're welcome. I figured I'd catch your dinner for you."

With a snort, he swung the bow onto his shoulder. "Yeah, I doubt you did all that for my sake."

Something snapped in the distance. We froze.

Luka put a hand up instinctively, then with carefulness, he pulled his bow down. I handed him the arrow and tossed the quail as he pulled it back against the bowstring.

My vision grew a bit fuzzy, my mind drifting in the fog.

A rotting creature stumbled from the brush.

Luka groaned and lowered his weapon. "Dave, you're causing more ruckus than there needs to be."

For a moment, the name didn't register. *Dave?*

“Why did you follow us?” he asked, dismissing him with the wave of his hand and a snort. “You can’t answer that.”

"He's a corpse," I let out in a rushed whisper. Was he coming after me? Why was he looking at me like that? Had I done that to him—made him into such a monster? Had I ended his life and he was coming for revenge?

"He's your corpse," the huntsman corrected. "Which definitely means I meant what I said about him.”

Like the ocean waves, it hit me when I hadn't been looking.

Did you forget, Little Raven, just how grand our power is?

"Dave," I repeated. "My corpse."

Turning away from them, I touched my face. A small knit of my brow. It had been just a *silly* fluke.

Maybe even the curse.

Ah, yes, because flukes happen multiple times.

No.

Because whatever had just happened didn't make sense otherwise, and I wasn't so sure I wanted it to.

“He just follows me everywhere,” came out so quietly I was sure Luka hadn’t caught it. “He’s lonely like me. Great company to keep.”

The huntsman’s brows shot up, letting me know he had heard me after all. “I thought I was your bodyguard?”

“I didn’t say that’s what Dave was.”

“No, but you implied it.”

“I implied he’s,” I paused. “He’s a friend.” I pressed my lips together. A friend I had somehow *forgotten* about.

The sun rays spilled through the trees, specks falling on the vibrant green grass I had so lovingly tainted with a dead bird, and another walking creation of my own doing.

"We should head back." My fingers wrapped around the hilt of my sword as I looked up towards the leaves waving at me courtesy of the gentle breeze.

The world hadn't always been so kind in Orsadia. It portrayed itself as such by giving us sunshine and warmth, as well as the most striking nature you could ever find on a morning walk.

But behind all the beauty on the surface, there'd be dry soil and crumbling structures. Decaying bodies. Ghosts forced to haunt what once was—forced to face the world and watch it grow and change without them. Their influence had no bearing these days.

I had been living proof of such deceit.

What a vile world we breathed in. A world in which we allowed into our soul to take root and promise to take back what it rightfully owned. Moss in the crevices. Weeds protruding from cracks in a gravestone.

When the sun would set and a new moon was beginning to turn, I was the one left with my memories. And sometimes, not even that.

TWENTY-SEVEN

Dave had been the first to knock the candle off the wall as it clattered to the ground. Clumsy as always.

He mumbled as he tried to right his wrong only to lose an eyeball. Then a hand. He could never keep it together.

Why did that provoke Luka to ask, "What happened after we kissed? I left. Then I return to everything I see here." His eyes danced around like a couple during the waltz.

"What is that supposed to mean?" I cocked an eyebrow. "Everything you see here?"

"Firefly, do you need me to answer that question?" His gaze darted to my dead friends.

Such distaste coming from a man who claims to love you.

"He does not love me," I muttered.

"Hm? What was that?" Luka shot me a puzzled look.

Instead, I said nothing.

With a shiver, I summoned Dave to grab me a cloak. The crisp spring air had been fairly cool this morning. Dew on the grass, a chill in the air. The wind had not been so nice.

When he dropped one around my shoulders, Luka waved him away before clasping the metal together.

It warmed me a little, but I gave most of the credit to his body heat radiating an inch away. "I went to find Mira. To get the battle over with. She informed me that I was supposed to die and the sins I killed were real human beings. She never expected me to go through with it."

"But you convinced yourself they weren't people," he added.

Nodding, I dropped my head. "I was supposed to die that day. The way to defeat the curse would have been to kill myself. To sacrifice my life for the good of this land. I didn't do that as you can see. I was selfish and stubborn. Instead, I killed Alexander—"

He tensed at that name but recuperated with a breathing technique.

"Then I took Mira's life. She told me I was a necromancer. Like my own grandmother, I am the curse. That's why I was required to die for it to all be over. I should have listened to her. I regret not laying down my life. I see now that I've only perpetuated the situation with so much death that I breathe it. It's because of Kiernan and Esmira that I see I'm an anthology of nightmares in the flesh. I wasn't made into a curse, was I? I was born as one. There is no hope for necromancers." I glanced at Mira and Aalia. "As much as I can, I'm going to help end it."

"What does that mean?" His brows knitted together. "Lana, tell me what that means."

If you end me, Little Raven, you will be nothing. You will have nothing. What comes after that?

I already was. And I'd already burned all my bridges.

Mira said, "She's going to sacrifice her life to make things right again."

He grabbed my jaw, fingers sliding up my cheeks to force me to face him. "No. Absolutely not. You don't need to die. Don't you dare suggest such a thing."

A humorless laugh escaped my throat. "What are my options? Have my magic stripped from me and allow the people of Orsadia to burn me alive instead? At least if I do it myself, I can restore some honor to my name."

Honor? Oh. No, dear, that's never going to happen. What you are is far more magnificent with that deadly magic at your fingertips.

A hand slid into my hair, fingers tangling as he rested his forehead to mine. "I won't let you do that."

"I'm not asking you."

"I should've stayed. I should have stuck by your side even when you shoved me away. That kiss...it meant far more to me than I ever let on, and I'd been anticipating it for far too long. I couldn't get you out of my head for more than two seconds. I can't keep you out no matter how hard I try."

"Apparently I can't shut you up in my own," I managed to joke, despite my voice coming out so small.

"So it meant something to you, too."

Let's focus on something as silly and miniscule as a stupid kiss instead of making sure we stay in power.

It wasn't silly. Or miniscule. Not to me.

But I wouldn't admit that to Luka.

"Even if magic somehow manages to weave its way back into humans, at least with my death, there will be a guarantee necromancers never return."

"Lana." His throat bobbed.

My warmth returned to the earth, my skin as pale and cool as a body fresh out of heartbeats. "I'm being serious. There is no other option here. I have to sacrifice myself. It's something I'm willing to do now that I've seen the error of my ruling. Allow me that."

A frown disgraced him. "You're avoiding talking to me about our kiss."

I shrugged. "There's no reason to talk about it."

He straightened his posture, his head now raised inches above mine. "I beg to differ."

"Beg all you want, huntsman. I'll give you zero satisfaction. I even quite like when you beg."

The hand that held my jaw slid a bit, his thumb running up the dip in my throat. "Why? What are you so afraid to admit?"

My eyelids grew heavy, but I kept them open just for my sake. "Who says I'm afraid? Discussing something as ridiculous as a kiss three years prior is a waste of our time."

His eyes narrowed, searching mine. Wading through secrets.

Don't let him in, Little Raven. He wants to rip you at the seams. Study you. Destroy everything you've worked hard for.

Luka couldn't truly care about me. Nobody could. I certainly didn't.

A popping echoed and my eyes glassed over as my back stiffened.

"What's so wrong with our feelings?" he asked softly.

Look at what you fucking did. Useless.

"Hey," Luka repeated, grasping my chin until I met his eyes. "Ignore him."

"The voice? I try." I tried to replay the exact moment Luka returned home. The way my heart squeezed, knowing he would always come back to me.

I'm still here.

I fought harder, closing my eyes to think only about that moment. That single memory of Luka.

"Firefly," he whispered. "I'm right here."

My eyes shot open as he grabbed hold of my cheeks.

My headache began to dissipate as soon as a familiar voice echoed inside my mind.

I'm here. He can't hurt you when I'm here. Listen to my voice.

"How are you doing that?" My heart swelled as my eyes widened.

His lips didn't move as I heard him again, promising, *I manipulate sound, Firefly. He's a sound in your head—my voice. He's our magic tethered together. I figured it was time I found a way into your thoughts before he fed you more lies.*

I swallowed, not sure how to respond to that.

"Within a certain distance, I'll make sure it's just you and me. Not the curse. Fair?"

I nodded just a hint before I heard it again.

At some point I stopped trying to keep you out of my mind. I let you take over. You are the queen after all, far more powerful than I ever imagined. I let you wreak havoc on my sanity.

I had to hold back whatever lump formed in my throat. Tears threatened at the brim. "Luka," I forced out in a choked whisper.

I won't let you go. You'll have to kill me before I ever let you out of my sight again.

"Stop," I breathed as a tear slid down my cheek.

"Stop what?" He wiped it, but more followed.

"Stop trying to guilt me. I'm trying to be the bigger person for once. Allow me that."

I'll never allow any decision that removes the happiest memories from my life. You are forever embedded into every layer of my body and soul. I'll let you have control however you wish. If I die, you can take my bones as your own, for I am entirely and undoubtedly yours until the world ends.

"I loathe you," I sputtered as the dam broke and my cheeks soaked in the pleas of my heart.

"And I'll be the one keeping you alive. That has always been my oath. You're my reason for breathing, Lana. *You* alone."

TWENTY-EIGHT

I hated that he put that responsibility on me. How dare Luka love me so deeply that I couldn't properly look in the mirror at the woman who'd ruined an island?

He needed a reminder, didn't he?

The huntsman had to know how ruthless and poisonous I was. My heart black as night. Soul as rotten as the corpses I dredged up. I wasn't worthy of his feelings.

I trekked in search of answers. I'd gather just a few more corpses, even, to show him that I didn't deserve his undying affection.

I should never have been loved that much.

"When he sees my army, he'll be horrified. I want him to move on from me," I mumbled.

"No, you don't. You cling to him. You breathe because he's always by your side. You want his soul to curl around you and keep feeding you what you want to hear."

"Is that so wrong?" I croaked. "He makes me feel something. But it doesn't change how I'm no good for him. Lana, we're *toxic.*"

My fingertips tingled.

I halted.

"Wait," I let out in a hushed tone. "Someone's...dead."

Allowing the tendril of death lead me to the body, I found a woman sprawled in an unnatural position. Seeing the berry stains in her palm and seeping under her nails was the answer. She'd eaten the wrong berries and lost her own life.

"Serves you right, Gemma," I spat on her.

Her skin paled in comparison to my own, bluish, her eyes rolled back.

Growing up, she was one of the girls in the village who had bullied my brother and made sure I went down with him.

"Now it's my turn." I snapped my fingers as her form straightened and she lifted to her feet. "Follow me."

Luka would see the extent of my corruption.

"What in the hell are you doing?" Mira's eyes bulged as she halted in the doorway.

I glanced at my new creation with the tilt of my head. "I'm having a little fun. Experimenting. Besides, I need a few guards. If Luka is going to take seriously the idea that I cannot sacrifice myself, then that means nobody is allowed in this castle. I cannot have any outside persuasion that makes the voice louder. Understood?"

Aalia yelped as she spotted my craft. "Lana." She stalked slowly towards me, hands out as if I were a child ready to flee. "We can talk about this."

"There's nothing to talk about." I grabbed the head, pulling the upper body up and sitting it against the wall. "Dave has been gathering me all the sand. They look much more human and life-like this way."

I'm utterly impressed.

"Snow, she's dead," Mira cut in. "She's a dead body. What are you planning to do with her? There is so much... Oh fuck. I'm gonna be sick." She turned from the room and sprinted down the hall.

I rolled my eyes as I wiped some blood from my hands on a cloth. "She can't get sick. We all know that." With a shake of my head, I faced the corpse. *Fresh* corpse, that was.

"Lana..."

"Lana, what..."

Now it'd been Luka's turn to question my sanity.

“I didn’t do it. I found her like this. I swear it.” But why would they believe me? “I can’t let her go to waste. She can right her mistakes this way. I didn’t take her life. That has to count for something.”

He came closer, but I ignored his presence, instead washing my hands of blood in the bucket while I pushed aside a bag of organs and waved Dave over as he entered with more sand.

"I can control her this way," I whispered. " If she’s my doll, I don't need to sacrifice myself for the greater good. You didn't want me to, right? I didn’t kill her," I repeated the last part over and over.

"This was not what I meant! You did not have to do this!" He came closer. "Look at me for universe's sake!" When I glanced up at him while sitting on my legs, he dropped to his own knees. "This is not you." He choked on a sob, reaching for my shoulders. "You can't use their bodies."

I clenched my jaw, scrambling back from his grasp. "Why? The same people who throw stones at princesses. The same people who have always painted us in a black light. These people look at my own brother as if he's the fucking abomination! Boys used to beat him until he was bloody and bruised! Fallon had never harmed anyone before that," I screamed. "Orsadia could use a fucking clean slate. I'm doing us all a favor and showing them what they can become, the people who've made this a miserable place to be. I will not apologize for that. I found her already slaughtered. You can join me or join them, but I will not sit here and be ridiculed any longer. You cannot straddle the fence, Luka."

He stood. "Fallon? You mean the brother you disowned because he did exactly as you are now? Stop being a fucking hypocrite! Do you support murder or don't you?"

Before he could intimidate me some more, I climbed to my feet, marching up to him. "Have you met me lately? You left for three damn years! You left me here all alone, and I'd killed at least nine people before I became the queen. I'm the one living with that! They made me this monster. If I can't beat them, I join them, don't I? I despise me just as much as they do, but without the strength to fight this curse, I've given in. I've already dug my grave and now I'll lie in it. Don't you see? I'm nothing if not the Poisonous Queen. That has been my destiny all along. I'm no good. I do not deserve your undying devotion. If I crave the taste of blood, I'll do it for a good cause. I will not apologize for mocking the lives of people who have never provided anything more than shame to this land. I'm not insane," I said in a quieter tone. "I'm not losing my mind. I simply want Zoe to have a better chance than I have. She cannot succeed if she rules over people who refuse to see farther than their own asshole.

"Mira was raised as the daughter of a queen. They outcasted her from the beginning. They made her feel as if she were lesser. Already a curse. Even if Mira knew what awaited her in this castle when her turn came, they made matters worse by treating her as such. These people do not believe in change. They do not have hope. They do not believe in the good of our future. They've convinced themselves that it will never get better to justify the way they live. The way they raise their own children to bully other children for who they might love. They do it without an ounce of guilt. What absolves them of that responsibility? Better yet, what makes them so special that they cannot be harmed for such actions? They're not untouchable. They're going to learn they should be absolutely terrified and begging me for mercy just so I might not use them after their death."

Extending my arm towards the body filled with sand, I twisted my fingers until my magic pulsed within her, bringing her back as she stood to her feet and waited for a command.

I'd scooped out her eyes first. Then, I drained her blood. Emptied out her insides until she'd been hollowed out for me to fill.

It had taken me hours to perfect, but now she appeared at least horrifying enough to ward off the rest of the residents. To warn them of what was coming.

"I think she's absolutely flawless," I mumbled as I fixed a strand of hair. "I never realized that dolls could be so much fun. Don't worry about your looks, darling. Being pretty isn't what we're going for. I just need you to cause terror until all I can hear are the screams of all those who ever wished ill on anyone innocent. You're my proudest creation yet." My frown deepened as I sent her out of Everinthian Castle and towards Ash Forest.

I'd never claimed to be a good person. I knew my lack of worth. Was it so wrong if I hadn't murdered her? Was it wrong when I remembered the way she'd scolded and hit her *own* child for speaking out of turn?

"Please don't look at me like that," I let out in a whisper. "I know I'm a horrible person, but what good is that if I don't use it to make right what was once wrong with the bad apples?"

Luka ran a hand down his face and let out a sigh. "What ever am I going to do with you?"

TWENTY-NINE

My heels echoed throughout the Great Hall as I twirled and plopped down onto my throne, a fist resting under my chin. "I've been...thinking a lot."

Fallon barely budged an inch. He said even less as silence hung heavily.

"Three years ago, I treated you poorly."

"Poorly is an interesting way of putting it," my brother replied coyly.

I released a sigh. "I'm disappointed in myself. And we both know Mother thinks the lowest of me. Father would be the one telling me that I fucked up. Not in those words exactly, but the same idea. He would be right." A frown dragged me down. "I saw you brutally beat those boys to death. It crushed me to see that side of you. I always believed that I could protect you and keep you innocent forever. It was foolish of me to think that. That's not me pinning blame, either. At some point, I needed to loosen my guard and let you be yourself."

Lifting his chin higher, his gaze honed on me. "I haven't killed anyone since. You thought I'd become a monster like you."

It certainly stung. But it wasn't anything I never deserved.

"I know. I kept comparing myself to you when I should have known we aren't the same. I might lose control. I might become bloodthirsty after my first kill. Or *seven...* You were never me. You were the mediator. You've always hated conflict even when it's necessary. That's why I had to protect you. I wanted to keep you safe. You didn't deserve to experience the hate and awful things those boys said and did. I'm sorry," I whispered.

He swallowed. "Don't you understand how difficult it is? You always pushed us away. Me, Mom, Dad. Do you ever think—" His face became a wreck as tears poured down his cheeks. He choked on a sob, turning away to try and hide it, or to recollect himself. Both, maybe.

I shot up from my throne, rushing over to him. "I do think, Fallon, all the time about Father. I think about how horrible I treated him. I wish I could take it back." By now, his emotions became mine. Together, we crumbled under the weight of every trauma ever placed on us. "I can't take that back," I cried.

"He loved you! He just wanted to see you do better!"

As I fought for air, sucking in breaths between wails, I nodded as much as I was allowed before my neck would snap. "I did, too! But I didn't do better, Fallon! Don't you see that? I'm no different than our grandmother. I'm what Mother feared I would be. And as much as I miss Father, I'm glad he can't see me now. I'm the stain on our family name, Edmilla and Regali alike."

He rubbed a hand down his face as he took in a deep breath when his breathing steadied. "I don't know what you want me to say."

"I don't want you to say anything specific. Just be honest with me. You deserve to at least open up about everything I've put you through." I wiped tears with the back of my hand, then onto my gown.

He swallowed the lump in his throat. "You never let us in. You locked everyone out because you believed you had to do it alone. Look at how that turned out for you, Snow." I shoved down the urge to remind him I went by Lana now. "Now you're a terrible queen and our villagers want your head on a stake. Better yet, your heart fed to the wolves."

Wolves. Orsadia's wolves had gone extinct about a decade prior. On an island so small with many people eating, we had little to survive off of.

It was a miracle that we had anyone left at all.

Maybe I'd talk to Luka when this all was over about importing foods from other places. That entailed making deals and trades. Zoe would fare better as the friendly face.

"I know," I forced out above a whisper.

"Do you know how that feels? To walk through the village and hear how badly people want my sister's blood smeared across the dirt? You're so damn lucky that I can't hold grudges when it comes to you. You're lucky that I've missed you far too much." He stifled a sniffle.

"What are you saying?"

"I'm saying I forgive you. If you'll stop trying to make me feel guilty for what I did." He stepped closer.

Nodding, I pulled him into my arms, fighting back the cries as I relaxed from the familiar warmth. It'd been a miserable three years without my best friend by my side. I didn't want to imagine the rest of my life without my own brother.

The rest of my life entailed the next few months.

When he pulled away, he smoothed his shirt.

A shiver crawled up my spine. "I'm a hypocrite. There's nothing more I can say about that than just admitting my faults. I villainized you for defending yourself yet I'm murdering people under the excuse that they raised their kids to bully you."

"But are you wrong?"

I paused. "No. I suppose not. Nobody else sees it that way."

I glanced over his shoulder to see Dave make his way inside the room.

Fallon looked back. "One of yours?"

"One of my corpses. Believe it or not, I didn't actually kill this one. Right, Dave?"

He nodded, his jaw clacking.

"If we're meeting friends..." He pressed his hand to his mouth. "I should introduce you to someone I've grown close with." My heart leaped. "I made him wait in the foyer just in case this went *poorly*," he joked.

As I nodded in agreement and asked him to bring him up, Fallon sprinted to fetch the guy.

Clyde.

Well...

"I'm Clyde," he said as he extended his hand.

Smiling, I shook it with a firm grip, biting back the urge to say, "*I know.*"

Pulling my hand back, I cleaned up my face some more with my sleeve. "I apologize for looking a little askew." I brushed my fingers through my waves. "So, what is this about you and Fallon being friends?"

He sent a look towards my brother. "Oh? Is that how he introduced me?" He twisted his head back my way. "I assure you we are more than that."

The blush that rose on my brother's cheeks was impossible to miss. "On the plus side, he's not from our world so he doesn't hate you, and he doesn't judge me."

Clyde chuckled as he grabbed Fallon's hand and tugged him to his side, placing a kiss on his cheek. "I could never hate you. You make that far too impossible. Your sister seems cool. I mean, Esmira spoke pretty highly of her. Kiernan agreed a little." He snorted.

At least not everyone despised my guts. It was simply a tragedy that they lived in another world. "You've decided to stay then?" I asked softly. "To stay in Orsadia?"

His brown eyes sparkled when he gazed at my brother. "I couldn't leave if I wanted to. What's left for me? I mean, I was a guard. That was a duty I took seriously. But I was always willing to change my plans for something—or someone—better."

My brother. Fallon Edmilla made a man who came from Anequeco decide to stay in Orsadia.

Maybe between them and Luka, Orsadia could grow in population, too.

I hadn't entirely destroyed my own home.

I just wouldn't be around to see it thrive later on.

"And you promise to take care of him? Protect him? You are a guard after all."

"*Was* a guard," he corrected.

Shaking my head, I repeated, "You are a guard. Queens need guards, and I suppose my dead company could use some...sprucing."

His eyes went a little wide before he adjusted his features and nodded coolly. "Yes. I'll take the position, and I promise not to hurt your brother."

"Good. Because seeing the awe in your eyes and the redness of his cheeks, I can tell that this means more to both of you. While I absolutely approve, I won't hesitate to make threats if Fallon ever comes crying to me because of you. Fair?"

"Yes, Your Majesty."

Fallon smacked his chest lightly. "I told you that you don't need to call her that. She's my sister. She doesn't need anymore of that ego going to her head anyway."

Clyde patted his shoulder. "I'm a guard now. Say, what is that..." His eyes drifted back to me.

"A doll. I didn't particularly end her life, but she'd reproduced for the sake of controlling someone smaller than her. She had nothing but insults for people like you anyhow."

Fallon grumbled.

"And the other guy? Who's alive?" he asked.

"Luka," Fallon and I answered at the same time.

"If he has a bow and arrow pointed at your doll." He shrugged.

I scowled as I gathered my skirts. "How fucking dare he." I hurried past them. "Excuse me while I go scold my huntsman for his crimes."

On my way out the door, Fallon muttered, "That's the same huntsman she has the hots for."

"Oh this ought to be good," Clyde said with a belly laugh.

When I made it to the garden, I yelled, "Luka!"

He swung around and dropped his bow with the arrow still taut against the string. "Firefly."

"I have company," I said as nicely as possible. "Get your ass inside. Leave my doll alone."

Laughing, he pointed. "We were only playing a game."

I shifted my weight to one leg. "Oh yeah? What was that exactly?"

He rubbed his neck. "She runs and I shoot her. Target practice? She's already dead."

Snapping my fingers and pointing to the door, I said, "Inside. Now. My brother and his boyfriend are here."

"Oooh. Time to meet the Mr. and acquaint myself with your family. Again." He jogged over, patting my shoulder the same way Clyde had Fallon. "I'm proud of you for finally saving the rest of us from the awkward reunion." He disappeared while I turned to follow.

Glancing back at my doll one last time, she stood in her respective place amongst my hellebores. Dried blood and decaying flesh with the scent of poisonous plants permeating the air.

Our creation, Little Raven.

Despite how much I despised the voice, I couldn't disagree this time. Part of the curse had made me crave more corpses than I ever had. But I'd only be lying to myself if I didn't admit that I also had a particular taste for decorating my world with the dead. They made for very obedient statues, and even more gothic décor as their bones littered my garden and allowed everything to thrive. Vines and belladonna sprouting from the ribs. A bit of hemlock peeking out of a skull's eye sockets.

I wasn't going to give that up even when this ended. I couldn't. I couldn't even be expected to.

Would anyone ask that of a necromancer?

Did people not wish to give back to the earth in which raised them?

Maybe Luka would accept me even with such a flaw embedded into my soul. I embodied death, and it wore me as its most intricate gown for the ball. Promising. Pristine. Purposeful.

I liked most of who I was, even if I could never say that aloud to another living person.

THIRTY

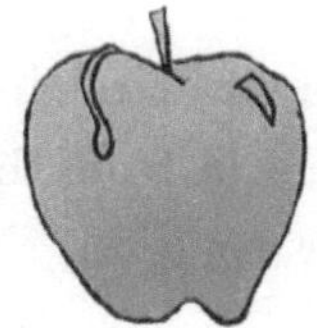

Panic settled into my bones the second I tried to lift my arm to roll onto my side but couldn't.

Eyes shooting open, I started to fight against the restraints that held me to my own bed. "What the hell is this?" I yelled out.

A shadow fell over me and I lifted my eyes to meet the hanging eyeball of Dave.

"Dave! I'm glad to see you. Get me out of this!" The leather straps dug into my skin, rubbing and creating a bit of a burn.

A familiar voice on my other side said, "Oh, he won't be doing anything of the sort. It's time you paid for your sins."

I met the gaze of Mira Sunder.

"My sins? What the hell does that mean? You can't turn against me! I own you!" I kicked, thrusting as much body weight as I could against them. Within minutes, I grew exhausted. How could I possibly fight back? Maybe it'd been a cruel nightmare.

"Oh, but Little Raven, you've committed crimes so far and wide that even your grandmother would admire your tenacity," Mira explained in a more cunning tone.

At that moment, I realized it couldn't be real. It had to be in my head, because that dark side of Luka had *never* once made it out.

I attempted to lift my arms to stretch, only to find myself still strapped. Moonlight poured in from the window. Then I found myself screaming out Luka's name.

"Oh, he can't help or hear you," that stupid dead queen replied.

"Why are you doing this?" I tried to slip my arm through the strap. It wouldn't budge.

She shrugged. "To teach you a lesson. You don't question me. You don't dismiss me. You do not get to lock me out, either. You and Luka both."

Racking my brain for answers, I concluded this wasn't Mira talking. It didn't make a lick of sense. It had to be that voice from inside my head. But how? Another nightmare? No, this felt too real. I never continued nightmares or dreams at a later time in the night.

"How have you been able to hijack my own power?" I asked more quietly, defeated.

She leaned back in a chair and let out a maniacal laugh. "Do you still not understand? I *am* your power. We are one now. Luka can worm his way in and try to quiet me, but at the end of the night, our magic is tethered. You. Him. I'm him inside your head, the side of Luka he doesn't want to admit. We've established that I got louder when he returned, correct? Because he subconsciously linked himself to you *that day* he put an arrow through your shoulder. With your magic coming from queens, the same source all leading back to Aalia and her magic fountain... I am him, a form of him he refuses to acknowledge exists. It had been far too easy for me to latch onto your necromancy and take it as my own. I manipulate sound, *Firefly*," she mocked. "And convincing your brain to release your magic into my hands is something I just do."

As leather rubbed against the raw skin of my forearms, I cried out. "What do you want from me?"

She pulled her right ankle up onto her left knee. "Oh. You think I'll bargain? Unlikely. No, this is all on you now. You and your pathetic little self. There is nothing you can say or do that will get you out of this, or that can convince me to relinquish control back to you."

"And Luka?"

"I manipulate sound—again," she repeated with the rolling of her eyes. "Meaning your precious toy can't hear a thing going on because he's deaf to the world for the night."

I glanced at the leather straps round my wrists. "Fine. I've handled many injuries before. What's a few more?" Grabbing my thumb with my other hand, I dislocated it from the socket and yelled out in pain, slipping it free.

“Bold move to remove access to your opposable thumb. Will it be enough though?” her words slid off her tongue with a seductive hiss—taunting.

Even with four fingers, it wasn't much help. I rubbed my ankle against the leather around my feet, biting into my lip as skin began to fade and a delicate layer appeared below that.

I made no progress in the five minutes that I struggled to angle my feet just right for the buckle. All I had done was remove a protective layer of my own skin.

“Remember the day you dived in to save Zoe when the bridge snapped?” she asked.

I went pale. “Why?”

"That, too, was my doing. When you weren't paying attention, I pulled a few *strings* with your Dave to cut the ropes." She wore a proud grin.

"You wanted it to look like I killed her. You wanted her dead. You just didn't predict I'd jump in after her." I scraped my bottom lip with my teeth.

"You've got it all wrong. I intended for you to end up on that bridge, for *you* to drown. Zoe was just unlucky."

"You wanted me to die? You'd cease to exist."

"Not quite. Zoe would inherit the throne right away. I'd leap from your head to hers. I'd live on after you've proven to me you're worthless," she spat.

I turned away out of habit before realizing Mira couldn't produce saliva.

"Tick tock, *My Queen...*" She hummed.

Wiggling myself down the bed just enough for the strap around my torso to slide up my forearms to my biceps, I lifted my hands to undo it, shooting up once I was loose. I groaned from the pain as my ankles twisted in a direction they didn't really want to go.

I reached down to undo the strap around my thighs, then I removed the buckle on my calves, yanking my ankles against the straps wrapped around them. No buckle.

"Fuck!" I tangled my good hand into the sheets of my bed, my cries coming out between breaths.

"What are you going to do now?" Mira asked, curiosity seeping through her teeth like venom.

I spotted a chamberstick sitting on the nightstand, so I twisted around and reached for it, before grabbing a pillow and throwing it over the top to pull it towards me. When it rolled onto the mattress, it started to fall off the edge but I reached over and grabbed it just in time, yelling out from the leather rubbing against fresh wounds.

Climbing back onto the mattress and facing my feet, I lifted the gilded object above my head. I hesitated, the pain running through my mind at a snail pace, giving me too much time to ponder. I backed out, dropping the object.

"You don't have any desire to break your own bones? Oh, but Snow White, don't you thrive off the bones of others? I figured you were more powerful than this. You're nothing worthwhile." She tsk-tsked.

Continuing to wiggle my ankle, the leather had just a little give until I pulled my ankle out at an uncomfortable angle. I let out a small cry.

Rubbing the strain on it, I then slipped the other leg free.

"I suppose not entirely useless," she commented with an amused expression.

I was, in the grand scheme of things.

I'd been better off dead from the beginning.

Mira reached forward, lifting my sword that had leaned against my nightstand above her head. Her eyes darted to the corner behind me. She hissed as my weapon clattered to the ground. "She deserves to die where she lays."

I glanced back at the dark pit in which she spoke to. Nobody was there. "Who are you talking to?"

The Evil Queen hummed as if she hadn't just been about to slaughter me in my own bed. "Run while you can. I don't stay compliant forever."

I contemplated lying on my bed and giving into exhaustion. But that hadn't been a smart idea. Instead, I swung my legs over the edge and grabbed my sheets, ripping strips and using them to bandage not only my foot, but also my thumb after I shoved it back into its socket.

A minute after gathering my sanity, I clung to the wall and other furniture around me as my ankle throbbed from whatever damage.

When had Luka's room suddenly become so far away?

Approaching the only door between Luka and I, I knocked. Too lightly, until I realized it was my castle and he was simply a guest.

I twisted the knob and stumbled into the room with a gasp.

The huntsman shot up with concern lacing his features. "Firefly?"

Before I could get a word out, he leaped from the bed and grabbed my cheeks without even considering my feelings.

Well... Maybe he was considering them and that was *why* he did it.

"Who the hell did this to you?" His eyes roamed my body, noting my thumb and ankle.

I tried to point down the hall, to get a word out. To say Mira. To utter Dave's name. To mention the curse.

I couldn't quite do it.

He picked me up without a second thought and carried me to his bed, laying me down. When he turned to go searching, I reached out, fingers wrapping around his wrist. He twisted back to face me, brows pinched together.

In a whisper, "Please *stay*," tumbled from between my lips.

He nodded without hesitation. "Let me lock the door." He slipped away to do exactly as he promised before sliding in beside me. His arm slithered around my waist before he tucked me into his chest. "What happened?" His low tone swept over my earlobe, warming every inch of my icy soul.

I'd managed to catch my sanity. "He... Mira." How did I explain to him the curse did this? "She strapped me to my bed. I couldn't move. I couldn't gain control..." I struggled to catch my breath. "She forced me to get myself out of it." I choked on a small cry.

I couldn't do this now. I would not allow tears to form—to let my vulnerability see the dark of night. Or in Luka's case, the rays of sunshine.

He planted a kiss to my temple, beginning to stroke my hair. "I've got you now. You're safe." His fingertips brushed the skin of my forehead. Soft and gentle. Grounding me.

The anxiety fled my muscles as relaxation settled in.

He was right.

For once, I felt utterly safe in my own home. From the curse. From myself. From my *fate*.

THIRTY-ONE

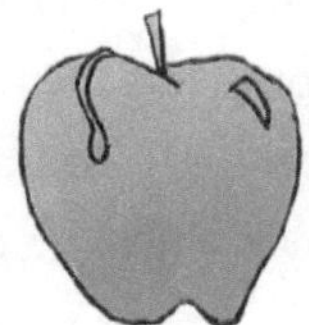

With thick cloth wrapped around my ankle to keep it stiff, I slid my sword from my belt as I approached the trees with a limp. Whispers grew louder, clawing at my eardrums. I needed them to stop. I would make them, too, and not just out of selfishness. I'd do it for the sake of these poor children who'd been trapped for decades inside of toys made just for them.

Now that I was certain I knew how to free them.

"If my own flesh and blood put you in there, it's up to me to get you out. As far as I'm aware, my grandmother used her necromancy magic. You're souls. We can manipulate you. Tell you to do whatever. I've never tried to take control of so many, and a child...but I suppose there's a first for everything if it's for a good cause."

I walked over to the first tree, careful and steady as I took note not to make my ankle worse. A large trunk, rotting from the inside out, with branches so dry, barren, and limp. They all appeared the same way, as if the children had been sucking the life out of them. I couldn't be entirely sure that was the case, but it was one theory.

I placed my palm flat against it and poured my magic through my fingers. It slithered through the wood—roots—latching onto every single tree first and encasing each soul hanging loosely.

My magic worked quickly as if it had been called to this, as if it knew its own purpose and fulfilled it perfectly. A snake burrowing into its prey, only I was using the tendrils to sink its teeth into the souls as I repeated, "Climb out. Use me to climb out."

The souls wrapped around the ends, warm and sorrowful, like a child clinging to its mother when he or she was ill. Small, sharp stinging ensued as they worked their way from the toys, yanking on my magic and testing its limits.

I didn't falter, however. I pressed my palm deeper into the bark as dozens upon dozens of tiny souls used my own strength to fuel theirs. When they'd popped out, I released my hand, whispering, "Be free."

Like so, the children all giggled and laughed, yelling out how thankful they were as they disappeared into the clouds or wherever it was that youngling spirits ended up.

But they were finally safe and sound. Free to be happy. To be children for eternity. I'd at least done one thing right in all three years of my reign of terror.

Then I screamed out as I stormed the trees, slicing every string as dolls thudded to the dirt.

Until every last one had been cut clean and I was assured they had no longer been caged up inside of objects made to bring them joy.

Falling to my knees, my sword clattered to the ground. The souls trapped in the dolls. Sacrifices my own grandmother made to spy on me. And when that didn't work, they became vessels for the dead, further proving that necromancers could not be helped. We were inevitable omens upon ourselves and everyone around us.

Still, Anne Regali did everything she could. Everything she

ultimately tried in the end had been for a reason.

I just hadn't been able to pinpoint what made her question how children's souls and dolls could be used for such things. Maybe because they were innocent.

Footsteps echoed behind me, and Dave grumbled when I glanced back.

Facing him, amongst Mira and Aalia as they trailed behind... What a show.

They hadn't entirely been in control. No, it'd been Luka's dark side.

But that meant nothing. Not to me, anyway. They had still been the ones who caused my injuries.

My foot still throbbed, thumb a dull ache. A warm bath would be my next move, as soon as I made it back home.

"I set right what my grandmother wronged. I set free the souls that'd been trapped for decades," I said in a quieter tone.

You disappoint me.

“But I didn’t disappoint *myself.* Not today,” I croaked.

"Lana!" Luka yelled as he stormed over from the bridge. Shoving aside Dave as he was the only one Luka could touch, he stopped just in front of me. "What's going on here?"

"They're free..." I gestured to the dolls that hung from the trees in dozens.

He glanced at Mira. "And them?"

Shrugging, I slumped.

Twisting himself until he faced them, he proceeded to plant himself between me and the dead. "If you *ever* dare touch her again, I'll make sure you never return anywhere remotely pleasant. That stunt you pulled? Abhorrent. We all know now I am very capable of taking control of her power and banishing you for good. Don't fucking test me."

He turned to me, grabbing my hand and pulling me to my feet. He reached for my sword and handed it to me where I then returned it to my sheath. Without even bothering to consult me, he scooped me into his arms.

I yelped a little, hitting his chest. "Put me down, you puke-green frog!"

"Your ankle is sprained, Firefly. And quite frankly, I don't think I really want to." He started our journey back.

"What the hell does that mean?" I swallowed, unable to sneak a look at Dave, Mira, or even Aalia as we passed them.

He pushed forward with a permanent scowl. "Just relax for once, you damn distress."

THIRTY-TWO

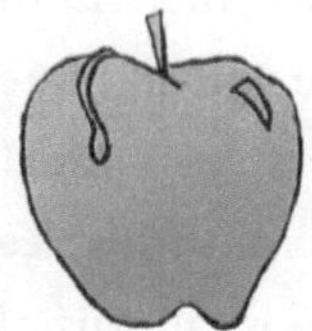

I slowly approached the village, spotting Luka with Zoe. They talked under their breaths, but I lifted a measly finger as a ghost nearby went stiff and inched closer.

After a few minutes, Zoe released a sigh. With a nod, she walked off. I beckoned the spirit towards me just as Luka turned to meet my gaze. We locked in.

Then the spirit relayed to me their conversation, "And so they agreed that maybe after his agreement with her parents is over, they can go their separate ways. For your sake."

"What agreement?" I asked, tilting my head as I fixated on the huntsman.

"Her parents pay him to be her bodyguard. The princess mentioned that if he really wanted, she could continue to pay him to be her knight or guard once she's queen, before questioning why your parents didn't offer the same to him when you were vying for the throne. He explained that he didn't think you'd ever go for it, and you made it abundantly clear that after the kiss, you never wanted to associate with him again."

Brows furrowing, I mumbled, "Offer the same to him?"

When the realization slammed into me, my face fell.

Luka's eyes widened as they darted to the ghost then back to me.

Before I knew it, I was storming over to him. "What the hell? Did my parents pay you to babysit me? All that time you pretended you wanted to help. All the time you all pretended you'd never met each other, but it was some big joke! A façade! I feel used!"

"Lana, I can explain!" He rolled his sleeves in a hurry.

I swallowed. "So, was the kiss all part of the deal? Did they tell you to try and make me fall for you or some shit? They're capable. My father agreed to Alexander's hand in marriage without knowing the man. Everything I ever believed was a lie. You were in it for yourself. Nobody trusted that I could do it."

Clyde lingered behind Luka, putting a hand up. "Slow down. A little dramatic."

Luka glanced at him, then released a sigh. "It had nothing to do with trust. Everyone trusted you, but you still needed some kind of..."

"Bodyguard, Luka. You were my bodyguard. Just admit it."

He ran his tongue over his bottom lip, pulling it in before releasing it. "Yeah. But I genuinely did feel things. It wasn't just one big lie. Yes, I was paid by your parents. But I was paid very little, and it was mostly in food. You can understand why I took the deal, as a man who lived in a cave at the time." When I didn't respond, he went on. "I do enjoy your company. I always have, even if you piss me off at times. So all those romantic feelings, Firefly, have always been my own. Your parents had nothing to do with that. A man doesn't kiss a woman with that much yearning without it being genuine." His green eyes pierced my dark ones. "I'm always fantasizing about doing it again."

Shit, he would be my ruin.

"We all knew you'd never agree to let me be your bodyguard, so that's precisely why we played the role behind the scenes. And given that you nearly drowned in the ocean the day I saw you again after we'd grown up, you needed me more than you'd ever admit."

"I never needed you."

"I beg to differ." He stepped forward. "Who helped train you when we were kids? Then I was there to help you with the seven sins. Now here I am, with the curse. You've always needed me, just as much as I've always breathed you in place of air."

I shook my head, dropping my chin. "You're just a sickness that comes back every season."

"I don't believe that," he said in a quieter tone. "We've always managed to come across each other. Our magic is tethered, but I think there's much more to it. There's no reason why my magic should be tethered to yours. I'm the first male with magic, but no two heirs have ever had that kind of connection. What makes me different, aside from my parts? I kept thinking. Velia, the way she longed for someone to understand her and be her other half... I sympathized with her. And then I came to realize that I already had that." His knuckle rested under my chin as he lifted it.

I pleaded with a whisper, "Don't say it."

"You, Firefly. Even if you'd pushed me away. I'd find my way back to you. We always try to deny what's right in front of us, whether we believe we don't deserve it or otherwise. In every life, we'd always be pulled to one another." His fingers trailed up my jaw before he pushed my hair behind my ear. "I'm quite okay with that."

My heart grew so loud I questioned if I needed a medic as he leaned in.

Then a scream tore through the village just in the nick of time to rescue me. I silently thanked Kiernan and Esmira wherever they were, too.

Until the screaming continued to make my ears practically bleed. Just my luck.

THIRTY-THREE

"Make way," Luka said as he moved people aside while leading us to the center of panic. When he stopped, he dropped his arms. "That certainly...puts a damper on things," he muttered.

When I peeked my head around his shoulder, intrigue seeped into my soul. "How perfect."

Luka shot me a look that told me to watch my tongue, whereas the people around me scowled. "She's dead." A villager, one who had gone by the name of Kera.

I rolled back onto my good heel as pain shot through the other. "Yes, I can see that. Hence why I said how perfect."

"You're too late, *Queen*," a man spat with such hatred.

"Actually I arrived at just the right time." I gestured. "The dead are my specialty." I stepped around Luka and squatted down. "So, make some room and she'll have some life restored."

"Life?" he snorted. "You call your wicked magic life? Don't you dare touch her. You've already managed to ruin everything else in our once beautiful home."

I stood. "Forgive me, Victor," I started in an all-too-pleasant voice, "but I do believe somewhere along the way you learned at least a little about Orsadia's history and our magic, correct? You are aware that we cannot control what we get? How is it my fault if I'm a necromancer? I did not ask to be born this way. In fact my entire family begged for anything else. My parents placed a spell on me as a young one to ensure I wouldn't be harmed or turn out like my grandmother."

He shifted his posture, cupping his elbows. "It didn't work."

"Oh, but you see, I'm far more dangerous if I have no control over my magic. Given the curse and what I know exists, you should be grateful I've managed to handle it. I may not be able to heal people. Again—that is not in my control—but I can offer the next best thing. Bringing the dead back."

He stepped over Kera, placing himself between me and her. "If you dare touch her, I'll ensure you suffer greatly."

"Whoa," Luka growled as he shoved his arm between me and the piss-poor excuse Victor was. "Watch your tone."

Even Clyde stepped forward, pulling out a dagger. He definitely took this guard thing seriously.

I rolled my eyes so hard I started getting a headache. "I'd be careful making threats. I'm still the queen, and quite frankly, I don't always have a desire to do the right thing. You all tend to be much more obedient when your heart stops beating. Why do you think I revel in murder?" I lifted my palm towards the sky, fingers curling inward like an old, withered tree branch in the dead of winter.

"Lana, you won't do that," Luka warned.

"Listen to your boyfriend, Lana," Victor teased with much malice.

"He is not my boyfriend," I said with a scowl. "Luka, stay out of this."

"Yeah, Luka, stay out of this." Victor shot him a twisted upper lip with a side-eye.

"Hey," Clyde started.

The huntsman stepped forward. "Fuck you, Victor. "

Regardless, the man folded his arms across his chest. "So. The huntsman finally works for the queen. The legends have made themselves true. What is it? Does she take her clothes off? Give you what you want? Pay you well?"

Growling, Luka quickly got in his face. "Watch it. I'm trying to protect your sorry ass."

He shrugged in response. "I'm not exactly sure what you see in someone so merciless."

The insults didn't bother me as much as I'd expected them to.

Clyde cleared his throat. "Excuse me, but does anyone around here listen to anything I say? Are we going to fight like children or can we go our separate ways?"

"I'm not exactly sure what your issue is, but in case you were a little too focused on yourself lately, you'll notice now that we've been working hard to break this curse that surrounds all the queens. We could use a little less backlash and a bit more understanding. There's far more you're unaware of than meets your raisin of an eyeball," Luka said with the clench of his jaw.

Clyde shook his head as he pinched the bridge of his nose, mumbling, "I signed up for this."

Victor guffawed. "Understanding? I've watched my community drop like flies because of her. I am not about to understand shit. Fuck you and your support. And what do you even know besides what she's told you? She could be simply feeding you so many lies to keep you complacent before she rips your heart out just to use your corpse as her puppet."

Releasing an exhausted sigh, I shook my head. "I'm not going to bring her back. This is getting ridiculous."

"Someone with some sense," my guard exclaimed.

Victor swung his arm in retaliation but before I was able to block, Luka caught Victor's fist with his own hand just an inch from my nose.

He stepped between us and proceeded to twist his wrist until Victor was on his knees begging for that mercy I never gave people. When Luka gave in, Victor then shouted profanities.

Clyde didn't hesitate to step closer, the tip of his blade pointed at Victor's vulnerable throat.

"She couldn't do that even if she wanted to, Victor, because you see here that we are a lot more alike than you think." Luka squatted to his level. "My mother, *Astrid Lockwood*, would agree that the curse needs to be broken if we are going to revive Orsadia. As Lana has proved with the death of Mira Sunder, murdering her will not be the cure. Zoe will fall into the same pattern relentlessly and she will be coming for you first because I'll be the one to tell her to." He patted his cheek before jumping back to his feet and turning to face me and pull me away. He ached to just scoop me up, but we both knew that was not going to help our case here in front of Victor. Even so, once we'd go far enough, I didn't doubt Luka would be right there to carry me home.

I despised it.

However, he paused, then faced the man still on his knees. "As the first man of Orsadia to be born with magic, I've concluded that Lana does not lie about this curse. I've witnessed it. I've heard the voice. I've seen what it can do to a person, Victor. It's not the magic that has made a villain of all the queens that ever ruled. It's the people who ostracized them since birth in the first place."

Spinning on his heel, he grabbed my elbow and guided me from the village with Clyde hot on our trail.

When we returned to the castle, Clyde greeted Fallon with a kiss while Luka led me up the steps cluttered with bones.

Just as Luka started to shut the door, a foot wedged itself to stop him from closing it. Fallon peeked in before knocking on the door. "Hey. Can I have a moment?"

Luka glanced at me, and I nodded for him to go.

Once he was gone, my brother shoved his hands into his pockets and scanned the room. "Clyde filled me in on what happened. I'm sorry."

"For?"

"You can't be that inept."

"Excuse me?"

"Snow, you're aware that the people despise you. They're not just afraid but disgusted by your presence."

My gaze landed on him. "No need to rub that in."

He shook his hands. "No, no, I'm not trying to rub it in. I'm trying to sympathize."

The cupid's bow of my lips curled. "Oh, don't start with that bullshit."

"What?" His brows knitted together. "What's so wrong with that? Snow, I'm trying to understand, and given what Clyde said, you need someone to."

I slapped my hands against my sides. "What the hell does that mean?"

"It means you deserve to be treated better. It means Victor is an asshole for antagonizing you and Luka. It also means Luka is just as childish for partaking." He snorted a laugh.

Dropping onto my bed, I shrugged. "Honestly, there's no reason to say anything at all. I've been used to it for a while."

He ran a hand down his face. "Just because you're used to it, doesn't mean it's right. It doesn't mean you don't feel some kind of way about it. And as your brother, I'm not about to ignore that. It's been three years without you around. I'm trying to patch up a relationship."

"We could talk about literally anything other than how the people around here treat me." I waved my arm over my lap.

"Maybe I'd rather talk about this." He came over and sat beside me. "You deserved better. And I'm not at all justifying the way you disowned me, or how you shut Dad out, then us. But outside of that, you'd never done anything wrong. Before this curse, it was always about helping the people. They just never had any compassion for you from the start. Before you became the princess, that was mostly because you're related to me."

"Fallon," I said as I swallowed. "Please, don't blame yourself for that. I don't love you any less. None of that was ever your fault. It was always theirs. They've judged you for ridiculous reasons. If they managed to just open their hearts a little and see how Clyde treats you well and makes you happy, they could understand. I wanted to change that for you, too. I apologize for never being able to."

"And now you're trying to take the blame." His laugh restored some hope to my heart. "It's not your fault, either. You can't control how people think, and you can't force them to change their minds. You've always been supportive and that's all I could have asked for growing up. You were my protector. You defended me like the good big sister does."

"That's my job. I'll always protect you. I love you, even if you do piss me off most days. I'm the only one allowed to tease you." I nudged him. "Remember that."

His laughter grew. "Not anymore. Clyde teases me a lot. Mostly about my blushing. But I guess I don't mind it all that much. And thank you, by the way, for giving him a purpose here. He might not tell you but he really loves being a guard."

"I'll need one. Even after my term is over, people will still be vying for my head. You can tell him that, too."

"Will do, Snow." He nodded in mockery.

"You know I go by Lana, right?"

An all too familiar grin flashed. "I do. But I like Snow much better." When he winked, I burst out with my own laughs.

Something tugged at my heart, like a stitch attempting to mend me back together. If I'd been corrupted yet Fallon could forgive me, why did I still loathe my entire existence?

THIRTY-FOUR

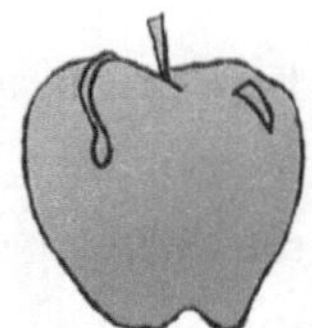

After the way Luka had stepped in, despite my previous protests, I wanted to thank him.

He'd just admitted to another human being that he had the same magic the queens did. He placed a target on himself.

At one point, it became so apparent how much people loved Luka's presence. He came with an aura about him that made others feel safe and at peace. I would tend to provoke the opposite.

As a man who'd grown up without that kind of support or family surrounding him, he deserved it.

But now they all knew he was no different. He had cast himself out of the village and that took far more courage than I would ever have.

So, I stood at the grave of Thomas Hawke. I'd bring him back, just for Luka. Even if he had been dead for so long now... The way Luka had come to my defense told me he supported what I did. It'd be my best gift to him—a chance to laugh and talk once more.

I considered the shovel sitting in the corner for a hot minute. But digging into the dirt wasn't exactly my thing and took far too long. The faster way was to let them dig themselves out.

They certainly did it so well.

I lowered to my knees and pressed my palms into the dirt, sending my magic on a journey into the grave. It wormed its way to the corpse and wrapped around bones, spreading and rattling the skeleton to life.

When the magic snapped back under my flesh, I stood as what was left had already seeped into the bones.

A hand wiggled through the dirt, fingers grazing the surface.

As the corpse clawed its way out, he stood before me, waiting for a command.

"Did you have a nice long sleep?" I asked.

Before me stood just a skeleton, seeing as the weather and the environment had deteriorated whatever else was left of his brother.

His jaw clacked as he grumbled. So, I turned on my heel and led him out of the cemetery and back to Everinthian with me.

Mira and Aalia both eyed him, whereas Dave frowned like a woman who noticed her husband checking out another woman's body. I brushed him off, and so did Luka's brother.

We headed up to his room and I knocked, waiting to hear feet shuffling across the hard floor. "Oh Luka, come on. I have a surprise for you."

He groaned from the other side before finally swinging the door open. "What's this?"

"Thomas. I hope this...makes up for the way I've been acting."

Thomas growled, and Luka stumbled back.

"This is my way of saying...thank you. For what you've done even if I don't deserve it."

Luka's eyes shifted to mine. "What the fuck is wrong with you?" He shut the door in our faces.

The skeleton looked at me as I swallowed. What did I do wrong? Didn't he want to see his brother?

When I eyed the corpse, it became abundantly clear.

I knocked again. "Luka, I thought you wanted a chance to talk to him. You gave me mixed signals the other day in the village when you came to my aid after I wanted to bring that girl back for Victor. Luka." I listened for movement, ear pressed to the door. Nothing. "Luka, I was trying to be nice. I wanted to do something nice for you. I thought it was obvious that I can't do much more with this kind of magic."

"Then don't use it at all, Lana! It's that simple!" he yelled from the other side.

Not using my magic was impossible.

And for him to suggest it, that stung a bit, right in the foot as if I'd stepped on a bee.

I turned to face his brother. "I'm sorry he doesn't want to see you." My shoulders slumped. "At least now he won't try to kiss me again."

Congratulations, Little Raven. He despises you. We've been waiting for this moment to rear its wonderful head again. It's my favorite part.

I waved for the skeleton to follow, taking it to my room instead. I didn't have the heart to put him back in his grave.

Sitting on my bed, I snuck a peek at Thomas. "There has to be a way to find your ghost. Maybe he'd be happier with that instead of the skeleton."

He grunted.

"I'm Lana." I faced him, pulling my good knee up on the mattress. "Luka helped me when I was fighting the seven sins so I could become queen. Now he's back, to help me break the curse."

His jaw clacked some more. I couldn't quite make out the words as he gargled them.

"We're going to find your ghost. Then Luka will *have* to thank me."

THIRTY-FIVE

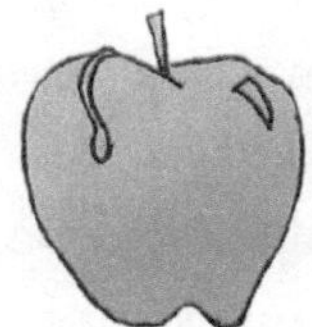

As the sun disappeared beyond the ocean, the moonlight shimmered over the surface.

"We're ready." I turned to face Thomas before we trailed down to the dungeons. It was as close as a necromancer could get to the other side.

I'd once told Luka I didn't really believe in anything after death but I didn't have much of a choice these days given how closely connected I was to their world.

So I knew where they went, or where they were supposed to go.

I led him back to the corner cell. "This should be easy access to the other side. You generally need a very thin barrier between our world and the world of the spirits. And granted this dungeon never sees sunlight anyway, but I wait for the sun to set just to be certain. And not everyone can access it. Being a necromancer, I can reach through the barrier. I'm going to go search for your soul. Wait here."

I pressed my palms along the bricks, feeling for the opening. Once my hands slipped through, I stepped into a very dark and grimy place. Moans and wails bounced around despite the lack of walls. It smelled of smoke, and a light odor of mold.

I called out his brother's name, but very few looked my way.

Grabbing my skirts, I grumbled, "Oh piss off," to a soul trying to reach for me.

I waded through the bodies, ignoring the despair that hung in the air. Eventually it weighed on me. So heavy, I had to stop.

My throbbing ankle thanked me.

Was this where we all truly ended up?

How cruel. How so very uninspiring.

It couldn't be *fair*.

There hadn't been that many people to wade through. Well, I said that but I meant it as there were less than I expected. All of Orsadia had been around barely a hundred years and without proper reproductive health, people either made lots of children or none at all. Or they started, only to never survive past the birth.

There'd been more babies than I thought would be here, but their incessant crying solidified me in my decision to never recreate that in my own home.

Mother would never have me to rely on for keeping the lineage going. Our bloodline died with me.

In a way, that'd been comforting. Knowing even if this curse never was broken, no necromancers would ever exist to wreak greater havoc.

"Thomas Hawke!" I yelled out.

The dead didn't make my job any easier. And as hard as I tried, I couldn't seem to control them here. Which made no sense. I could access this place, yet I couldn't use my magic otherwise.

I eventually began to shove spirits. Some gave me looks, but nobody really did anything about it. Did anyone down here have feelings or a purpose? Did they truly not mind being pushed around, or was it because they hadn't been alive in so long that they stopped caring about anything at all?

I continued to call for him, eventually spotting the one spirit who reacted by turning all the way towards me. "Got you," I breathed as I hurried over with my poor excuse of an ankle, ignoring the cold air nipping at my pale skin as I brushed through ghosts.

When I found him, I grabbed his wrist. "Come with me. You won't regret it."

He didn't have much reason to protest. Could his situation get worse? Precisely my point.

So he trailed behind, and as we approached the barrier that faintly glowed, I faced him. "Not sure how memory works as I've never brought a corpse to life then snatched its soul. I'm Lana."

"Lana," he repeated with furrowed brows. "Sounds so familiar..."

I didn't bother elaborating. Instead, I took in how different he appeared compared to Luka. Luka's hair had been darker, wavier, with bright green eyes. All derived from his mother, the fifteenth queen.

But his brother had lighter hair. Dark eyes. It'd been too short, like he had recently cut it. I'd never met his parents but I assumed he got his genes from one of them, or both.

"I've got Luka on the other side. Just...trust me on this." I turned to step through. As I did, hands and boney fingers grasped my arms. I shouted as a foot hit the back of my knee, sending me forward. It took pressure off my sprain, but that wasn't my point. "What the hell is this?" I asked Mira as she stepped in front of me. Aalia stood to my right, Dave on my left.

She bent down to my level, gripping my jaw. "Oh, Little Raven, did you not anticipate I might come back thirstier than ever? I'm out for blood."

As soon as her eyes met Thomas', his form stiffened. "On her stomach. Now. I want to hear her beg for mercy."

He grabbed a fistful of my hair and sent his foot to my back, forcing me down onto my frontside with an umph. With his knee digging into my spine, he leaned forward and rubbed my cheek into the dirty stone floor. "Start begging, Queen."

"No," I spat.

Mira whistled. "You heard her."

As Dave pinned my wrists to my back, Thomas dug deeper. I groaned, but it was the blow to my side that made me cry out.

I wiggled in their grasp only for another cry to escape as Thomas pulled my head back by my hair and slammed it into the floor.

"Beg."

"Fuck you!" Blood pooled in my mouth.

"Wrong answer."

They sent punches and kicks into my sides, arms, head, and everywhere in between. I couldn't even get my magic to wake up. I couldn't take back control.

"I've got a better idea," Mira said, causing Aalia and Thomas to pause. "Get her to her feet."

As they hoisted me, the blood from my mouth dribbled down my chin and stained my rich green floral dress.

With her in the lead, they guided me through the castle and out the front doors. Stopping in front of a tree, Mira instructed their every move, and they shoved me back against the trunk, palms pressed against my shoulders. Once Mira found the rope she needed, she had Dave wrap it around me and the tree, knotting it.

"I like you this way." She tilted her head as she stepped closer.

I leaned my head back into the bark, swallowing. "What way is that?"

A new, unfamiliar face appeared a few feet behind her, beside Aalia. Someone who emitted far more power than anyone I could have fathomed on my own.

"Powerless. Covered in all your own sins." She stepped back. "Allow me to do the honors." She grabbed a few stones, bringing them to my feet. Aalia fixed the bottom of my dress. Mira struck the rocks together a few times until sparks caught my skirt, a flame roaring to life as oxygen fueled it.

The heat grew unbearably, and so much so that I started to beg. Despite my pleas, they didn't douse the fire.

"Lana!" Luka sprinted out screaming bloody murder—and he hadn't been wrong about that.

Mira stepped back just as the dark side subsided and magic tingled at my fingertips.

I didn't use it, however, given I had no energy left to exert.

As he used his dagger to cut the ropes that broke too easily due to the fire, he pulled me to the grass and put it out by rolling me, despite the flames nipping his skin.

My dress was left mostly in tatters, and I a bruised and bloody mess.

He held my face tightly in his hands, using the sleeve of his tunic to wipe the dried blood. "Who the fuck did this?" His eyes lifted to Mira who widened hers and shook her head vigorously.

I coughed up a bit more crimson, blended with smoke. "Your dark side...or whatever."

I glanced over at the ghost I had the pain of witnessing.

Slick black hair. Sharp features. Lips pulled tight, and eyes that bore into the soul. A style that screamed *old money* here in Orsadia.

Who was this woman? Where did she appear from?

He began scooping me into his arms but halted. Eyes lifting to meet a familiar pair, he cursed. "You found his ghost?" He scowled. "Nevermind. We'll talk about this later." He jumped to his feet, tucking me against his chest. "After you're cleaned up. I better not hear a single protest about anything I may see. You've turned me into a damn medic, Firefly. I don't particularly like it."

I gazed up at him. "It's a useful skill..."

"It's as useful as your glow-in-the-dark ability during the day when I'm torn by the sight of the woman I'm in love with fighting for her life. They tried to burn you like a witch."

Was that what I was? I'd expected this after my term but I supposed the curse wanted to get in his turn before the mobs did.

"I had hope for you," the woman said. "I thought maybe being strapped to your own bed would show you who had the power and which side you should have been on. I was poorly mistaken. You're a disgrace to the queens of Orsadia."

Luka's eyes narrowed at her. "What makes you so important?"

"That's the wrong question to ask. What makes *her* so important?" She nodded towards me.

As he prepared to respond, I forced out, "You were the one Mira was talking to in my room that night. Where did you come from? How could you slip through without me knowing?"

She stole a glance from Mira. "I'm formidable everywhere I go. Don't look so surprised you couldn't sense my presence. I might be dominant, but I am also as quiet as a mouse when I'm determined to get what I want."

"And why hadn't you let Mira kill me then if that was your goal here today?"

"I wanted to watch you squirm. I wanted to test you—warn you. You simply failed. Although, don't be saddened by that. I still got a good show. Unfortunately, not all of the characters make it to the end alive."

Luka started walking, not allowing me to get in another word. That didn't stop *her*, however.

"I'd be careful, Lana, and I'd certainly watch my next move if I were you. I'm not done. Neither is the curse." She straightened her posture, chin high.

If she wasn't controlled by the curse, who was she and just where had she come from?

The huntsman lowered his voice as we headed inside, "What just happened out there?"

My chin fell as I grumbled, "I lost control. Your voice, tethered to *my* magic, has figured out how to take it into his own...form. He knows how to turn the dead against me." My head began to throb as my eyes fluttered shut. "The same way he turned us against one another."

"I could never turn against you," he replied, lowering his voice. "As hard as I've tried... Never you. Anyone but you."

THIRTY-SIX

Luka took care cleaning the blood and checking for internal injuries. Not quite sure how he knew, but I winced as he pressed on certain areas.

I lifted my hand, hooking my middle finger around my pointer. "Me and death are in good together, like this. I'm fine."

He rolled his eyes as he ran the hot water in the tub. "You always say you're fine but you're not really fine. You pretend to be. I know you well." Curling his fingers around the seat of my chair, he pulled me closer. "A hot bath should help. Then we're going to have a little chat about why the hell you brought my brother back."

I choked on a snort. "You really should be thanking me. I've seen the other side, Luka. It's bland and miserable."

"And what's your idea of misery, Firefly?" He pulled the chemise over my head. His eyes dilated a little, and it had been fairly noticeable given how light they were, but he resisted whatever temptations swirled around in his pretty head.

As he lifted me up and set me into the tub, I released a comforting sigh. The hot water eased the aches throughout my bones.

"My idea of misery is wandering a dark void with no purpose. So many souls. Maybe my purpose as a necromancer is to change the system. Sending both hateful assholes and good guys to the same place after death doesn't make a whole lot of sense." I glanced up at Luka as I leaned back against the rim.

He swallowed. "Is that what you plan to do?"

"Well, my magic tends to only hurt people when I use it in Orsadia. Maybe this is the one good thing I can do. Promise to people the afterlife and what awaits them. You always wondered what else was out there. You wondered what would happen when we died. Now you can get that confirmation. I can make it happen." I wrapped my fingers around the edge. "I know you're pissed off that I did this, but I won't apologize. If you just talk to him, he can tell you what it was like. I refuse to send him back there. It resembles being forced to eat dirt for the rest of your life while everyone around you feasts upon fresh meat roasted over a fire with steamed vegetables and baked bread. Would you wish that on anyone?"

"I'd wish that on anyone who dares lay their hands on you," he spat without hesitation.

That flutter in my chest could've been due to the flattering. Or, it could have been a serious sign of something wrong with my heart.

These days, the two were impossible to tell apart.

"Bringing ghosts back doesn't make me feel like a terrible person," I paused, eyes falling on the surface of the water. In a quieter voice, I asked, "am I still the villain of your story?"

Instinctively, he brushed his fingers through my hair. "You were never the villain to me. I've explained to you that no matter how hard I tried, I couldn't kill you. I didn't want to. You've always been my beacon."

A small smile appeared. "That's extremely cheesy."

"It put a smile on your face."

I held back my laugh. "Fine, I'll give you that one." I shook my head in disbelief. "Remember when we met all those new people, like Remy?"

"Impossible to forget something like that."

"He made jokes about Dave and his body parts always falling off. Now I constantly think about it. Every time one of my corpses bumps into something, I say things like: *Oh your eye fell out again.* And then I burst out with laughter. Damn Remy. He put all these jokes into my head. I make fun of the walking dead, my own creations. How horrible can I be? Dave is a good sport about it."

"Remy was fun to be around. I'll admit that." He chuckled.

I let out a sigh. "It's not the first time this happened. A week ago I woke up strapped to the bed. And the voice had managed to take charge of my ghosts, and Dave. I feel like a useless puppet when he does that. Your dark side is a real ass."

He let out a groan. "I really wish you'd stop calling him that. It's not like I did it on purpose."

"But it's true. He is your dark side. He's the side of you that wants to kill me." I attempted to shift positions but it hurt far too much.

Luka reached out, resting his hands on my arm and shoulder. "Careful." After I settled, he continued, "I have a hard time believing there's a side of me that wants to kill you."

"You conveniently forget you put an arrow through my shoulder."

His face reddened. "I had no choice. I had to at least stop you. And I wasn't about to kill you. I simply wanted to warn you not to mess with me, because you were certainly about to take my eye out without hesitation."

I grumbled, "I wouldn't have killed you."

After clearing his throat, he leaned forward. "Then we need a new tactic to ensure this never happens again. He can't take control of your ghosts or Dave if I'm around, right? Because I have control. So, with that said, I need to always be around."

My eyes moved from the bath's surface, to my arm, onto his fingers wrapped around my bicep, then up to his face. "What are you suggesting, Luka?"

"I'm suggesting I never leave your side. When you eat, sleep, pee, bathe. If that's when he gets you, then I need to be with you at *all* times. It's not up for debate, either." He sat back, letting go of me first. "Is that enough bath time?"

Once I agreed, I climbed out with his help, gritting my teeth at every movement.

He grabbed my chemise, and I lifted my arms halfway as he slipped it over my head.

The second I took a step forward, an arm wrapped around my back, and before I could protest, he bent down and wrapped the other under my knees to scoop me up. "You once told me that queens never have anyone to look after them. Well, I'm here now. We're changing that ridiculous thought." He pressed his lips to my temple. "Everywhere you go, I go."

THIRTY-SEVEN

"Well?" I tilted my head, eyebrows raised. "What's your verdict?"

Luka snorted as he threw a pear up and caught it again. "You care about my verdict now?"

"I trust you, yes. I'm only going to say this once, so please tuck it somewhere safe. You've been right about a few things involving Fallon before, given you are the younger brother yourself. So, what's the verdict? Is Clyde trustworthy?"

He glanced back. "You know Fallon would be upset if he knew what you sent me to do."

I waved my hand. "He'd get over it. I have good intentions."

Nodding a bit, he said, "He's trustworthy. Genuine. Everything he did is no different when a man does something to impress a woman. Buying flowers. Looking around for ingredients to his favorite meal. Really, you've got no reason to worry."

My lips curved upward. "Good. Just have to make sure my brother is not getting his heart broken out here. So, did you learn anything else about Clyde? Aside from the fact he comes from Anequeco and was a guard over there."

"Well..." He chuckled. "No. But speaking of brothers..."

As we began walking, he attempted to help but I smacked his hand away. I gazed at him. "You want to finally talk to yours?"

"I think I'm ready." He nodded, rubbing a hand through his dark waves.

"I'll give you privacy, too."

"You can't."

"Luka, yes I can."

"Nope. I won't allow it these days. Really, it's fine. I can introduce you to him, properly, and not just as the necromancer queen that brought him back to haunt Orsadia. Or in this case, Everinthian Castle."

I shrugged. "He likes my garden a lot more than that void. I'm still not apologizing."

He nudged me with a small grin. "I didn't ask you to."

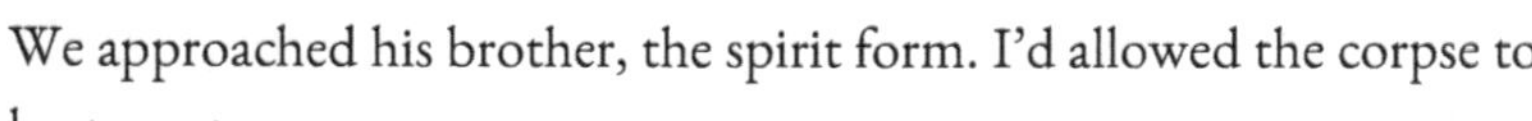

We approached his brother, the spirit form. I'd allowed the corpse to lay to rest.

At first, Luka hesitated, but within another few seconds, he tried to pull Thomas in for a hug only to come up short. "Shit, I missed you so much. And screw you for dying like that."

Thomas laughed. "We have a lot to catch up on. Starting with how long I've been dead for and what has happened in that time frame."

Jerry squeaked as he poked his head from behind Luka's shoulder.

His brother barked a laugh. "Leave it to my little brother to carry around a squirrel. You always did love the animals, didn't you?"

Luka snorted. "This one belongs to Lana, technically, but I adopted him when we separated for a few years."

He sat down, patting the seat beside him on the bench. Thomas followed. "Well, it's been...quite a while. A lot has happened. But the two biggest things I'll talk about are about Lana, and the time I visited another land."

When Thomas stole a glance at me, my cheeks grew warm. He wanted to talk about me to his brother? Why? Damn him for forcing me to stay. And to make matters worse, I had to listen to him talk about his adventures elsewhere. I'd been avoiding it for a good reason.

No doubt the universe was trying to tell me to finally listen.

"Lana is the current queen, as you can see," he continued, explaining my position and all the major events that had happened involving me and this damn curse over the last three years.

His brother barked out another laugh as he leaned back with his arms folded across his chest. "I guess I need to also add: leave it to my brother to fall in love with a woman who's destined to a life of horrid events." His eyes met mine. "No offense."

I shrugged. "Takes a lot to offend me." Well, that wasn't entirely true. But I didn't want him to know that. I was essentially Clyde trying to warm up to a version of me. Except in this scenario, I didn't have any plans to date Luka.

Despite the growing feelings...

"And how did the adventure go?" he asked him.

Luka lit up, eyes lightening as a grin appeared. He grumbled as he failed to grab his brother's shoulders and pull him close. "Well let me tell you! Okay, so I went to this land named Faitore." His eyes wavered on mine, before I nodded for him to go on. I liked the way he looked when he was talking about something he got excited about. As much as I didn't enjoy hearing how much he loved being away from me and

Orsadia, it made him happy.

"But I specifically visited the place called Ravenshire. It's covered in snow and a massive castle, and I'm talking way bigger than Drecose or Everinthian. It was run by this cruel woman named Medriana, right? Anyway, past all that nitty gritty... I met Velia. She's taller than me, actually. But she...has dark magic of sorts. We were still learning about it when I left. It was a lot of adventure where I stayed in the castle with her and Melusine, but I couldn't be caught by Medriana, and then I met Martell, right?" He rambled on about all these people I'd never heard of.

For the first time, I didn't envy him or loathe him for ditching me. I simply smiled because he had been able to get a sense of self and explore more of the world. He achieved a part of his dream, and could I truly blame him for that?

I had the urge to ask him more about it, even. But later. After he and his brother caught up. Later—when we were alone and heading to bed. When nobody would be listening but Luka himself.

THIRTY-EIGHT

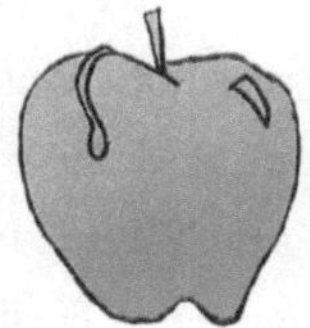

As Luka went on about Velia and Martell and Melusine, I smiled and nodded. He certainly fell in love with that place, and nobody could deny that in the way he talked about it.

Now here he lay in my bed. I'd never shared it with anyone, let alone a man. It'd been different. The pit of my stomach warmed while chills crawled along my skin. Beds were for intimate people. What had we done to end up here? Nothing romantic of the sort. He'd only fallen asleep last night, here, fully clothed. Regardless, why did I allow him to?

"Why did you come back?" I asked quietly.

He rolled onto his side, propping his cheek up with his palm, elbow on his pillow as he faced me. Something fluttered in my gut. Maybe it'd been a bad meal. Yeah, that had to be it. "Because the one thing Ravenshire didn't have, Firefly, was you. And without you, there was always something missing."

I frowned. "I hate when you say things like that."

"Why?"

"Because I don't deserve it." I pushed my head back into my pillow some more. "I should have heeded the warnings. All the signs were there, Luka. I kept telling myself I wouldn't kill humans, that Mira wouldn't do that. But she did, because she had faith that I wouldn't actually kill them. I'd sacrifice myself. I should have, too. I should have spared everyone the misery over these last three years. I was a necromancer, and the signs were obvious. If I had asked my mother or father more about the spell and the curse on the queens and my grandmother, I could have saved lives. Instead, I've taken them for my own gain. And the worst part of it all is that I enjoy it."

"I don't entirely believe that," he said. "I mean, you can't enjoy it if you also feel remorse. And given the way your brown eyes glass over as tears well, I know better."

"I don't cry."

He chuckled. "Tears might not leave your eyes but I know that's what happens. I can read social cues, body language, and facial expressions all fairly well."

I swallowed the lump in my throat, as if to prove him right, and my eyes began to water. "Is something so wrong with me?" I turned my head to my right to look at him.

With his free hand, he pushed hair from my cheek and shook his head. "It's just...a lot. It's the curse. My dark side. Your grandmother's lifestyle. It's a mix of it all. Like you've said, your environment as a whole made you who you are today." He brushed his thumb across my cheek and over my nose, wiping a tear I'd let slip. "You can't be entirely to blame."

I loathed him for the way he could cause my skin to dance beneath his touch.

"But I am. I'm a grown woman. There's only so much I can pin on everything and everyone else before I have to take responsibility.

I know better. I just won't do it."

His eyes sank. "Because that's my fault. Because my dark side is convincing. Because he's me—and nobody can blame you for wanting to please the voice of the very man who stood by you when everyone else doubted. You're being manipulated." I opened my mouth, but he shook his head. "Don't. Don't tear yourself down any further."

When I forced the rest of my tears back, I turned to stare at the ceiling. Regardless, Luka took it upon himself to wrap his arm around my waist and pull me into his chest. "Don't fight it. Don't fight me. Just accept love, okay?"

I whispered against his chest, "Okay."

THIRTY-NINE

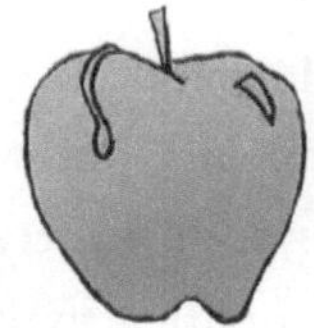

Fallon walked in on Clyde's arm.

Fallon wore a simple suit made of common fabrics such as polyester and cotton. Black slacks paired with a white shirt and black jacket.

Clyde complemented him in his sharp white suit and crow-dyed button-up. His curls had been left tussled and his brown eyes did a great job of melting the heart of my brother.

Mine soared for his happiness before plummeting because of my own. I tried hard to ignore it. I knew I was better off alone. Going through life with only myself to rely on, numbing myself to the idea that a happy ending would ever be in my fate—that became my normal. I started to accept it.

Luka would have scolded me for ever thinking such thoughts.

"You are damn right," he said from behind me. "Nobody should have to go through life alone."

I shrugged a tad as I watched guests flood Everinthian Castle with skeptical looks. I'd decided to host another ball. This time I wanted to do it in my own home and hopefully make amends. If I could still do that...

"I go through it alone because I'm better off that way. All I tend to do is hurt the people around me. I'm more of a bother than I'm worth. Don't deny the truth."

"I'm only denying lies." He grabbed my wrist, spinning me to face him. He reached out to grab my waist and steady me before my sprained ankle ruined whatever he was trying to do.

His muscular form was amplified tonight by the black pants and crisp shirt. White. Top few buttons undone, left to show off a bit of his chest underneath with some hair peaking through. Cuffs rolled to his elbows. This man was truly sculpted by an artist of the highest rank.

I despised when he looked at me that way, like he wanted nothing more than to sink into my soul.

I swallowed the lump beginning to form. Again. "Luka, I'm not trying to hold this over your head anymore, seeing as it was a good thing for you to do—but you were gone for three years. You cannot speak about what happened without you around. I truly am a bother. I do hurt people. I am better off alone. Have you ever noticed how when I'm not around, people cheer? Even before I was queen, before I was the princess... I didn't have many friends. Or any friends at all, really. Nobody wanted me around. They got along a lot better without me because all I did was put a damper on the mood. I was the downer of the group due to my obsession with death, so I stopped trying to fit in.

"Eventually, I noticed how they got along better without me. They thrived without my presence. Nobody ever noticed when I wasn't around, and they certainly didn't care that I wasn't. I faded into the darkness. I made friends with animals and I explored my magic. I explored Ash Forest. I began to train because I found I was better off that way. By building up those walls to protect them from me. I supposed I was trying to prepare for the inevitable, but I am the villain around here. When all of this is past us, who will I have? I don't have friends. I barely have family, and that's being generous after the way I treated them. I'll have to let Mira and Aalia go. Dave will return to his grave. I return to what I know, a life where the only person who enjoys my company is me."

Luka's eyes roamed over mine before flickering behind me.

When I turned around, Esmira and Kiernan waited.

Esmira's throat moved as she gulped down whatever it was she wanted to say. "I..."

Kiernan squeezed her hand, the tie around his neck matching the exact shade of crimson that her silk gown cascaded in.

I wasn't sure of what else to say. Given their expressions, I was certain they overheard everything, or at least most of it.

Esmira dropped his hand and stepped forward. "We enjoy your company. A lot."

"But it's not the same. You live in a different world than I do. I rarely get to see you."

As if on cue, the music group started to play a different melody, one much more filled with sorrow and despair. Longing.

"But I'll try. Don't you know that I'll try?" her voice cracked.

I lowered my head to hide the tears that began to stream down my face. I became a splintered toy, or a chipped plate. I hated being vulnerable. I hated breaking down like this at all.

"I have all this space, but never friends to fill it with." I attempted to wipe away the tears. "Guess I became a master of disguises."

She grabbed my hands, slipping her fingers through mine. "Tell me how you feel. You know you can do that, right? I want you to vent to me. I want you to let it all out because if you don't, you'll eventually explode. I don't give a shit if it's a ball."

A sob racked through me. "I...just get so lonely. Those three years, I had nobody but myself, and the dead who I had to control to obey. It was me in this big castle. Nobody visited. Nobody said hi. And I had so many horrible thoughts about how if I would have taken my own life, nobody would have found me for days, simply because they would wonder why I hadn't come to terrorize them." Nobody understood the kind of heaviness that put on me. To know that if I died, I had nobody to care enough to find me in time to save me.

Nobody ever saved the queen. We were expected to be the savior of everyone else.

"I was raised with all this responsibility that nobody else ever had. Everything fell on me. Maybe that isn't what I wanted. Maybe I had other dreams. Maybe I'm tired of being expected to put everyone first. *I'm tired of being the afterthought.*"

Esmira fell silent, slowly pulling me into her chest.

I told myself she was only here for the evening and it was okay, because once she went back home, she'd take all this vulnerability with her.

The moment I got a handle on my emotions, I stepped back and cleaned up my face. I smoothed my hands over my green gown, courtesy of Luka. Something about him wanting me to match his soul.

She released a small sigh. "Did that help?"

I nodded as I glanced at the doors to the Great Hall. "I suppose now that it's not locked away inside my head, the curse can no longer use it against me." After a minute of quiet, I gave her a hint of a smile. "Thank you..."

"It's not anything I haven't...felt before myself. I know the importance of having someone around to support you."

Kiernan leaned in and kissed her head, his eyes sinking. "I hope you don't feel that way anymore."

"No." She smiled up at him. "Not with you." She spotted Clyde from the dance. "Oh! How is he doing here?"

I followed her gaze. "Great. He makes my brother happy, and I've made him my guard. He fits right in."

Clyde's hand was tangled with Fallon's as he spun him. Fallon laughed before being pulled back to his partner.

"Fallon has always been such a pure soul. He deserves this. I'm just glad to know that I didn't ruin my own brother's future."

Luka leaned down near my ear. "You could never. You love him too much, and he knows that."

Esmira cleared her throat as she slipped her hand in her husband's. "Then we should go join them."

"We?" I asked with my eyebrow raised.

Her eyes sparkled and she grinned. "Yes, *we*. As in you and Luka, too."

I scoffed. "No." And I even had my foot as an excuse this time.

"Oh come on! Everyone sees it." Her eyes grazed over the few guests and dancing skeletons. "It is so obvious. Stop trying to fight it."

I wanted to curse her out for that one, but I stuffed it down into the pit. Luka took that as his sign and grabbed my wrist, pulling me with ease through the double doors.

Everyone was staring. I didn't mind being feared or the center of attention on a good day, but this had not been that. And with Luka on my arm, I was desperate to crawl into a corner and hide my face from the world.

When I opened my mouth to tell him we didn't have to really do this for Esmira's sake, he stopped smack in the middle of everyone and spun to face me, yanking me to his chest. After he placed my arms around his neck, he slid his down to my waist. "Put your feet on mine."

"Excuse me?"

"You can't dance with a bad ankle, Firefly. So, let me take that pressure from you for the night." Figuratively and literally.

I wore a scowl, but we both knew from the thoughts lingering in my mind that I wanted more from him. I'd been too afraid to ask. And I hated him for ever bringing these kinds of feelings out of me.

Regardless, I lifted my feet onto the toes of his boots.

Nobody ever really looked away. We had no privacy here.

As he swayed us side to side, he leaned into my bubble. "You don't have to be alone anymore."

I lowered my eyes to his collar. "I already know where this is going."

"I'm not leaving your side. Ever again. You're going to have to kill me first."

"I can make that happen," I said as I lowered one hand, fixing his neckline.

All eyes lingered.

He laughed, shaking his head. "You might be sick of me, but I'm not sick of you." He raised his hand, grabbing my chin to stop me from looking elsewhere. "I mean it. You admitted you're lonely. You have nobody to go home to, but I promise you that's never going to happen to you again. I'll be there every night when you go to sleep, and when you wake up. If you have a nightmare, I'll console you. If the dead try to kill you, I'll be the one to prove you can obliterate a ghost into nothing."

"You don't have to give up your freedom just for my sake. I've always survived just fine." I tried to ignore the flutter in my chest from the way his fingers held my jaw.

The world revolved around us. Orsadia. The ball. Why did they make us their entertainment for the night?

"I'm not giving up my freedom for you. People always assume that choosing love over a dream is a terrible idea, but I don't see it that way. I can just as easily convince you to sail with me." He choked on a laugh. "But loving you has never been one of my terrible decisions. It's the reason I keep fighting. You've given me a purpose because at the end of the day, life is about making connections, a community, and surrounding yourself with people who make you feel alive and free." As the music slowed, he breathed, "And I'll be the first one to save a queen from a cruel fate."

FORTY

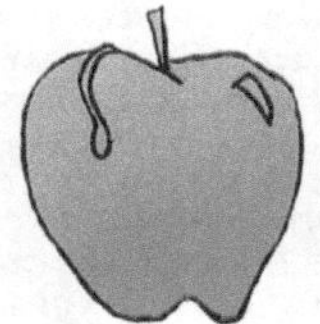

After sifting through the letters from my grandmother a million times, I yelled out in exasperation. Nothing changed. Nothing ever changed.

Did I expect it to?

Then something caught my eye.

The corner of a paper poked out from underneath one of the letters, and when I pulled it up, I realized it'd fused to the back probably due to lots of humidity and then sudden heat drying it out.

I peeled it away from my grandmother's letter, finding my name scrawled across the top.

Snow White Edmilla (or Snow White Regali as soon as you find this),

We met once, when you were younger. I knew your future. I knew mine. Although I don't know the outcome, I write this anyway. I beg you to make the sacrifice. It wasn't a decision I made lightly, as I would never want to advocate for a young life being cut short. Regardless, I had to make that the answer, as the curse needs to end with us both. We need a fresh start on the throne. You and I won't make it through this war if we play our cards right. That's the goal, anyway. You're probably pissed off at me, and rightfully so. But if you'd seen the future like I have, you would know just how dark it is. You would know that Orsadia is on the brink of dying. If we don't survive, Orsadia can.

It's not ideal. I'm aware. I know that choosing to sacrifice yourself is not a decision anyone wants to make. But you won't have your father waiting for you if you take the throne. I have plans to send Luka away, to give you further incentive to give up your life for others just as I will. What's so great about this path? You and I both know the kind of pressure put on us as princesses. We know it wasn't a fate we asked for.

Do you want to be the reason Orsadia crumbles into nothing?

I apologize for pulling the guilt card on you, but I have no choice. I knew you'd go looking here once you discovered who your grandmother was, so I figured this was the best place to stash this letter.

Please. For everyone else, I beg you to lay down your life for a good cause.

Your Evil Queen, Mira Sunder

"I was hoping you'd get it before you died. But it appears I wasn't able to deliver it properly," she said from a chair. "And I'm sorry I was too late."

"You weren't too late. You still told me in person, to an extent. You warned me. I just didn't listen."

She dismissed me with the wave of her hand. "All I forgot to say then...was that the magic didn't choose me. None of us were picked that way."

"What are you referring to?" I furrowed my brows.

Luka turned his gaze our way, but said nothing as he promised to pretend he didn't have to be here.

"What came with it? The curse, of course. All magic came with the curse. So in reality, I was not chosen by Magic Law at all, but by the curse in itself."

We'd always hoped it would be played off as something innocent. Magic had been like a gift, but instead it came with a price. If she was picked by something sinister... It meant the rest of us were, too.

FORTY-ONE

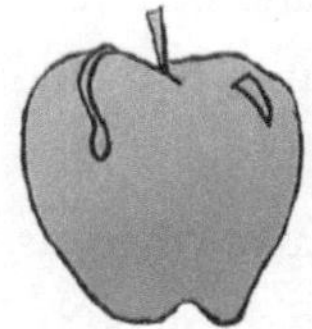

"I saw you, walking through the forest. I saw you moving along," Zoe said, peering out of my garden. "So I told Luka, because I had no other choice given his position. I assumed that he knew who you were before he went out there. He informed me when he returned that he had no idea it was you, yet he should have suspected. It took him off guard." She turned to face me. "Once I saw you, I knew you were going to kill me. It's how every destiny goes."

I leaned against the tree. "And? Did I meet your expectations?"

She shrugged, humming a little. "I thought you'd be more creative, honestly. Poison is a boring way to go out."

Luka choked on a laugh from the corner.

I rubbed a shiny leaf between my thumb and forefinger, knowing this plant was one of the few nonpoisonous ones. "You came to tell me that my choice of murder is bland for your taste."

She let out a laugh. "No, I actually came to tell you that... I want to help. I want in."

"In what?"

"In this." She gestured. "Whatever it is that you and Luka are trying to fix. Granted, I can't sleep in the castle because Magic Law won't allow me inside. But I can still come and try to help where I can. Whatever you need, ask it of me. It affects me. It affects my future and maybe any children I have, or their children." She straightened her posture. "It affects you, and believe it or not, I do care about you. I empathize. Everything you've had to deal with, I understand. Let me help."

When I glanced back at Luka who was waiting near the wall of the castle, my eyes dragged along the grass and back to Zoe. "Well, maybe your magic will be a wonderful key. If we can combine it with mine, and Luka's. None of the past queens ever worked together to defeat the curse. That was a mistake on my part. Now, we can set it right."

A smirk appeared on Zoe's lips, slow and steady. "Oh, this will be the turn of the century."

FORTY-TWO

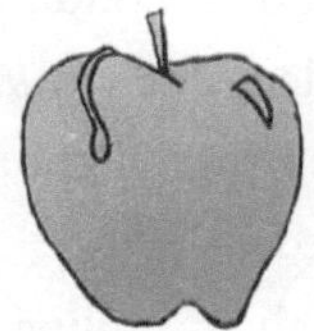

I leaned over the book, shaking my head. "So you made a wish, and the magic fountain granted that wish. But as far as we know, it was also such a strong wish that giving you and all future heirs magic ultimately drained it from the fountain. And what could it do, deny the wish?"

Aalia dropped into a seat across the table, letting out a sigh. "No, it could not. Wishes at the time were hard to break. Impossible to deny. Set in stone, literally. You could ask it to bring someone back from the dead. You could ask for endless wishes. You could ask for someone to fall in love with you. You could do whatever you set your heart to." Even if it brought someone back, we knew it could only animate a dead body. It could not restore a soul to its vessel. It certainly couldn't change fates. "And that was what I did. I wished to have magic, and so it happened, and I got to take the crown. Magic Law came about. I became Queen. Everinthian Castle became my home. Drecose was named after me when the next princess got her power. Gaia Quillen."

I swallowed. "Quillen. As in Zoe Quillen."

She nodded. "Indeed. That's right. Gaia Quillen had been very strong-willed. Bold. No fear in her bones. I admired her for it, given I didn't get many of those traits." Yet everyone else who ever knew Aalia knew she carried those exact ones.

"Wait!" I gestured to Luka, who read my thoughts and handed me Gaia's journal. I flipped it open, nodding as my finger landed right where I wanted it to. "Quillen. Zoe's *grandmother.*"

"Have we not established that? I thought it was obvious by the name alone," Mira mumbled.

Luka grabbed a wooden chair, pulling it out and spinning it as he sat with the backside in front of him. As he rested his arms across the top, he furrowed his dark eyebrows. "Grandmother? Gaia was the second queen. If my math is correct, that'd make her eighty-seven. Zoe is twenty-one."

"Yeah. Zoe's older sister, Wendy Quillen was a queen, too. The twenty-first queen."

Luka shook his head regardless. "No. I mean, yeah, it could happen. But given the poor health, there's no way Zoe's mother could have Wendy and Zoe in twelve years."

I snickered. "Are you trying to say that women can't have kids that far apart in age?"

"Yes, that's exactly what I'm saying. When has it *ever* been done?"

Putting my hand on the book to hold it open, I nestled my chin in my other palm which had been propped up by my elbow on the tabletop. "I'm sure it's been done. Doesn't Zoe talk about her family? Mira mentioned her mother quite a lot."

He tilted his head. "But that's just it, Lana. It has never happened for two siblings to both end up as heirs. One sibling gets magic. The other doesn't."

"Bold coming from the first man on Orsadia to possess magic."

"Will you please listen to me? I spent far more time around Zoe than you have. I'm telling you, it doesn't add up. When you moved into Drecose, you brought your brother and parents."

"Correct."

"Zoe doesn't have a mother. If you're insinuating that her mother was Gaia's daughter, who would've been roughly twenty to twenty-five when Wendy was born, that'd mean she would have had to give birth to Zoe at thirty-seven."

My gaze lowered to the book. "Women don't survive giving birth at that age. Medicine isn't advanced by any means. So maybe her mother died giving birth."

"Zoe has never once talked about her mother. She definitely didn't know her. But Wendy lives there, too. Her sister, and she doesn't seem to talk about her either. When I asked about her once, I got the strangest response."

I stifled a laugh. "Which was?"

"She said that her mother never got the magic. Shunned Wendy. Died when Wendy was just eleven years old."

Aalia's eyes slowly rose to meet his. Mira's snapped up. I focused, stating, "Zoe wasn't even born yet."

He swallowed. "No. Wendy never corrected herself. Never pedaled back, nor did she realize what she had admitted. But living with both Wendy and Zoe, I see the resemblance. Not the resemblance you'd catch between sisters, but that between a mother and her daughter. Wendy is protective of her. Caring. Treats her exactly like her own child."

My breath caught.

Mira replied, "Because she is her own child... I rarely knew Wendy then. But I remembered how all the boys looked at her, and how Wendy craved that attention. Her mother didn't want her. Wendy was forced to grow up. How tragic, a baby forced to have one herself.

With no support? The fear she must have experienced. The pain. The despair. It's truly... There are no words. She made it through all of that and then became a queen."

"A queen with a daughter of her own," I whispered. "Zoe grew up in Everinthian, in Drecose. This isn't her first time walking the property. She was raised inside all these castles only to watch her mother be forced out into the dirt." I began to chew the edge of my thumb nail. "She's going to be a bigger key than we've suspected. She knows things we don't. She's been through this all before."

"So have I," Mira said with her eyebrows raised in offense.

"Your mother had you after her term ended. She taught you. But this is different. Zoe has already been through the whole process. She was there when her mother became princess. Trained. Practiced magic. She was there when her mother took the throne and succumbed to the curse. She watched Wendy deteriorate for three years." I widened my eyes. "And now Wendy is watching her own daughter go through the same fate."

Luka choked on water. "You know, I'm surprised Wendy didn't come to me about all this, or ask me to come to you sooner, given what she knows is going to happen. We need her on our side. She knows how this works."

"She and Zoe both do." I straightened my back. "They hold a lot of information that could help us. We're going to go to them, tell them what we know, and then we're going to figure out just who the hell created the wishing fountain that gave us all magic. I need to know who started this and why exactly the curse came about so we can finally end it for good. Considering what we're trying to do for Zoe, I don't have any doubt Wendy will be willing to work with us." I drummed my fingers across the page. "Which makes Gaia Quillen Zoe's great grandmother. Third generation of an heir. And exactly the person who has all the secrets we've been digging up from the grave, only to find an empty coffin."

"Get to the damn point," Mira said with a scoff and roll of her eyes.

"Zoe might be the one who can break our curse."

FORTY-THREE

Wendy tapped her foot, arms crossed. "This is taking too damn long."

Zoe hissed at her to shut up as we dried up the stagnant water from the fountain.

Mira eyed the once Wicked Queen. She'd given that title strictly to herself. When Wendy ruled, she insisted on picking her own. Something about the alliteration...

"If you want Zoe to have a shot, you'll shut your yap," Mira spat.

She intentionally dodged calling Zoe her daughter. Made us promise.

As Luka stormed over the bridge and up to the castle doors, we spotted Wendy attempting to shut them in his face, but she decided to change her mind, heading right for me and my deadly friends.

When her foot landed on the soft dirt on this side of the bridge, she huffed. "Fine. You got me. Zoe is my daughter. However, if you want my help, it's under one condition."

Mira rolled her head.

Aalia's gaze flickered to Drecose. "Zoe doesn't know, does she? She believes you're her older sister."

Wendy shrugged. "It's easy to play off when she was too young to remember that my mother wasn't alive when she was born. I don't want her to know. She's better off not knowing that her mother was a whore because her breasts developed early."

Luka frowned. "That doesn't make you a whore. Boys took advantage of you. You didn't have anyone else to love you. Your mother had just died, Wendy. You're hardly to blame for doing what any young girl would do."

"Yet I'm the one who ended up with the kid, didn't I? Nobody was there to take the responsibility from me when I got pregnant, so it's now mine to carry to the grave. Enough of this. You won't tell her, will you?" She lifted a finger in a threatening way.

We all shook our heads as she wiggled the tensions from her muscles. "Then what is it you need from me?"

"Found it!" Zoe screeched as she rolled over the edge of the fountain and into the base where water once sat. "Right here it states who created the magic fountain. Kit Strahm."

Not to be confused with Kit Holloway, the eleventh queen.

The huntsman and I both groaned at once.

"Fuck," I muttered.

"Say it ain't so," he begged.

Zoe's eyes darted between us. "What's so wrong with that?"

"He's the ancestor of a man we had the recent pleasure of running into," he began.

"And neither of us are too fond of having to go ask him all kinds of questions," I finished. "Victor *Strahm.* I imagine this creator was his great grandfather? How much would he know?"

Luka shrugged. "Probably as much as his parents and their parents were able to learn and pass onto the future generations."

"Which means Victor has good reason to despise every single one of us," Mira said so nonchalantly. "Given that we're all products of his ancestor's pride and work ruined. Let's go find the prick and beat it out of him I say."

I shot her a warning, making her promise to simmer down. What had gotten into her lately?

Zoe glanced at her mother. "This is the man whose own family created a wishing fountain that we ultimately stole all the magic from. Just how well is that going to go over?"

Wendy mumbled, "Not well at all."

And we set out towards the village.

"Get them away from me!" he yelled as he stumbled back, tripping over a basket. "I don't want a single thing to do with any of you!"

Victor Strahm cursed us. Intentionally, too.

"Victor," Luka started, placating him. "We're not going to harm you. We simply want to ask a few questions regarding a man from your lineage. If you help us, you could end an almost-century-old curse. Orsadia could flourish."

Victor scowled. "What exactly does that mean?"

I released a sigh, throwing my head back. "It means the queens won't be terrible people. It means Zoe will be able to save us."

His beady eyes narrowed on me. Damn, he despised me to no end. "Who do you want to know about? Could it have anything to do with Kit, my great grandfather?"

Victor hadn't been all that young, but not entirely aged, either. He'd been about ten years older than me at the very max. Younger than my parents, by far, but not quite as young as us. His hair had been dark—short—beginning to gray, lines defining features such as his grayish eyes and tight scowl.

"It may," I said in a softer tone.

Victor had been ready to tell us to piss off when Fallon shouted my name and came running. Clyde wasn't too far behind. And so, Victor studied the couple before grunting and gesturing us inside.

We piled into the tight home.

Victor poured himself a steaming cup of water from the kettle over the fire, then poured herbs into a small bag and dropped it into the drink. "I hate to admit it, Queen, but I do admire you more than I'd like you to know."

"Admire me?" I asked, taken back.

He met my gaze. "Of course. You've always stood by your brother and who he's been born to love. I never had that, unfortunately." He frowned as he started to stir the tea after removing the herbs. "My great grandfather was a private man. But private men also tend to document most of their life, and I happen to have evidence of that in this very house. You might want to take a seat and get comfortable. There's a lot you're going to learn about this man."

Once we took our seats, he sipped his tea and started, "Kit was one of the first as you all know. Not magical, no. But he had great ideas for Orsadia. The wishing fountain was one of them."

Kit had been alive with the giants then.

Not many had been left, of course, as the fourth queen, Willow, had been the one to wipe them out completely. Kit had existed only a decade before Aalia came along and wished for the magic herself.

Meaning Aalia had been just a youngling when he was planning his great idea for the structure.

He had the idea for the wishing fountain to help Orsadia grow and thrive in its own way. He wanted to help the people, to give back.

Little had he known that it would cost us far more, stealing everything that was left of us.

So Kit came up with the idea that he wanted the wishing fountain to be filled with magic. He wanted wishes to come true, no limitations. At the time, he trusted everyone to use it for good.

Poorly misguided.

Kit got to work on sketching his brilliant idea. Once it had been finished, he picked a location right in Ash Forest. It'd been the perfect spot, away from the village so people weren't always abusing it. People were required to do a little exploring themselves to attain something so magical.

Then he set to work, drilling into the ground to find a well of some sort. It wasn't all that hard to find. Assuming it was accessible given its distance from Keenain River as well as the underground cave full of that glowing green water. I wasn't sure what the green water looked like then, though.

Once he tapped into a source, he began with his plumbing. He started filling in material around it before he formed the structure of the fountain that we saw today.

Victor couldn't recall exactly where the water flowed from, but he assumed it had been from the river that came from the ocean. I had added in my own guesses that maybe along the way, the green water from that cave somehow flowed in just a tad. Maybe the bones of the dead seeped through the damp earth to find the fountain. Maybe ghosts had been curious.

Maybe. Just maybe...

Once it had been built and water began to fill up the base before pouring out of the top and recycling itself, Kit searched for a new idea. Magic, and how to ensure wishes would come true.

The giants didn't live in the village with the people. No, we'd still been too afraid. The giants lived further out, in the underground cave and throughout Ash Forest. Kit found himself venturing out to find them himself, and when he did, he mentioned his fountain and how he had plans to make wishes come true. He needed the magic to fuel it.

The giants agreed to help, only under one condition—that their kind be a protected species. They wanted to be able to roam freely without being outcasted or feared.

Kit agreed to those terms without issue, seeing as he'd had enough interaction with the giants to know they were anything but dangerous.

The giants led him to that green water I'd discovered. He was in awe, mesmerized by the way it glowed, curious if he could touch it. The giants ensured it was safe to touch. But it had magical properties to it, and they were certain that if it were used in the fountain, it would enable wishes to come true.

Kit thanked them as he managed to find a way to reroute a little of that water to the fountain. Mapping out the locations and ensuring that more plumbing was done in a discreet kind of way. It certainly took at least another year to make happen, but when it did, Kit stood back with pride as he watched his greatest creation come to life. Tossing in a silver coin, he made a wish and it had come true by the next day.

It worked.

And news began to spread to the village. People would wish for food, and for money. For bountiful harvest, and to never have to live in such poverty again. For a while, that fountain kept Orsadia thriving in all the right ways. Until years later, when a teenage Aalia had wished for something different from everyone else. When she sat at its edge and tossed in a coin, she wished for magic to flow through her veins. By the following morning, it came true. She had become a dream walker, and when people discovered it, she never told them where it came from. She relished in that glory and became their queen, the first ever of Orsadia to exist in the history books.

The ghost who sat beside me had asked for too much. The giants hadn't anticipated anyone taking it that far. They begged Kit to close off the valve that led to their supply of enchanted water, but Kit refused. He didn't believe it'd lead to worse things.

Using up all it could, that fountain gave her magic, and every queen followed shortly after.

It had been drained of all the wishes.

And with that, came the curse the giants promised would arrive as a result.

But that magic could only go so far. After Aalia's reign ended, her magic vanished. And she had been murdered by the people, suffering the consequences of her own actions.

"So the magic that fueled the fountain came from that glowing river underground. Where the giants lived," I said. "Which means the giants know the most about this curse and how to end it. But what do we do if the species was wiped out decades ago?"

Everyone turned to face me.

I groaned. "You want me to go into that void and find giant spirits to bring back here so we can get it out of them."

Luka shrugged a little. "You'll get to use it for good, right? Is that what you want?"

"We can't reverse what happened," Mira stated.

Victor finished off his tea. "But we can find a way to fix it. And not all magic needs to be used for the wrong reasons. It can have a purpose."

"And if we're lucky," Zoe began, "Maybe we can even keep our magic beyond our ruling."

FORTY-FOUR

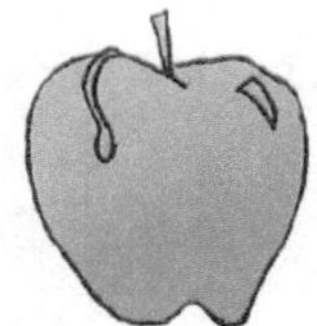

Most of them followed me to the graveyard. I insisted on going to the dungeon but Zoe wanted to be there. So, we waited for night to drape over Orsadia and then I had to break into the mausoleum that had a secret tunnel to the giant's cave. Not everyone could fit in here, so Luka took the honors of waiting just inside the door while the rest of them hung out in the dampened grass.

Victor didn't want to partake any further so he stayed home, and I silently thanked *someone* for that.

I slipped through the thin veil and became overwhelmed by the spirits wandering back and forth.

Spotting giants was too easy. But I couldn't leave all of them here.

An idea came over me, and I whistled to gather the attention of many. As I started sifting through the ones I recognized first, I was able to pick who belonged here and who didn't. Those who didn't, I shoved out of my doorway. I could only imagine Luka's face when random ghosts began popping out.

I came across Alexander, stopping just in front of him to study his appearance. "You."

He didn't say much as his head hung low and he attempted to move around me.

I blocked him again, grabbing his shoulders. "Do you understand the seriousness of what you did? Do you understand how justifying your actions can lead downhill? If you start to say one thing's acceptable, where do you draw the line?"

Behind him, a familiar face flashed, causing me to gasp. I dragged Alexander by the wrist over to Kali, pulling her against my body. So much coolness in one place. It was almost a wonder why it didn't look like winter.

"Kali. You're coming with me. Okay?" I spotted Aelin shortly after, beckoning her over. When the three of them surrounded me, I exhaled. "Listen, this void is...unfair. Unusual. I've got a better idea for people like you, if you'll trust me."

Neither of them said much, and I realized that most of the spirits here couldn't muster up enough energy to say anything at all. This void had nothing. Darkness engulfed all of them, weighing them down as they trudged on.

At least the life in Orsadia could radiate energy for them to roam. It wasn't ideal, maybe, but I was the necromancer. I'd be the judge of what their ghosts deserved—and it wasn't this.

I dragged all three of them with me through the barrier, watching as they started to return to their former selves. Personalities became apparent in their expression and body language. They might have been just ghosts, but I had at least given them some purpose.

Zoe warned me the sun was peeking above the horizon, and so I hurried back beyond the portal, searching for one last spirit to take with me.

"Father!" I shouted as I tripped over my gown on the way over.

After I scrambled back to my feet, I gathered my skirts and caught up with him. The ghosts here moved at a snail's pace. They couldn't exactly outrun me.

"Father," I breathed. Before I could even hug him, I grasped his wrist and yanked him behind me as I sprinted to the cracked portal that barely glowed, slipping through just before it became that of a speck.

Falling to my knees, I expected Luka to catch me. Nobody did, however.

I slowly stood, stepping out of the mausoleum and facing everyone who now waited before me. The ghosts. All of the queens, past and upcoming. Dave, as well as Luka.

Oh, but your time is over now, Little Raven.

He shouldn't have been able to invade my mind while Luka was here, but he had. And Luka didn't notice... Had his dark side managed to lock him out without him knowing?

I swallowed as I stumbled back. "I need to go." I turned and ran from the cemetery, avoiding every pile of bones and headstone imaginable. My ankle throbbed, but I pushed on. I hurried towards Ash Forest, attempting to lose everyone who wanted to follow.

I mostly managed, grabbing onto the trunk of a tree as I halted and breathed heavily.

Glancing back, I saw no one.

A twig snapped and I whipped around to find the source of the sound. "Who's there?"

Nobody answered, and I started to question if it was the very man who loved to play coward.

As soon as his chuckle echoed, I stiffened, yanking my sword out, peering up into the trees. "This is so typical of you. You can never face me like a man."

When a soft thud landed behind me, I spun to face the huntsman who knew this forest better than I ever could. His eyes lingered on my weapon. "It's called making like a predator and hiding to stalk your prey."

Don't you hear how he talks to you? He doesn't love you. He sees you as his victim, and you so easily give in.

Swallowing, I pointed my sword out in front of me. "I'm your prey, now?"

His laugh bounced. "No. But if I must, I will. It's a useful skill, and you're only pissed off that I'm using it on you. Firefly, what is all this running about?" He gestured around us, a small frown beginning to form.

He'll kill you if you don't do it first. You know I'm right, because I am *him.*

I swung at him just as he jumped back to dodge me. I sliced again, nicking his arm, my heart swelling. He hissed as he reached for his dagger, but I lunged forward and shoved him back into a tree, pressing the blade to his throat while a scowl escaped. "You should have known better than to trust me, Luka. I never earned the title Poisonous Queen from befriending a huntsman like you."

Do it. Kill him, he said in a more seductive tone. *You ache to watch his blood trickle down your blade.*

"Is that so?" His mouth twitched as his gaze fell from my eyes to my lips. "I'd say we were more than friends for a moment." His arm snaked around my waist, yanking my chest to his as the other hand tangled itself in my hair and pulled me into a kiss.

A kiss so promising, and sweet like honey. Smooth as it dripped from a spoon into a cup of piping hot tea.

That's how his lips moved against mine.

Kisses are a distraction. He's just using you.

As I pulled away, pleading, "This is wrong, you callous asshole," he ignored what I had to say.

It wouldn't have been Luka if he hadn't entirely shattered my soul.

It's what he does best.

Carefully slipping the sword out from between our throats, it clattered to the ground. He took that as his opportunity to spin us until my back hit the trunk, my head cushioned just by the vines snaking their way up and around.

For a minute, we both caught our breaths as he whispered, "You say it's wrong, Firefly, but what's stopping us now? Don't say the curse. It'll always be something with you."

But it *was* the curse. He had managed to break the barrier. Luka had no idea.

My eyes roamed his face, searching for a tell of a lie. If I could spot a weakness...

It's just you, Little Raven.

Before I finished trying, his lips came down on me again, this time far hungrier. Begging to be let in.

My walls crumbled around me. I'd allowed my guard down just as he slipped past the gates the second he got the chance.

He tasted of spices—such things I never got a chance to try.

Just as he gave us some room to fill our lungs, I swallowed whatever I'd wanted to say previously. "I shouldn't be fraternizing with you, given that you're sworn to kill me when my one mission is to murder Zoe before she has a chance. But..." I slowly reached my hands to his tunic, fisting his collar. "I suppose these days I like to give into what harms me. I'm nothing if not a queen who allows herself to be filled with poison, and you Luka Lockwood, are the most addicting kind that I will happily drink. I invite you to be the death of me."

I adored the way he quieted the voice that wanted to take control of my power.

He placed his forearm against the bark just above my head, leaning in close but too far for my liking. In one breath, he uttered, "That's my girl." And then I succumbed to his power all over again, our kiss melding into one.

Everyone had fled, leaving me and Luka to handle the way his dark side managed to take hold without him noticing—with Luka a few feet away from me.

"Imagine me at my ripe age, never having been with a man." I brushed my fingers along the sill of the window. "Twenty-four years. I'm certain many out there are probably thinking to themselves that if I were to just let my hormones take over and get a little something, I might not be so hateful towards the world."

I don't believe that's the answer.

"Is that supposed to be a terrible thing? Having waited longer than other queens? I believe everyone knows when they are ready. And if you're not there, who has any right to shame you?" Luka stopped just a few feet away, shoulders broad and expression made of stone. "If they so much as believe you're better off taking leaps you aren't ready to, what would they think of me? I'm simply a few years older, and I've never been with a woman. What would it say about me?"

"You've never laid with a woman before? Hard to believe given..." I swallowed my words along with my laugh.

It's easy to believe.

"Given what? My physique? My charm? My personality? I might be as bold as the sun when it comes to making my moves or saying what I think, but that does not translate to being so in love with a woman that I'm ready to share all of me. Even so, she's not ready to share all of her. I'm not one to push."

As bold as the sun yet as mysterious as the moon—picking and choosing when to show more or less of the darkness swirling around his skeleton.

"I hear their whispers, Luka."

Use them to fuel you. Wipe them off the face of Orsadia.

His arm shot up. "Ignore those whispers! They're far too concerned with the intimate lives of strangers anyway."

My voice quieted for a moment. "I'm no stranger."

As he stalked over, footsteps careful and calculating, he captured my jaw with his hand and tilted it up. "They will never know enough about you to consider you otherwise." His thumb rubbed over my bottom lip. "I know so much more than you ever wanted me to. I'm not going anywhere, even if it ends in my bloodshed. Not this time, Firefly. You'd have to take my life to get rid of me."

Yet you refuse to. How irritating.

"Who says I have the power to do that?"

He leaned closer. "Who says you *want* to do that?" As my lips parted just barely, he claimed them, and I so easily gave back.

Then someone burst through the door. "The giant wants to see you, Lana," Aalia said.

The giant got what he wanted, too. I exited the room, Luka trailing behind, and found the giant's spirit perched on a step while admiring the vines that hung from my walls. When he spotted me, he twisted back. "You want to know just how to stop this curse. I have the answers."

FORTY-FIVE

"Poisoned apples are easy. I can do poisoned apples. I've done poisoned apples. Shattering a mirror, done." I swallowed as the spirit tilted his head. "But death. Who has to die? Is it me? Do I finally get my second chance just to have to sacrifice myself after all?"

Befitting for a poisonous queen.

He shook his head. "Doesn't have to be anyone specifically. But it needs to be someone. You can decide that amongst yourselves. Those three things are needed, and once they're done, the curse will be enacted, and something will need to be sacrificed after the fact."

"Cool, so someone has to die and then we have to give up something on top of that." I shooed him away, turning to face Luka.

You should be the sacrifice. After the failure you've become.

"I know what you're thinking."

"Of course you do. You're reading my mind all the time."

He can't hear me.

"Lana, don't do it." He rushed forward, grabbing a hold of my face.

"It can't be you. That's not fair."

"But it is fair. I was supposed to sacrifice my life at the beginning of all of this."

He shook his head. "We'll find another way if we have to. It cannot be you." He kissed me longingly, pleading for my life. Was I really supposed to just take the selfish path again? It hadn't worked so well the first time.

When he pulled away, sorrow poured from his expression and into the air surrounding us. It drenched us in despair. "You're not going to listen to me at all, are you?"

I shook my head, wrapping my fingers around his wrists. "I can't. I've saved the ghosts from being stuck in the void. I've done the one good deed. If I sacrifice myself, necromancers won't exist again. My bloodline dies. Everyone is safe, and Orsadia has a chance to grow."

"Sleep on it. Please. At least allow that." He grabbed my hand, dragging me to the bed.

As a shiver crawled up my spine, I started to undress with his help, down to my chemise. I slid into bed just as Luka removed his boots and shirt, getting in beside me.

Tugging me to his chest, I forced my muscles to relax.

"I'm a moth to a flame, Firefly. You burn and all I can ever do is follow," he whispered, his hot breath fanning my ear.

Little did he know I burned because he lit the fire.

But I'd sleep on it. I just couldn't promise to him that I'd change my mind about what needed to happen.

Arms wrapped around my stomach, pulling me back until I hit a hard chest. I twisted my head to find Luka's spring-filled eyes glued to mine. I waited for a kiss. I counted on it, too, but his lips planted soft promises along my neck and shoulder, and in their path my skin had been left scorched.

My eyes fluttered closed, and I relished his touch. The moment they shot open, I couldn’t feel him anymore.

As I turned back to find the bed empty, I felt the sheets and grabbed my own aching head.

Nothing but a silly dream.

My own mind had betrayed my trust. I’d never allow him in again. He’d been nothing but a speck of dirt that hit my cheek. Maybe he’d been planning my demise for months now and I had so carelessly asked him into my home. But I’d have the upper hand this time. I’d never let him best me.

I’d do what needed to be done.

I stiffened when a familiar presence stopped behind me.

"Lana," my father's whisper echoed through the Great Hall.

Turning around to face him, I swallowed. "Father."

Luka slipped just outside the doorway to give us as much privacy as he could.

My father rushed over, pulling me into a hug as sobs swept over me. His hand smoothed my hair as he kissed my head a million times before pulling away to look at me. "You can't."

"What?"

"I'm telling you that you can't do it. I know you want to be the death, but you can't. You've gone all these lengths to right all your wrongs. You should live long enough to see the good it results in. Do you understand?"

"Father, I—"

"Lana Edmilla," his voice boomed. "You will grant me this one last request after my own death. Do you understand?" he repeated.

With a nod, I slowly replied, "I understand.”

FORTY-SIX

When I woke, I found my legs tangled in another pair. My cheek rested against a chest as fingers threaded themselves in my raven hair. The part of me plagued with sleep absorbed all it could from this comforting position.

The other side screamed at me to move.

One could easily guess which side I obeyed.

As I tried to roll away, his grip tightened, chest rumbling as he said in a low tone, "Firefly, don't go anywhere. Just let a good thing be." That voice became the lullaby to my ears. Smooth as honey and as hot as a red pepper.

"Luka," I started, but he cut me off.

"No. Don't say it. Just relax. Sleep. Enjoy the moment. There's nothing wrong with finally enjoying a good moment after all the shit we've had to go through." His fingers began brushing through my waves.

I could hear my father's voice in the back of my head, saying, *"Lana, just listen to him. You deserve to experience something pure."*

Listening was dangerous. Obeying—promising—it would make it that much more difficult to leave them behind.

Slowly, the tension dissipated from my muscles, and I focused on his heartbeat—steady, but a little chaotic from time to time. I wasn't sure if I was meant to be worried or not.

"Just like that," he whispered.

"Luka," I asked more like a question.

"Yes?"

"What do you think of...acknowledging my grandmother's name?" I drummed my fingers on his bare chest.

A chuckle vibrated through him. "Like taking her last name?"

I nodded a tad, careful not to move too much as to disrupt his fingers so carefully knotted in my hair.

"Hm. I think it's brilliant. Brave. Boisterous, like she would have wanted." He shifted, bringing his other arm down around my waist and hiking me up until my face hovered inches from him. "There's no reason to be ashamed of your roots."

He made it far too difficult to focus or form a coherent thought with his warmth wrapping around me.

"I'm glad I can be of service," he said with a small laugh. "Your brain is far too overwhelming anyway." Hand still in my hair, he brought me in for the sugary kind of kiss most women dreamed of but rarely experienced. His lips took charge, and for once in my life, I didn't mind not being the one in control. I was along for the ride.

When he pulled away, his smile sent flutters from my heart to my stomach.

"Then that's it," I said in a quieter voice. "They can call me Lana Edmilla-Regali." I'd wear the name with pride, too, for Anne Regali and all she fought for. I'd be the one to make a name for us again.

FORTY-SEVEN

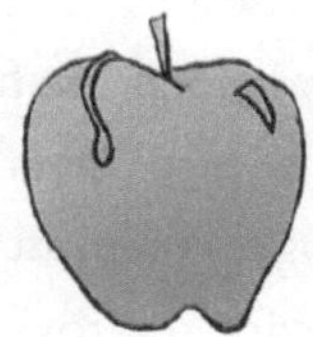

My fingers smoothed over the shiny leaves of the complementary plant to my garden. Monstera.

Large, vibrant green leaves. They paired fairly well right next to some of my more harmless flowers. Peace lilies.

They bloomed vertically, with one white petal at the backdrop of its pollen stem center. I thought maybe if I had planted something with peace in its name, it might inspire or invoke something calmer in me.

Somehow, I still admired my deadly nightshade with more vigor.

I hoped to the universe or someone that Zoe kept it thriving, or allowed me to. My garden had been my safe space lately. A place I could go and feel like maybe I had done some good. I'd brought life when everywhere else I went was a world of decay.

"You have a lovely garden," a deeper female voice stated.

"Mother," I whispered.

When I turned to face her, she stepped forward in all her glory. Her hair flowed, left in its natural state of waves while she wore a white blouse with dark pants and brown loafers. Anyone who knew me at all could see I never picked up my mother's fashion sense.

"I'm proud of you."

When I met her eyes, I searched for a speck of resentment. A white lie. Anything that called her out for saying such a thing.

Swallowing my urge to cause a rift, I asked, "Why?"

Her eyes cast about my garden as she furrowed her brows. "Why? What's not to be proud of? You've been fighting this curse."

"I'd hardly call this fighting. I've almost wiped out Orsadia because I'm obsessed with playing with my toys." I grabbed a fresh pail of water, pouring it over some of the soil. "In fact, we're standing over a graveyard of my own making right now." I glanced at her as she stepped back, scanning the grass. "Corpses really help nature flourish."

"Uh-huh. Seeing what my mother went through, it's understandable. I know this kind of responsibility can't be easy to take on. You've had to do it all on your own. I can't quite blame you for doing the best you can with no support and a voice putting you down." She reached for a plant.

"Stop!" I reached out, eyes wide.

Mother jumped back in shock. "What? What did I do?"

"Those are poisonous." I hurried over, wincing from the sharp pain in my ankle. "Touching them can make you really sick and mess with your heart."

"Snow, why on Orsadia are you growing such kinds of plants?"

I released a sigh. "Do you understand now? I'm not someone to be proud of." I set my pail down, seeing as most of the water sloshed out. "And they protect against insects and pests pretty well."

"The better question is: why are you surprised that a necromancer is growing poisonous plants?" Fallon stepped out of the castle door. "I thought you saw what your mother went through." He shot Mother a mischievous grin.

Mother dropped down onto a small stump. "I thought maybe the spell would have helped. But I suppose it didn't do much good other than ensure you survived to be able to take the throne."

I lowered my chin. "So you're not proud of me."

"I didn't say that."

I shrugged. "You've implied it."

Mother shot up and grabbed onto my shoulders, forcing me down where she'd been sitting. "Stop. Don't you dare say things like that. Listen to me." She squatted in front of me, slipping her fingers into mine. "You still hear that voice, correct?"

"From time to time..." More often once it figured out how to escape Luka's cage.

"You came back and let us into your life. You've taken the time to bring souls out of an afterlife that didn't entirely make sense for them. You're still searching for answers to fight a curse regardless that it's in your head, persuading you that you mean nothing."

Father stepped out, eyes roaming the little world I'd created for myself when I moved into Everinthian. "She's right. Your mother always is."

"Father," I said, trying to leap from my seat only to have my mother hold me down. "Let me go see him."

He came over to us, shaking his head with a chuckle. "I'll come to you. There's no need to disobey your mother."

"Her ankle has been sprained, and she refuses to stay in one place," she explained.

He lifted his head. "Ah, so your mother knows best."

I grumbled.

After a few moments of silence, I rubbed my sweaty palms onto my skirt. "You hired Luka to be my bodyguard."

Mother's fingers slipped from mine. Father frowned. "Were we wrong? You needed the help, whether you admit that or not."

Mother's smile brightened the garden. "And we all see how he looks at you. We can't really call that a failure on our part. Finding someone to understand you on a level nobody else can, that's special. And I'm not downplaying the importance of family or friends. Those relationships are crucial. But something about a romantic companion, it hits differently. You have someone to wake up to. He always promises to be by your side, even when your parents die, or your brother finds his own husband."

"Mom," Fallon said under his breath. "We aren't getting married."

"Not yet." She winked.

"You hired Luka to be her bodyguard and didn't think she'd find out or get upset?" My brother crossed his arms. "Really?"

Meeting his eyes with a puzzled look, I asked, "You didn't know?"

Father chuckled. "We didn't feel a need to tell him."

"And Mother? She knew?" My father had certainly come up with the idea, and asked Luka to follow through with it.

"Of course. You could never keep anything a secret from her."

Mother's smile eased. "Speaking of secrets, you need to stop pretending you're fine. Your ankle is throbbing, Snow. It's not going to heal like this."

"I can't rest. Not now when we're so close."

Father's hand landed on my shoulder. "Yes, you can. And you will. For us."

I wanted to argue. But I didn't have it in me to quite do that anymore. Not with the idea that I was conversing with my father's ghost and we were already running out of time.

Fingering the hilt of my sword on my belt, I inhaled, prepared to ask what I didn't want to visit at all. "I've been...having trouble lately. Here and there. With memories. I'll forget things that shouldn't be easy for me to forget. Three years ago, Luka told me that I forgot an entire night. And sometimes, I'll forget my own corpses. I'll forget details I may have known. Father, I'm terrified."

As he gulped down some air that he didn't need, he bent down to my level. "Lana, my daughter. To enact the spell, we had to...deal with a few consequences."

"What does that mean?"

Mother reached for my hands again, grasping them. Warming them. Preparing me for the worst news of my life.

"The protection spell came with a price."

I almost choked. "Is that price my memory?"

My mother squeezed my fingers. "To keep you alive until your term, we made a deal with Magic Law that you'd have to...sacrifice something eventually."

"And what does that mean?" I croaked.

Fallon circled, standing behind my right shoulder. "What does that mean, Mom?"

She opened her mouth, but Father cut in—I supposed to save her the backlash from what she was about to say, "Your mind will fade away over time."

"Until I don't remember who you are," I finished.

Their faces sank.

Just not as deep as my security.

Someday, my memory would cease to exist.

FORTY-EIGHT

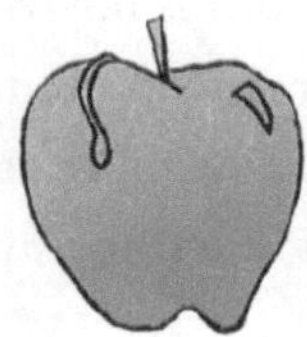

I didn't leave my bed for a few weeks.

No, it wasn't entirely to blame on what my parents told me, although it played a role.

I stayed in my bed per their request to heal my ankle.

Luka took great pleasure in waiting on me hand and foot—pun intended.

"Do you want to talk about it?" he asked as he set my tea on my side table.

I rolled onto my side with a shrug. "What's to talk about? I'm stuck in this bed."

He scooted closer and leaned forward, placing a hand in front of my body as if he wanted to force me to give him attention. He was so *needy*. "Exactly. So talk to me, Firefly."

When his nickname slipped from his tongue, a sob locked into my throat.

Luka's eyes caught on, darkening as his brows began to droop. "Hey. Please, talk to me."

Swallowing the lump, I twisted back to look up at him, meeting his gaze. "Someday I'm not going to remember why you call me Firefly. I'm not going to remember how to use my magic if I get to keep it. I'm not going to remember my mother or father. I'm not going to remember my own brother, or his boyfriend. I won't remember the queens, or my grandmother. I won't remember when we were kids and you trained me. I won't remember you, or your name."

He leaned forward, threading fingers into my dark waves. "What are you talking about?"

"When they put that spell on me, it came with a side effect. A bad one." A tear slipped. "My parents told me that I'm going to lose more memories, Luka. When I forget things, it's because my brain is starting to fade."

"Hey," he said as he grabbed my cheeks. "I'm right here. I will always be right here. And even when things get scary, I will be there, too. If you forget, just ask me. I won't judge you. I won't tease you. I'll simply remind you. I'll hold memories for the both of us if I have to."

I wanted to pull away from his touch, but he held me firmly to prove that he wasn't going anywhere.

"Firefly," he repeated, "I won't leave you. I will help you whenever you need it."

"Why?" I asked in a quiet tone. "Why do you love me so much that you're willing to spend your time filling in the holes in my mind? Why do you love me at all?"

He lifted me towards him, his lips hovering less than an inch from mine. "For one, you don't choose who you fall in love with. Two, because my life means nothing if I don't have someone to spend it with. Three, you keep my ego in check." That last one had been meant as a joke. Everyone knew my ego had been bigger than his.

"Luka," I started, my breathing growing shallow. "In case I forget someday, let me say it now. You're the one voice that even if they were insults, I was glad to hear for three years. You drive me mad, but I will only ever crave you. I hang around the dead quite too much. I forget how to feel things. You remind me that I'm here—breathing. You make me feel more alive than anyone else has ever felt. An electric type of feeling—addictive in all the worst and best ways. You're mine, Luka Lockwood, just as much as I am entirely yours."

With that, he devoured my soul.

FORTY-NINE

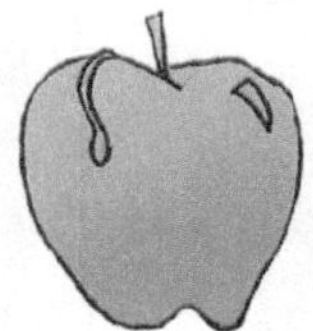

"I have never said this before but I think I'd like to simply not be a necromancer for a day." My eyes flicked to the ghosts waiting by my door. "You are all acting like I've become your servant. I could still send you right back to that void."

"You love us too much," Kali said with profuse excitement.

"What do you guys want?"

"Is it not obvious?" Aelin dropped onto the bed, her eyes wavering on Luka standing by the window as if he wasn't also my... Well, I wasn't sure what we were. Lovers? No, that implied much more intimacy than where we went.

Clearing my throat, I turned my head towards her some more, far too comfortable to lift it from my black pillow. "Is it supposed to be?"

Aelin leaned forward. "Have you kissed?"

"Excuse me?" I shot up as she moved back. I couldn't really hit her. I mean, I certainly could. But not anything that'd cause any real harm. "Are you all here because you want to know if I kiss and tell?"

Aelin squeaked. "That means you did!"

Kali leaned forward. "For the record, no. I just wanted to come say hello while I had the chance. And your father insisted."

He gave a small nod.

Aelin flopped onto her stomach and propped up her cheeks with her fists, elbows digging into my mattress. "So, tell me all about it."

Luka snorted. "Which time?"

"There were multiple kisses!" Aelin shot a look at my father and Kali. "Did you hear that?"

Father's lips twitched. "I really wish I hadn't."

"Hey, piss-colored toilet water, can you not give out our business like it's free bread?" I scowled at Luka.

He crossed his arms. "The unique insults turn me on way more than you'd like." Unfolding them, he threw his hands out, waving his fingers in sync towards himself. "No, really. Keep them coming, Firefly."

"Please, not while I'm in the room," my father raised his voice.

"Then don't be in the room, silly!" Aelin grinned as she kicked her feet behind her. "So? What does he taste like?"

I widened my eyes. "Taste...like?"

A smirk slowly crept up on Luka's lips. "Oh, pray tell. What *do* I taste like?"

Father turned away. "Why did I bother coming in here? I should have suspected this was going to turn into some type of romance talk." He glanced back, eyes moving from Luka's head to his toes. "With Luka."

Aelin shooed him. "No, no, we are not brushing this under the rug. Answer the question."

"What was that again?" I asked quietly.

"What does Luka taste like?" she repeated.

Even Luka himself had stepped closer.

"You don't have to answer that, Lana," my father said.

He said that. But Aelin wouldn't leave me alone, and Luka would take it upon himself to tease me until the end of time to get the answer.

"Honey."

"Honey?"

"Yeah."

"Int—"

"And spices." I chewed my bottom lip. "Like a honey glazed ham with a side of seasoned, roasted vegetables. But the honey glazed ham is also coated in natural sugars to give is a sweeter taste. You get all the best flavors in one simple meal. And when it's really late, and unsuspecting, he tastes like the funnel cake from the carnival. Powdered sugar with fresh strawberries. Whipped cream. All to top off a fried pastry."

When I met their gazes, I forced a laugh. "Not that I've been thinking too much about it or anything."

Aelin slipped from the bed. "My work here is done. It's Kali's turn." She waved her fingers individually before disappearing from the room.

I refused to make eye contact with Luka.

Kali stepped forward. "I'm not here to pester you about your love life. I'm thankful that you pulled me out when you did. And even if you beat yourself up about my death, please, don't. You had to do what you had to do, and Mira came to me with the proposal long before you found me. I knew what my fate was going to be." She approached the window, overlooking the land. "I lived in a tower that had been crumbling. It was never going to get better than that. Especially knowing how things would have turned out here anyway." When she caught a glimpse of my apologetic expression, a sorrowful smile appeared. "That's not a jab at you. You shouldn't take that guilt upon yourself. I like to believe things happen for a reason."

"What reason is that?" I whispered.

"Maybe I would have been the cause of a disaster. We never know. I could have been the one who started some kind of plague." She shrugged with a smile. "It's good to see you again, Snow."

She took that as her cue to leave.

"Father, I suppose that leaves just you," I said as I rolled onto my side.

He ran a hand down his face. "You know, I think I'm okay for now. I'm a little tired."

"But ghosts don't sleep."

"I'm still tired." He put a hand up before dipping out of my room.

Luka pressed his legs against the side of my bed. "I taste like all the flavors in one simple meal, hm?"

Rolling my eyes, I scoffed. "Don't flatter yourself."

His laugh still made me smile anyway.

Once it faded, I let my eyelids fall shut. Seconds later, a body lay beside me. "Can I flatter myself now?" he asked in a low tone.

I cracked my eyes open to find his beautiful juniper irises boring into mine. "What are you blabbing on about?"

"You aren't that naïve." He flashed a smile.

Tangling my fingers in his dark hair, I laughed. "You're right. I'm not." I closed the last of the gap between us and tasted the funnel cake that belonged solely to me.

Damn Aelin for asking such a question and feeding Luka more of my weaknesses.

FIFTY

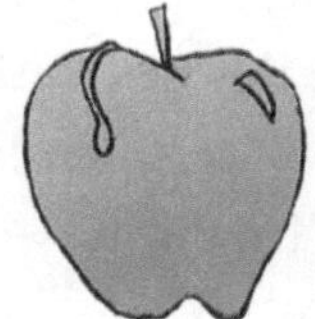

"What are we here for again?" Zoe asked as she slapped a tree branch out of her face.

"Since we've got what we need between the poisoned apples and a handheld mirror, I'm just here to see if I can gather anything about my grandmother. If I lose my magic, I don't want to lose access to her."

And when I'd sacrifice my life, I wouldn't have a chance to come back here.

Luka whistled as he trekked beside me. Dave, Aalia, and Mira all lingered behind.

Clyde and Fallon tagged along, too, because we had to make it a family affair.

She says sarcastically, he hissed.

As we began crossing the bridge, familiar music drifted our way, courtesy of the wind. Fast-paced. Child-like. Fun.

"What..." We halted in our tracks on the bridge. I lifted my arm to keep everyone behind me as my eyes danced around the colorful lights. Tents stood on every corner, vertical stripes of red and white, purple and white, blue and white, and so forth. Characters strolled from one gaggle of fun to the next. Laughter bled into the skies. The scent of fried foods, buttery popcorn, and sugary funnel cakes wafted by.

Mira floated past everyone, stopping near my shoulder. "It's back."

"I didn't do this. How is this here?" My jaw clenched as I turned my chin down over my shoulder, towards her.

A chuckle escaped her. "I was a forseer in my life. How do you think the carnival existed, Snow? I was able to conjure it up because it came from the future. Well, now the future is here," she whispered the final sentence.

Starting the slow venture into the carnival, Zoe's eyes wandered in awe.

"Okay. Well, change of plans," I said as I turned to face the others. Nobody listened.

"Yeah, yeah," Zoe gave a thumbs up.

"Be careful. Do not converse with fortune tellers! Beware of the tents!" I shouted after her as she took off.

Fallon hurried over to a stand of games, and Clyde hesitated to follow before pleading with me. When I shooed him away, they were gone.

Mira and Aalia decided to take a stroll, letting Dave stumble behind them. Which left just Luka and I.

"Fuck," I muttered.

Luka reached for my hand, slipping his fingers into mine as if I was about to disappear forever. It shattered my heart knowing what I would eventually do to him.

I call it karma for the way he left you for three years on your own. Albeit you did do wonderful things then, before you turned on me.

Now you're useless.

He tugged me against his side, pressing a kiss to my cheek. "This carnival is not the same one. It's still different. Why don't we enjoy ourselves?"

"How do you figure? Mira was able to tell the future but we could never change it."

"Precisely. But also, this is Hypnotic Arythe. Magic is both weaker and stronger here. Flexible. You may bend it in ways you couldn't do before." He smacked his lips together.

Glancing at him, I cocked an eyebrow. "When the hell did you get brains?"

He reminded me of his own magic and how he was able to practice. Even if Hypnotic Arythe was ultimately controlled by the queens, it amplified magic for others who had yet to take the throne. Luka took advantage because without control, magic could be used as a deadly weapon.

Well, in Orsadia it already was.

Luka began walking, his grip tightening.

"Wait." I pulled him back. "There are a few questions plaguing me. One that pertains to you."

He spun on his heel with a grin. "What might that be, Firefly?"

"If you were born to a queen, why did the curse skip making you the heir?"

His features softened. "I never wanted the throne. It was between you and Mira, but she'd already moved into Drecose by then, so coming out with my own magic seemed pointless. And when she became queen, you immediately stepped up. When I saw you announce who you were, my heart skipped a beat. I trusted you more than I trusted myself."

"Grave mistake," I said in a quieter tone.

"No." He reached for my chin, lifting it. "I still believe you could handle it better. This death thing, I mean. Me? I could never. My light would have been snuffed out because I don't consider myself strong enough for any of this. And before you dare say you're not, I've seen you. Making it through three years of ruling with a poisonous tongue and still managing to turn it around, that's strength. You're brighter than the sun, and far more courageous than you'll ever know."

Just how many others were born to queens but never took the throne because of us? How many more carried magic? If Luka had forgone the throne and still carried magic at twenty-six, then there had to be others.

I cast my eyes downward.

"What's the second question?"

"Hm?"

"You said a few questions plague you."

"The first queens. Aalia. Gaia. Willow. None of them were born to a queen. We know how Aalia attained magic... How did the others, before it became a part of their DNA that then began getting passed down?" I tilted my head, brows pinched together.

Luka opened his mouth to answer before a hand slapped his shoulder. "Hey!" We both burned gazes with a familiar face. Remy.

I think Luka mentally groaned, because I heard it in my own head and it wasn't mine. At least this time.

Damnit Zoe. It was almost like she couldn't entirely help it when she came here.

Behind Remy was everyone else we ever met over there, too.

And someone we didn't recognize this time.

When she stepped forward, she threw her hand out. "Hi! I'm Zhyire!"

Well, holy fuck, color me surprised.

"You and me both," I uttered under my breath.

The way she'd been talked about, I knew she meant something

more to Remy. But this woman was adorable. I hadn't seen anything like it before. She reminded me of a teddy bear in human form. The one I'd willingly gave up as a child that night in Ash Forest when I came to discover just how comforting the darkness was.

Subtle waves, strawberry blonde hair, and bangs the way Zoe had her own. She wore blue pants made of a thicker and rougher material, with some sort of pink extra thick tunic with a hood on the back and pockets on her abdomen. What was with the style in their world?

Luka nudged me and cleared his throat. It was then I lifted my gaze from her teeth-white shoes and to her hand that still sat in front of me. "What do I do with this?"

"You...shake it." Her head tilted as she laughed a bit. "Do you not shake hands here?"

Remy leaned in, coughing. "We're not in Smarioe anymore."

Nivian snorted.

We did. But to think others did it, too? Did Luka teach others when he traveled?

"No Calum? Or Ambrose?" I asked.

Zhyire dropped her hand as she shook her head. "Calum said he didn't need to be here this time. We let him stay back with Ambrose. They deserved a cozy night in."

Swiveling to face Kiernan and Esmira, I gestured around them. "You never bring friends along."

Esmira smiled softly. "We don't have any friends to bring along."

Kiernan slipped a hand around her waist, planting a kiss to her temple.

"What's this?" Esmira pointed down at my hand.

When I followed her attention, I realized it was the one Luka held.

Luka took that as his cue to yank me against him, to which I threatened to stab him with a fork later. "That's our business." While he had said it with a grin, there'd been bite to his tone.

I knew there was a reason I'd kissed back.

What were we? What did this really mean—us?

I made note to tuck that in for later.

"You have funnel cake, right?" Zhyire asked, looking back at the food stands.

"We do. Although it might be drugged."

"I might be okay with that."

Remy shot her a look. "No, you are not okay with that. As your bodyguard, absolutely not."

I nodded as Luka who then quietly pulled me away from the group. "Which ride first?" He pointed at a few different ones.

The tall one was a no-go. It made me sick thinking about it.

Before I could get a word out, Luka was leading us to the first one of his choosing.

I silently thanked Zoey for providing me a new dress after my last one had been covered in my own blood. I did not want to be riding all these rides in a gown when summer was peaking.

This one had been white and blue, with floral patterns and a cinch in the chest to accentuate my cleavage.

Growing up, being a woman had never been something I wanted to hide from anyone. I wore dresses and gowns. I wore corsets. My chest was no secret because I appreciated what I had. I'd be damned to let anyone make me hide it from the world.

Luka certainly liked the color of this dress, too.

Light. Breathable. Feminine. A muted hue, a few shades darker than that of the ocean.

I yelped as Luka ripped me towards a ride made of sky blue and pink. The color of the teddy bear woman if I were to compare at all. I totally was.

As we waited in the short line and seated ourselves beside each other in a pink pod, a metal bar came down on our laps. Loose enough for us to climb out if needed. Was that safe?

I pushed against it, but it wasn't going anywhere. A little wiggle room and nothing more.

Luka sat back with a sigh. "I know we've got a curse to break but it's nice to get away for a bit. If we're forced to enjoy the carnival that comes to Orsadia, I'm not going to complain." His eyes fluttered shut.

"I will," I mumbled.

An eye popped open. "What was that?"

"Nothing, dear," I mocked.

The ride started, and the entire platform the pods sat on began to spin, and our pods started swinging around based on the momentum and force. I hadn't anticipated how bad it was going to get. The ride went so fast that Luka flew into me, pressing against my left side, and I was pinned between the side of the pod and his buff ass.

I grabbed for the bar and struggled to pulled myself away. He tried to do the same, but the ride had been too strong. Too much spinning.

When it stopped, I was the first to leap off when the bar came up. I ran to the fence and hunched over, dry-heaving.

Luka pulled my hair back, stifling a laugh. "No more rides like that. Understood."

"I think my brain is stuck to the right side of my skull." I groaned.

His arm slipped around my waist as he pulled me into his side, guiding me away. "What about food?" When I shot him a glare, he snorted. "Okay, no food. A game, then?"

"As long as we don't go into any tents." I refused to put myself through that again.

We approached a booth full of plush toys and what looked to be targets. Red and white circles alternating until they hit the red center.

"I'm good at this." Luka sat me down on a blue cushioned stool that'd also been made of silver.

I glanced up at the awning that had been stripped in the same colors as the targets—clown crimson and seafoam white.

The man behind the counter explained to Luka he had three tries to make the skullseye and win a prize. Luka practically dismissed him, but as soon as he started throwing the darts, he cursed under his breath. "This game is rigged."

I pretended that was the case. It wasn't as if throwing darts with your fingers and shooting arrows with a bowstring were entirely differently things.

"Don't you use a bow and arrow?" that damned voice asked.

Remy.

I hated this guy most days.

Luka scowled at him. "It's different."

I'd almost piped in to come to Luka's defense but it was not only adorable to see him jealous and flustered, but I wanted to see his ego be pegged down a notch.

From Remy of all people.

"Maybe in a sense." Remy shrugged. "But you should angle it up a little. Think about the trajectory."

Luka paused to twist his body a little his way. "Are you some expert now?"

"Well, I don't mean to toot my own horn, but then again I kind of do." He patted Luka's shoulder and moved around him as Luka grunted.

The poor huntsman wasted about half an hour of our time before he finally hit the center enough to win something small. The man behind the counter handed him what looked to be a small turtle.

Luka then handed it to me, which my eyebrows shot up for. "What do I do with this?"

"Take it home and display it proudly. Cuddle it. I don't know, but I won it and now I'm giving it to you. Have you ever seen a turtle before, Firefly?"

"I haven't seen a wolf either. Some crows. A raven. Definitely squirrels. Rabbits. The rare deer. Never a turtle." Not even a fish. "It's a miracle our ecosystem survives at all. I've no doubt Zoe will change that. Orsadia will flourish under her ruling."

And I'd never be around to see it.

"Take it." He placed it in my arms. "I have seen many on my ventures."

I opened my mouth to protest, but Luka's sparkling eyes shut me down.

Damn, I hated when he did that. He had such power over me.

Remy wandered off and I assumed it'd been because his guardee went first. She stuffed her face with cotton candy and funnel cakes and all the fried foods one could imagine.

"I'm hungry now." But was it safe to eat?

Luka gestured over to a stand and I swiveled on the stool before hoping off and jogging to catch him. I grabbed onto him and sidled up, wrapping my arm around his bicep.

When we approached, I decided to let him pick.

He picked roasted corn, although it was still on the cob. He took a bite first, eyes falling shut as he groaned in bliss. "That is the best corn I've had since I've existed. It's safe to eat." His gaze locked on mine. "Go ahead."

I took my first bite as juice exploded on my tongue along with the flavor. Spices. A hint of sweetness. "Fuck," I muttered. "This *is* the best corn ever."

We devoured our cobs of corn in minutes. When we'd picked them clean, we tossed the center.

"We should go on something easy, to settle our stomachs," he suggested.

I agreed, and so we headed over to the Ferris Wheel.

Again, the line had been short and we were on in seconds. I spotted

Fallon and Clyde in a cart up ahead, my brother's head tucked into my guard's shoulder. My heart warmed at the sight. All I'd ever truly wanted was happiness for him. Seeing him achieve that, it gave me better reason to say my goodbyes while I was still their hero.

Seeing as Luka hadn't been able to catch the cursed voice of himself inside my mind, it came as no surprise that he couldn't hear the heinous and disturbing thoughts of my own.

The ride began, and this was the moment I looked over the entire carnival. With an ocean backdrop, it'd been breathtaking.

Storm clouds rolled in. The ocean crashed against the base of the cliff as if it'd had a vendetta against our island.

It almost replaced the horrid memories of the first.

Almost. Not quite, though.

"Luka, what are we?" I turned my head towards him.

"What are we?" He furrowed his brows. "As in: relationship wise?"

"Yeah. I suppose."

He savored the question, smacking his lips together. "Well, I could ask you want you want us to be, but then that would beg the question what I want us to be. Since you're curious of my perspective, I suppose it's fair to give it." He leaned back. "You, Firefly, are the flame when someone needs a little light to see in front of them. You pave our future. That would make me the candle itself. Wax, wick, and chamberstick. I give you something to burn. I melt in your presence. I support you. I'm yours as much as you'll have me, and I hope you feel the same."

My lips parted a little as my breath hitched. Damn him for saying shit like that.

"What's that look for?" He rested a hand on my knee. Warm, firm, strong. Everything he was that I wasn't.

I'd been the cold breath on an early winter morning. Unsteady, wavering to whichever way the wind blew me. Weak. Easy to manipulate and convince to do terrible things.

I envied Luka, and I admired him for everything he was.

It was a shame I had to be the one to take the heart he so willingly and carelessly gave to me to the tomb.

For now, I'd let us live up in the clouds a while longer.

"Everything you are is inviting and promising. I adore it about you." I rested my hand over his before bringing it to my lips and pressing a tender kiss to his knuckles. "That's the kind of man I've fallen in love with. I don't regret it. I don't regret meeting you, or kissing you, or falling for you. Not a single second of it has been wasted. Do you hear me, Lockwood?" I held his gaze as my heart pounded in my ears. I would never return from this. "You can have my heart. Have my soul. I trust you far more than I trust myself with it. I am forever indebted to you because you've given me something to lose."

"Is that a nightmare?" He leaned close, his hot breath fanning my lips.

I pressed them together. "At times. I want you to have every piece of me until there's nothing left of me to give."

His fingers came up to cradle both sides of my jaw. He inched closer, and I craved the very taste of him.

The wheel stopped. "Ride's over," a worker said.

"Until next time, Firefly," he whispered with a tiny smirk as he leaped from the seat and dragged me with him.

The world had changed. Colors saturated every nook around me. Details sharpened. Senses heightened, and smells blended together to create the perfect delectable treats.

Love did not make one blind. It simply showed one what all the world had to offer.

To give ourselves a little bit more time, we stopped to sit on a bench painted in stark purple. Hunter lingered just a few feet, like he wanted to come say hi, but he decided against it. Probably the best call. That was what made Hunter one of the easier ones to get along with.

My eyes followed as he went to go hop on a ride. His screams and laughter could be heard over all the chatter and whimsical music.

In the way he enjoyed himself, I wondered if he got to be a child like this. Did carnivals exist in Arizona? Had Hunter ever had the chance to get away from the harsh realities and just relax?

With a sigh, I twisted my body, pulling my knees up and laying my head in Luka's lap. "So, about your magic."

"You always want to know about it."

"It intrigues me, Luka. *You* interest me. Is that so wrong?"

He shrugged a bit, instinct kicking in as his fingers began stroking my hair. "What do you want to know?"

"What else can you do? Is that it? You manipulate sound into something sinister?"

Despite the uncomfortable question, tension dissipated. Maybe it was because he had someone to open up to. Someone who understood dark magic.

I certainly wasn't one to judge.

"I've attempted to turn horrendous sounds into something soothing. It doesn't work. As hard as I've tried, I cannot. I've discovered I cannot create new sounds. I must use those I've heard before. Sounds that might invoke fear or anxiety or dread." He threaded his fingers through strands of my raven-colored hair. "Screams. Sirens. Children crying."

"And... Dare I ask, can you mimic the voices of people that have died? Do you have the power to make them hear their dead loved ones?"

He swallowed as his eyes glassed off. "Sometimes. If it's enough to terrorize the person still alive."

The way I terrorize you, Little Raven. Because even if his blood spills over this land, I'll never leave you. You'd never let me after that. I'd be all you have left of him. We may be tethered now, but I came from the curse before I sensed his magic.

"I'll get rid of you," I whispered. "Anyway I have to, I swear to it I will."

Luka frowned. "Firefly, what does that mean? Who are you talking to?" Concern seeped into the wrinkles between his brows.

"Nobody. Nothing." I grabbed his free hand, pressing it to my lips. "Just let this moment be."

He did. He allowed it even if he craved to know the truth.

Soon we wouldn't have memories like these to make. Eventually, we couldn't create pockets of time where everything stood still and gave us something to live for.

I was going to destroy all of it simply for Zoe's future. For Orsadia's. It was a sacrifice I was willing to make to ensure we didn't lose everything. I only mourned Luka having to be the casualty among it all.

Turning my head to the left, I watched the carnival in all of its glory.

Clowns maniacal laughter. Popcorn tossed about. Screams of fear and awe soaking our skies. Mischievous and offbeat tunes flitting from one tent to the next.

At some point we gained the energy to continue on with our night while it was still young. Dusk had only passed an hour ago.

We passed by a dark building in which I yanked Luka back as I halted. "I want to go on this one."

His eyes darted to the structure plastered with ghouls and skeletons and other creepy creatures. "Only for you." A shiver ran down from his head to his toes.

We circled around to find the door and headed up the steps. We were seated in a small cart connected to a track. It jerked forward, and we began rolling beyond dark double doors that opened up to swallow us whole.

My huntsman attempted to appear relaxed, but that man could not fool me.

As the cart threw us around sharp corners and right into dead ends, lights flashed. Smoke poured from crevices. Creatures made from two-dimensional materials popped up and screamed at us. Luka jumped, and I snorted.

"It's okay." I patted his thigh. "I got you."

He took that as his cue, grabbing my hand and sliding his fingers between mine. "For your sake."

"For my sake," I repeated with a grin.

The scares and horrors eased my racing heart. The hair on my arms laid flat. Nothing filled me with more content than the darkness that made us question what else was in the room with us.

When the ride ended, Luka was practically sprinting to get off. I laughed as we stepped outside of the building, my boots landing in the grass with a soft thud.

He whipped around. "Do that again."

"What?"

"Do it again."

"Do what?" I furrowed my brows. "Laugh?"

"Yes."

"Luka," I said with a small chuckle.

He closed the gap between us in mere milliseconds, pressing me against the back wall as his hands cradled my face. "That. Your laugh. It fills me with..." He searched for the right word but never found one. "I don't get to hear you laugh often enough."

"You were pretty panicked in there," I noted.

He rubbed his thumb over my bottom lip. "That's your scene more than it has ever been mine."

"But you went on it for my sake," I chirped.

"Just for yours." He closed the last of the space, erasing all of his own fears. His lips moved with my own. Slow and sensual.

The man made of brass pining for the woman branded of silver.

He was all my own.

I'm gonna be sick.

My fingers carefully wrapped around his wrists, but in one quick movement, he slid them away and turned on me, pinning my wrists above my head. His palms met mine as our fingers locked together.

I could live in this moment forever.

"I knew it!" a woman gasped.

Luka parted from me but hovered about an inch away. "I said it wasn't your business."

Esmira crossed her arms. "Oh, come on. I just wanted to see it happen. Listen, I was once the kind of woman who had nobody but longed for someone. Watching everyone around you find love is heartbreaking. I just wanted to ensure Lana found the same."

I freed my hands from his and pressed my palms to his chest. "We should get going."

After another moment of hesitation, he grumbled.

Kiernan came and dragged Esmira away, quietly questioning why she had to butt into our private life.

Regardless, a small smile crept up.

Happy endings don't exist for people like you.

And like that, it faded.

Luka turned to follow, but couldn't entirely make up his mind. The toe of his boot pivoted and he twisted back towards me, placing a few fingers under my chin. He stole one last kiss—the flickering flame finding the fuel to burn bright.

Luka Lockwood plunged that knife into my chest and took what belonged to him, for I allowed him to take every last bit of me.

FIFTY-ONE

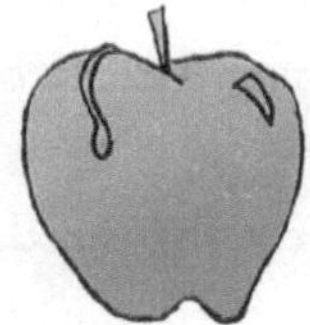

My gaze locked on a large structure behind all the tents and booths, a gasp escaping me. The mansion.

Not the run-down, skeleton of the home, but the lively version. The one my grandma had lived in before or after her term. I couldn't be entirely sure, but I assumed it had been once her ruling was over where she needed to hide from the people. Rarely did they want to take a trip over the long and unstable bridge.

Despite how close the village had been otherwise.

Orsadia was an island filled with people who'd rather surround themselves with others. Community. The only ones who had to accept a fate of solitude were the queens. And when my grandmother moved in, I doubted anyone was rushing to visit her. They'd rather her leave them.

Until they assaulted and murdered her, that was.

"Luka," I choked out as I smacked his arm. "Look."

When his eyes landed on it, we both weren't sure what we could utter under our breaths in the isolation of the night.

Why had it been there? Hypnotic Arythe was a force to be reckoned with, and not even the queens could entirely control it.

"Isn't that where we first met?" Remy asked, grabbing our shoulders as he squeezed himself between us. Luka growled in response. "Pipe down, lover boy," he replied with a scoff.

Something faded by in a window upstairs where a glow illuminated what I assumed to be a silhouette of a woman.

Someone was inside.

Immediately, my heart squeezed. Was it possibly my grandmother?

Before Luka could stop me, I was rushing up the concrete steps and ripping open the black double doors. I hurried inside, halting as a chill nipped at my skin.

The silence hung so heavy I'd almost questioned if I'd gone deaf.

"This is the place we so lovingly became like a family who only see each other at reunions," Remy said with a sigh. "Tragic."

No, I definitely was not losing my hearing.

Flames flickered, candles lighting the way up the grand steps. Beckoning me. Calling my name and tempting me to follow.

"If you want to stay down here, be my guest," I shot back before I raced up, palm sliding along the wood railing, skipping every other stair.

When I landed at the top, I skidded. The hallway lengthened and the doors doubled—from eight to sixteen.

A scream rattled the walls.

I quite enjoy this, he purred.

I marched forward, throwing open doors and coming across bedroom after bedroom.

At the end of the hall, another door creaked open. A woman exited, never showing her face but rather fleeting so quickly all I caught was the black hair left in her...death?

My fingers tingled, magic at the ready. Certainly a ghost.

"Grandmother," I forced out as I sprinted over to the room she disappeared into.

Entering, I found it vacant. Where had she gone?

A low moan filled the halls as if the mansion had been on fire and smoke billowed out along the ceiling.

It suffocated. I couldn't seem to get a full breath into my lungs, my chest constricting.

Maybe you'll die this time.

Wallpaper peeled as if I were the one spreading the demise. Maybe. I wouldn't have doubted it.

"Firefly?" Luka asked in a softer tone.

"She was here, Luka. She was. I saw her. My grandmother. I swear it." I didn't dare look him in the eyes for I knew he'd see me as delusional.

As if to make me look sane, a woman's wail echoed through the halls.

She was here.

"Anne Regali is here."

"Did you say your grandmother?" a gentle voice asked. Ah, the woman of the night. Remy's guardee, Zhyire.

I exhaled, embodying a shaky mess. "Yes. She's dead."

Her bright eyes widened as she glanced at Remy who carefully tucked her behind him. "I told you, Lana is a necromancer. She deals with the dead. And Orsadia isn't anything like our home." His eyes burned holes in my soul. "But we must not do anything rash, right, Lana?"

Run, Little Raven. Your grandmother is waiting for you.

I brushed them off, searching for the source. "It's her. Those are her cries." Door after door swung open until I located it. A woman whose face hadn't been recognizable. A blur, features not entirely prominent. I could make out black locks and a luscious gown in the same shade if not darker.

She stood over another woman who kneeled before her, the one whose power pulsed in the air around us.

The woman with a smeared identity screeched as she brought a sword through the other's chest. Blood splattered her skin.

As the woman dropped dead, I caught sight of her face, and I nearly collapsed with her. She had been the one who watched me burn.

And in an instant, both spirits vanished as if they'd never been here at all.

They hadn't, either. Not really. Not tonight. Just memories of this mansion left to rot in the bones.

I still had no idea who they were, but I suspected they had been queens, and I had an inkling one of them had been Anne.

Something disappeared behind me and I whipped around to follow. The wails began once again, and the woman defined by the night evaporated beyond the corridor.

Find her.

I started to run as Luka yelled for me to stop.

As if I'd listen to him.

When I rounded the corner, a cry in the opposite direction bounced down the hall. I turned my head towards the eerie atmosphere, not fazed by the way darkness engulfed me.

Sconces took their last breath. Doors slammed shut. The walls hummed and if I listened just right, I could almost hear its beating heart. I was left to rely on my senses which had not always been entirely useful to me anyhow.

Howling shook the floorboards beneath me.

"She's here," I whispered. My skin began to set off a glow. Subtle, but enough for me to not run into doors or smack my head into sconces decorating the walls. I could only truly see about the length of three skulls in front of me.

Following her cries, I wrapped my fingers around the cold metal of a knob. I pushed it open, slowly.

The room had been empty aside from one single chair. Intricate details carved into the wood, the back and seat lined with the most plush and luxurious blood red fabric known to Orsadia.

Shadows danced around the room before slithering into the corners never to return.

"She's not here. I don't understand." My eyes darted from wall to wall. Spinning on my heel, I ran into Luka.

"I had to," he said in a strained voice. He wouldn't meet my gaze and his posture slumped forward.

"Had to what?" My eyebrows knitted together.

"Distract you. Turn you around." He reached up to fix a strand of hair to which I retracted from.

"What?" I forced out, swallowing.

You Ridiculous Raven. Prey to the huntsman. A fool no wiser than a child.

He ran a hand down his face, pinching the bridge of his nose as if I were the one who disappointed him. How dare he? "You were following a ghost who mercilessly slaughtered another. I wasn't about to let you walk right into your own murder."

"She's my grandmother, Luka! She wouldn't have harmed me!" My back hit the wall behind me with a thud, air dissipating in my lungs.

"How can you know that?" He placed his palms flat on the worn floral wallpaper on either side of my head. "I'm not saying your grandmother was as dreadful as her title claimed her to be. All I am saying is that maybe she wasn't your grandmother. The way she moved around here tells me she wasn't aware of us at all. If this mansion is living in the past with its gore and glam, she may have been a memory just playing before our eyes with no ability to recognize you. We are far too close to ending this for you to make any grave mistakes."

"He's right, Queenie."

I groaned at the damn nickname.

Remy stepped forward, and Luka for once didn't wear jealousy. He gloated in being the sensible one. "You were treading in dangerous waters. It wasn't worth the risk." Darkness wrapped itself around his arms, gliding along his skin before seeping into his soul. The shadows... The shadows in the room had been from *him.*

Luka had recreated her weeping.

They worked *together* and I'd be a fool not to be sickened by it.

Slow and steady, the others emerged from the pits of the circus and its untimely slumber. Hunter. Zhyire. Nivian. Even Esmira and Kiernan.

"You used your magic against me," I said in a quieter voice, gaze flicking to the huntsman's.

His frown deepened, eyes searching every inch of my face as if he ached to kiss away the hurt. He wouldn't do that in front of our...allies, would he? "No, Firefly. I used it to protect you."

I choked on a sob.

He dropped his arms and pulled me into his chest, a hand landing in my hair and kisses to my temple. He was attempting to shield me, to save me the humiliation of shattering in front of all these people.

It wasn't fair.

Being chosen as the heir. Being given magic so powerful, so poisonous that I couldn't use it for good. Forced to give up all dreams. To watch my father die for my existence.

Life is never fair... Neither is death.

All to have to sacrifice myself and doing so simply because I truly didn't want to feel like the blemish on everyone's complexion.

I fucking loathed myself.

And Luka, for trying to piece me back together.

FIFTY-TWO

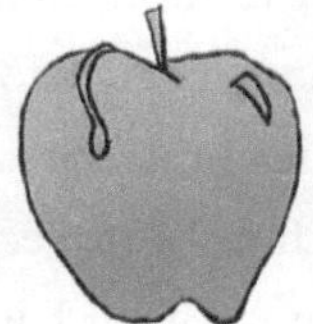

"This is it." I pointed at the dirt. "The spot we found Aalia's bones."

Zoe shot me a look. "And how did you know they were hers?"

Aalia's gaze fixated on it. "Spirits have...a sense. I can't find my bones but when I do stumble upon them, I know they're mine. They have this aura that nobody else can see."

"And...you have no idea how they ended up here?"

"I don't. I can't remember much about my death. I know she killed me. She poisoned me. But..."

Zoe's eyes met mine. "But you need definitive proof. Which is why I'm here, isn't it?"

Zoe and I both wondered what it was that always made her magic more powerful given her status. The conclusion we came to was simply that her being the first queen to be a third generation had more magic coursing through her veins than any of us could fathom.

I straightened my back. "I was thinking you and I could combine our magic. You warp reality. I play with the dead. Somehow, we can awake a dead memory about Aalia's death and see what actually happened to her. That way she can get the closure she needs."

"Sure. But I have a question."

"Shoot."

"How do we combine our magic?"

I snorted. "That's what we're about to find out. Luka and Clyde are here to stand guard in case something happens. What I'm going to do is try to reach into Aalia's dead memory and tug it out. When I do, I expect you to try and catch it, to project it somehow and warp the reality in a sense that we can see what happened that night."

Nodding, she stepped back and shook her hands, her black hair falling over her shoulders. "Great. Then that's what we'll do. I'm ready when you are, Lana." She blew a puff of air up towards her bangs to brush them from her dark eyes.

I swallowed and reached towards Aalia, sending my magic from my fingers and into her soul, slithering through her limbs to her head. I had to sift through so much, picking apart what I could—until I found the nook of her mind where the trauma and hidden memories lay.

I began to beckon them out, carefully, and slowly. I had a small grasp, pulling until it was free, and then I threw the magic towards Zoe who threw her hands out, palms towards us. Magic twirled and danced as reality began to warp around us, taking us from the present back to Aalia's death.

Zoe yelled out as she projected the memory that encased us, bringing us center stage.

Black hair fell down her back as she paraded down the halls of Everinthian. At first, we couldn't see much but the front view of a woman dressed in the finest gold Orsadia had ever seen. Intricate details with lace and decorative stitching across the waistline, but below that she wore a pair of gold pants. A suit in one piece. A queen who did not fancy gowns herself.

I almost stumbled, almost lost sight of our plan here as a gasp escaped me. She was the same woman who'd helped the curse—helped Mira and convinced her not to kill me that night they strapped me to my bed. The one who had watched me nearly burn at the stake, warning me.

"Please, stop! Let me go," a familiar cry echoed down the corridor behind her.

The woman flicked her wrist that hung at her side back and a chain sounded against the concrete. "I told you not to speak, you despicable girl." It was then we noticed the way her fingers were wrapped perfectly around a large chain, dragging it behind her.

As the angle panned out, we caught sight of Aalia following, restrained at her ankles and wrists.

This queen stopped for no one as she marched down the steps to the dungeon, and poor Aalia tripped on the stairs, scraping her legs.

At the end of the line, she stopped, facing Aalia. "You belong here." She opened the door and tossed Aalia to the dirt before locking her inside.

Aalia shuffled against the floor and rushed to the bars, wrapping her skinny fingers around them. "What have I done to you?"

"It's not what you've done. It's what you will do. If I'm going to keep the throne, I won't let anyone stop me, and certainly not the first queen." Her eyes roamed down Aalia, as if she had come to the conclusion she didn't like what she saw.

"My term ended! I'm not coming after you!"

"I don't believe that." She turned on her heel, heading back up.

"Damnit, Gaia! You can't do this! The only reason you have your magic and got the throne is because of me!" She continued to yell at who we now knew was Gaia headed back up to the main floor. The

heavy door swung shut, encasing Aalia in both darkness and silence.

Zoe and I caught a glimpse of Aalia as her eyes drowned in sorrow.

Gaia Quillen had been the second queen, just after Aalia. Zoe's great grandmother. As far as we'd figured, she didn't need much persuasion from the curse. Gaia had been truly sour. That had been evident in the way she raised her own daughter who then abused Wendy until Wendy searched for love in men as a youngling.

The scene skipped ahead, and here Gaia had been carrying a tray of food. When she opened the cell, we caught sight of all the other trays Aalia refused to touch. Her bones were beginning to show as her figure slimmed down.

Gaia set the tray down. "You should eat, Aalia. Nobody is going to be looking for you."

"Your plan is to just keep me down here? For how long?" her voice came out frail—weak.

"As long as I see fit." Gaia locked the cell door.

"You're a fool to believe I got magic because of you." When the first queen met Gaia's gaze, she went on, "I'm the reason I have magic. When I discovered how you got it, I knew it was only a matter of time before that fountain stopped providing. I went in search of the owner. I forced out of Kit where his magical properties came from. The giants had been hoarding water that could do unfathomable things. Unfortunately for me, a few more women overheard. I could have killed them. I desperately wanted to, but they'll be much more fun later on. It won't be much longer until the giants are wiped out and their source is all ours. Magic is mine. I will never let you take the credit for that." She disappeared back up the steps.

Aalia eyed the food, kicking it away at first. But as her stomach growled at her, she crawled forward. When she reached the buttered toast and eggs, she took a bite before shoving the rest of it in her mouth. She scarfed down every bite with her hands, crumbs scattering along the floor around her while the yolk dripped down her arms. She licked every last bit she could before her eyes widened as she clawed at her throat. She collapsed, struggling to yell out for someone. She wanted to crawl to the bars, but as she choked, she grasped her chest, eyes glossing over.

As her last breath dissipated, so did whatever hope had been left in her bright green eyes.

Aalia swallowed as Zoe and I dropped to our knees, energy depleted.

Zoe shook her head. "No, it can't be true. My grandmother? She killed you? But..."

She'd tried to murder me, too.

Seconds later, the first queen screamed as she lunged for Zoe, tackling her to the ground.

Luka went to pull her off, and I reached out for my magic but I couldn't find it. I didn't have anything left in me to search for.

The moment I've longed for, Little Raven.

I rushed over as I pulled my sword from my sheath, swinging and slicing the air. It did no good, and Luka figured that when his arrows would zip through Aalia's ghost and just barely miss Zoe.

Corpses started to rise, and I stumbled back. "Oh, shit. Luka, Clyde. Zoe. We need to run!"

Clyde rushed forward with his dagger. "Lana, stop them!"

"I can't!"

"What?" Luka's eyes almost bulged. "Firefly, please tell me you're lying. You're pulling my leg."

I dove for Aalia, throwing her into the dirt. "Run, moronic lover!"

Luka grabbed Zoe by the wrist, giving her to Clyde. "Take her somewhere safe! Take her to Drecose! Now!"

"What the hell are you going to do?" Clyde shouted back.

The huntsman growled as he sent a kick to the ribs of a skeleton.

"I'm staying behind to fight with *my queen.*"

Clyde wrapped an arm around Zoe's shoulder and rushed her away from the castle and into Ash Forest.

Luka sent more blows to the corpses walking around, and they mostly shattered into individual bones once more. I silently thanked someone that this curse couldn't quite grasp my magic as well as I could.

If I'd learned anything at all about spirits, it was that they were easier to manipulate without their vessels. That was what made me a necromancer after all. Aalia had been a loose cannon, and seeing the ancestor of the heir helping us murder her for no reason other than to keep her power, it set the first queen off. She hadn't deserved to die like that. But Zoe was far more innocent, and she was not her great grandmother. Nor was Wendy. I believed the apple so easily fell far from the tree.

"Aalia, stop!" I wrestled her to the ground, pinning her arms.

She screamed at me.

Something grotesque knocked into my side, throwing me at the base of the castle wall. My head slammed into the bricks. Groaning, my vision began to grow blurry.

Luka picked up my sword and began swinging around at the dead, sending them back to the ground where they rightfully belonged.

The unrecognizable monster growled at my feet as I scrambled up the wall. The same kind of monster that had cornered me in my own castle the night Luka had to come save me.

Out here in the light, I made out exactly what it was. It had been a young wolf at some point, though mostly bones as the rotting corpses of other small animals protruded from his belly. Its eye sockets bore into my very soul as it stepped forward before snapping at me.

"You sick fuck!" I yelled at the curse. It took innocent animals and used them as its weapon.

Rage boiled in my blood as my limbs began to shake.

In an instant, I kicked its jaw and sprinted for the bow and quiver Luka had left by the garden.

As I dropped and grabbed them and threw the quiver over my shoulder, I rounded a tree at the edge of the forest and pulled an arrow against the bowstring. I peeked out from behind the trunk and let the arrow fly. It pierced the creature but hardly slowed it down.

Grinding my teeth, I ran to another tree, tossing the bow over my other shoulder as I gripped a lower branch and hoisted myself up. Now perched, I pulled out yet another arrow and aimed right for the gut. "Try me. I own you now."

The creature screeched as he charged for the trunk, only I kept my word. The arrow shot through its ribcage as it jumped up, exposing its belly full of other disturbing carcasses. The tip lodged into the gut, and then a blade came slicing its head clean off. The cursed creature collapsed into the dirt. Lifeless—returning to where it belonged.

I panted as my eyes locked in on Luka's who gripped my sword. Clearing his throat, he stepped back and gestured. "I told you we'd need to use each other's weapons someday. Not bad, Firefly. Not bad at all."

FIFTY-THREE

Turning to face Dave, I waited for him to begin. He never did. He swayed, unsuspecting, hoping I would say something.

"Dave, if you're asking for a favor, the answer is no. I've got all the things needed to enact the end to this curse." I pulled my basket of apples—freshly poisoned—and brought the handheld mirror with me. "We have no word yet on who's going to die but I suppose I'll bring it outside where everyone else is and we'll find out then. We have to hurry or Luka is going to freak out. You know how he gets."

Nobody had to know what my real plan was.

Dave tilted his head, throwing his hands out.

"You want to carry it?"

Nodding, he grabbed the items from me and I followed him down.

We passed by the kitchen, where I stopped for a moment. "Let me get everyone some fruits we can eat." I grabbed another basket, filling it with pears and oranges and anything else imaginable. Dave and I headed down the stairs, flames flickering in the lanterns hanging on the walls.

"I'm going to miss this place." I admired the gilded décor. "Wherever we move, do you think Luka will let me decorate in my taste? I might have embraced a dark side of my own, but I'd be lying if I didn't admit that haunted castles full of gold and plants were more my taste. A green thumb. If I can't keep people alive, at least I can my own garden."

I brushed my fingers over the vines. They rustled from the movement, I liked to believe it was their way of shivering from their immense love.

I reached for a pear, admiring the greenery and catching a glimpse of my beloved garden just outside the ornate glass window. "I'm really going to miss this *castle*."

Dave grumbled.

When we paused on the steps, I called out to Dave. "You need to do something for me, okay? No questions asked and no objections. Understood?"

When he agreed to my terms and conditions, I reached out for the basket of apples in his bony fingers. The pear rolled from off my palm, contrasting the red fruits surrounding it. I switched it out for an apple, feeling the shape beneath my fingers.

Taking a bite, sour exploded on my tongue, sliding down my throat hastily.

It'd been the right thing to do.

I stopped to pull the fruit up to the light, fear flashing in my eyes as the red skin of an apple laughed at me. Death terrified me even if we intertwined fingers on most all occasions.

But as my foot slipped down a step and fruits went tumbling, Dave turned to hide himself from my fate which he'd deeply disagreed with.

Mira's form flickered. She waited in the corner, her voice low yet bitter as she said, "You turned on us, Snow. How could you?"

Because you deserve to die for all the lives you've destroyed.

Dave lifted the mirror above his head and brought it down against my temple per my wishes.

My vision blurred as I choked, the taste of iron coating my stomach, throat, and tongue. I rolled over to spit up blood, fingers loosening as hope began to fade from my soul.

That had been the last thing I remembered before the curse swallowed me whole, its clutches forever promising to never let me go.

"Lana, darling, you can open your eyes," a soft, feminine voice said.

I obeyed, glancing at my surroundings, far more confused than I had been with them closed. "Am I dead?"

"Yeah." Another woman nodded, shrugging. "Like the rest of us here."

As I scanned their faces, I noticed how every woman here looked familiar in ways I couldn't place. Familiar, yet not recognizable. They'd died before my time. Until I noticed one who looked so much like Mira I could have sworn it had been her mother.

But her mother had died.

The woman who stood before me looked oddly like my mother, but even moreso like me. As if I'd been standing in front of a mirror.

Although I must have been standing inside *the* mirror that'd been my doom because a small window in the distance flashed with familiar faces, a crack running through it, right where it'd hit my temple. Blood streaked across it.

My breath caught in my throat. "Are you..."

She tilted her chin, a crooked smile glued to her lips. She'd been so stunning. A few laugh lines that seemed to take me off guard, reminding me that her life hadn't been all dreary.

Her short dark hair had become streaked with silver, her brown eyes having seen so much of the world in her days, crinkling when her lips curved upwards. She wore a simple gown, black, with no pattern on it. It was her beauty and kindness that paired well.

After everything she'd been through, she could still look at her own granddaughter like this.

Without thinking, she stepped forward, brushing a few strands back from my face. "I always had faith someone would eventually do it. Pride doesn't begin to cover the intensity of what I feel. My own flesh and blood..."

"I still fell under the same curse. I'm the one who killed so many people. Orsadia has less residents, if that. I'm no good."

A frown weighed down her joy. "That's not true. You freed the children I so cruelly trapped because of my own careless magic. You've made Orsadia a safer place for people to love. You broke the curse."

"Broke..." Furrowing my brows, I studied the way her skirt swayed. "I'm dead, Grandmother. Against my father's wishes. Against Luka's. Luka must be so heartbroken! The curse—it killed me. I killed myself because I deserved to lose my life out of everyone on the other side. I broke a promise to my father to protect those I love."

"But?"

My eyes cast to the side, to that small window into the living world. "But I was never going to be able to redeem myself. Forcing people to face the queen who terrorized them for three years seemed too cruel a fate. I belong here—trapped. They've always been better off without me." I choked on a sob. "I wasn't adding value to their world. I didn't just sacrifice myself for the end of the curse. I truly wanted to terminate it all. I wanted to make my vow to death, and that's why

I'm here."

Her hands, though cold as they were, cupped my cheeks as she forced me to focus on her words, "Everyone asked you not to die. You refused to accept your second chance. Never had a queen willingly sacrificed herself for her people or the princess." Her breathing came out steady. Anne Regali knew what she believed, and she poured her whole morale into it. "A man's dark side is never the same as the light. It was never meant to be this tethered hue that laid in the gray matter. It's exactly as it sounds, darling. His dark side feels no love. It's all his worst parts, set to destroy you. It feels *nothing.*"

I forced the lump down my throat. "Is that what you felt? Is that what you heard during your ruling, after all those unanswered letters? I am so sorry."

"My dreams were silly then. I've done horrendous things in my days. That doesn't make me regret having your mother or being able to watch my own granddaughter have a chance at love. The one good thing I achieved was raising such a wonderful woman for the world, who then in turn raised you. I took that with me to the grave. I held onto that and I'll certainly never let it go. Listen to me." She lowered her hands, grasping my fingers to remind me that I was loved even from this side. "You're going to go back and earn your second chance. You're going to love that man who so clearly adores you because it's the very least you deserve, and I want you to own the whole world. You are going to say *fuck you* to the curse. Do you understand?"

Shaking my head, I stepped back. "I'm dead. There is no such thing as a happy ending here. You've lost your power. I've lost mine. Nobody can bring us back anymore. We're caged monsters—and rightfully so."

Mira's mother, Imogen and the fourteenth queen, cleared her throat. "If I may, you've achieved the one thing none of us could. You *broke* that curse."

"So."

My grandmother chuckled as she watched the woman with wonder.

"So, Lana, there was always one little loophole to this game. The curse was tied to Magic Law in the sense that it knew of your presence the moment you were conceived. Now that you're dead, it has no idea who you are. It's connection to you has been severed. The curse was the part of Magic Law that also forced every queen to lose her magic as soon as she fulfilled her term. You've done both. You've also broken the curse itself. There is nothing holding you back from returning to the living."

"Except my lack of necromancy," I stated.

"You sacrificed yourself."

"Pardon?" I choked on a laugh. "I might have done that but it wasn't without more than one reason. I wanted to end my life and I did so. Who says I want to return to that world where they despise me and I deserve every ounce of it? Maybe I quite like being dead."

"It's in the escape clause," my grandmother piped in. "Nobody knew about it because it was always meant to be something pure. A sacrifice that someone made of their own choice."

"Only because someone had to die for the curse to be broken! I wasn't about to let it be another innocent soul. I had to poison myself, and I don't even like apples!" I threw my arms up.

"Suicide is too permanent a decision." I knew that. Did she not think I was aware? "Not even a villainous queen deserves that fate. The curse made us who we are."

"Not all of us," I mumbled as my gaze darted to Gaia. The queen—Bloodthirsty Queen—who my own grandmother had killed, and most likely for a perfect reason. Such as Gaia's given title.

"You're not a monster, my dear. You're a woman who cried out for help when nobody was around to listen." Her eyes mourned. "It counts, because you died. Because you made that decision of your own free will, when you shouldn't have had to at all. Because all the signs were there with the poisoned apple that blackened your insides to the point of death, and the mirror that drew blood from your temple as it cracked your skin." She admired the way I clenched my fists. "Because of what we consider the moth effect, it trickled in just the right ways for you to finally get what you need. To end the curse, and to reverse your own sacrifice. You don't belong here with us, darling, and you never have."

"But I just met you! I can't go back!" I rushed forward, clinging to her arms as I yanked her into my own. "Please."

"All you have to do is find me..." She pressed a kiss to my temple. "I know you will, as resilient as you are." She pulled away, her eyes wandering to the one-sided mirror window, something slipping through the tear in the void. Voices, and a little bit of light.

Luka.

With wide eyes, I reached for my grandmother and clawed the air as I was ripped back into the world once again.

"I'm so fucking pissed," my brother said. "Why would she do this?"

"Because she's stubborn. I love her but damn, why does it have to hurt this bad?" Luka stifled a sob. "I can't believe she's dead. I can't breathe. I can't eat. I can't sleep. My entire heart was torn from my chest, ripped to shreds, and then they shattered the pieces from there. But I can still feel it. How can I still feel it?"

"We'd just begun to patch things again," Fallon said in a lower voice, a cry forming I'm his throat.

Gasping, my eyes shot open, and I threw my hands out as I gripped the edge of my...casket?

What the hell?

"You did all this for me?" I asked as I sat up, eyeing the surrounding people, everyone seemingly amazed. Wide eyes, *unhinged* jaws. Or so I kind of hoped. "Is this my funeral?" Did I deserve such a thing? Nobody would want to mourn me or celebrate my life. They'd never forgive me at all.

When I met the fragile green eyes that gave way to Luka's soul, he raced forward and grabbed hold of my cheeks, peppering kisses over every inch. "I thought you fucking died! Oh, damn, Firefly." He pressed my face into the crook of his neck, squeezing me tight. "Please never do that again. Why would you? Why would you do that to me? You promised you weren't going to take your own life!"

How long had I been gone? Time didn't appear to pass the same in that void.

"I'm sorry," I whispered against his skin. "I couldn't let it be one of you." I swallowed as I pulled back. "You..." With the shake of my head, my eyes searched for another answer. "I've done unspeakable things and I wouldn't expect the people to accept me with open arms even with the curse finally over. My father made me swear not to do it, but how could I take his advice when our other option was someone who didn't deserve to die at all?" I halted, eyeing the crowd. "Father. Where is my father?"

Climbing out of the wooden box lined with such lush bedding, I ran to the front doors, skidding to a stop when someone said, "They're gone, Lana. When you died, the spirits vanished. Aalia. Mira. Her brother. Your father. The corpses dropped dead."

Something would have to be sacrificed...

In this case, someone. All those I'd brought out of the void.

Scanning the area, I spotted a chair made solely of bones.

"We turned Dave into a chair. Thought it was...fair, for a piece of your friend to be useful to us. Now that you're here, it's whatever you prefer to do with him. Maybe we can still toss his body to the sea," Clyde said with a curious tone.

I turned to face my mother. "Why aren't they here?"

Zoe's eyes darted from the sparkles that drifted along the trees, rustling their bright green leaves. "Because you stopped the curse. Magic is still here. I can still use my power and I suppose I have you to thank for that."

As the chair wiggled with the tingle of my fingers, dread washed over me. My necromancy...hadn't entirely disappeared.

"Where are they?" I grasped at the dark corners, searching for that thin veil to the void. I couldn't even feel it. I couldn't feel any of their ghosts. Even if my skin glowed... "I can't access where they've gone. Is that it?"

Luka slipped his hand in mine, his fingers locking between mine. "Maybe it's for the best. Maybe wherever they are, they're happier and at peace now."

"How can I confirm that?"

"Where did you go?" He rested his chin atop my hair.

"The void. Where all spirits go."

"Did you see anyone there that didn't truly belong?"

Aside from the queens, no. Very few people had been left.

Was he right? Had I made a change to the afterlife that gave ghosts a better chance? As a necromancer, I had to believe it.

"What's on your mind?" he asked in a gentler tone. "I want to know if you sacrificed yourself for a darker reason."

"Luka, I..." I didn't know how to explain to him.

"You're worth the world to me. Please, *stay*. You're not corrupt. You're simply just a queen who fell victim to a curse and now you can live on as the one who finally ended it. *Allow yourself that.*"

Even outside of my head, he was convincing. His voice soothed me and allowed me an inkling of raw emotion. How much Luka adored me had to be a crime. How could he look at me with such yearning?

What did I do to deserve him at all?

Nothing, Firefly. You don't need to earn my devotion. Your existence is enough. We can't help who we fall in love with, and if you deem yourself unworthy, what does it say about me vowing my soul to you? You don't need to loathe yourself for my sake, My Queen.

"You're going to love that man who so clearly adores you because it's the very least you deserve, and I want you to own the whole world," she whispered in my memories—those I could still recall.

But my grandmother was still there, and I'd go pull her out the second I got the chance. When the sun had set and the shadows loomed just right.

Until then...

"You're never going to believe who I finally got to meet."

LUKA'S POV

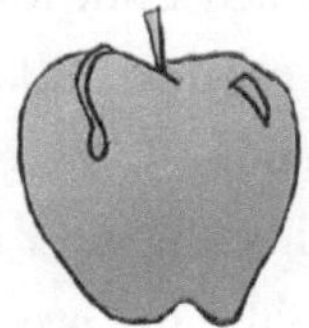

When you lived one life, it sped by in a blink. Even before I'd met Lana, nothing lasted forever. We fought hard. Dared to hold on as tightly as we could.

We could just never quite get it. Even the dead she played with weren't exact copies of those lives they'd lived to tell. The legacy they all left behind. Her legacy.

She feared—like all of us—that her memory would eventually wither like that of a flower just before the winter storm.

Because in the grand scheme of things, our lives were ephemeral.

We strived. Fought. Created. Everything we did was to ensure our purpose and leave our impression before we faded into nothing. My dreams of traveling always played into that, too.

By visiting what else might exist there, I could make my name last forever. I could be a story told to future generations, and maybe then those people could take it upon themselves to explore and stumble upon Orsadia.

After all, a home did not thrive without a community to water it.

When all of this ended, I'd take Lana out there to explore. She tried to reiterate to me that she never wanted to travel. What she couldn't quite hide was the jealousy when I talked about my adventures. Her sarcastic remarks would fizzle out, and sorrow would seep into her hazelnut irises. A piece of her had been too curious.

She was a queen, having ruled alone for the last three years because I had ultimately broken my promise and trusted Mira when I should have trusted my gut in the end.

But queens knew that alliances with other lands were crucial to survival. Traveling was crucial if she was so certain that a queen was going to make deals and trades to fill in the resources we could not otherwise provide on our own.

Lana wanted to travel. She would, and I'd be there to admire every wide eye and dropped jaw as awe filled her expression. It would be something we could finally enjoy together.

The door behind me closed, and I turned to find Lana stepping out of her bathroom with a surprised look and just a robe. A caught-off-guard version had definitely been one of my favorites, and I tucked this memory into the corner of my mind for a rainy day.

"Hello, Firefly."

"What are you doing in my room? Forget I asked." She waved me off with her hand. "I hadn't been able to properly bathe in over a week. Don't give me that look, Luka." Her eyes roamed from my head to my toes.

"What look?" With confusion laced in my eyebrows, I grabbed her nightgown from the wardrobe and laid it out. On cue, my mind took a trip back to the night she'd called me when something went awry in Everinthian. How much she loathed my existence yet couldn't keep herself from asking for my help. She'd worn the same flimsy fabric.

"That!" She pointed. "The look you wear right now. Like you want to—" She went silent.

As my eyes shifted over to meet hers, the corner of my lips tilted up. "Like I want to what?"

Her throat bobbed. "Like you want to marry me."

"And what is so wrong with that?" I stepped closer.

"I don't *do* marriage." Her hands flew to her robe as if I'd been about to peel it off her. It was cute the way she shied away from the more intimate things. Lana Edmilla-Regali had been a bold woman. She spoke her mind on most occasions. The moment the idea of sex popped up, a blush brought color to her cheeks.

I'd never push her farther than she was comfortable.

"Hey," my voice lowered. I closed the last of the distance between us, taking her face in my hands. "You're the light in my eyes."

A small laugh slipped. "I'm death in the flesh. I am hardly anyone's *light.*"

I pressed a finger to her lips to shush her. "Just listen." As she went quiet, I continued, "you give my life a purpose. You bring meaning to everything I ever thought I knew. And I know the idea of marriage has never been on your mind, but I vow to support you and never dim your power. May I ask what it is exactly about it that turns you away?"

Her eyes softened. "The idea that once a man achieves it, he wants to control everything about you. He believes he owns you."

"I would never—"

"But you," she started, "you don't believe that. Regardless of whether it's true, I'm your equal. You..."

"Yes?"

Her tongue slid over her bottom lip. "You worship me, Luka Lockwood. That makes me yours, doesn't it? I'm yours, and I'll be damned that I want to marry you, too."

My heart pounded against my ribcage as I captured her kiss. I'd never let her go, and I'd never be able to leave her again for as long as we both lived. If she dragged my soul from the grave, I'd happily oblige. Not even in death could we part.

ALSO BY MONICA SHANTEL

THE FEATHERS AND FLAMES TRILOGY
Beauty of a Crimson Soul
Beauty of a Burning Flame
Beauty of an Undying Love

THE TO BELIEVE DUOLOGY
To Believe in Peter Pan
To Believe in the Demon King

STANDALONES
Blissful
37 Nights
The Goddess in the Shadows
Tainted

THE QUEENS OF ORSADIA DUET
Seven Deadly Sins
One Poisonous Queen

ACKNOWLEDGEMENTS

I want to say thank you to my mom for always supporting my dreams. Thank you to Ashly for reminding me that my writing is always amazing. Thank you to the friends I have made along this journey and who have supported me through the thick and thin. Thank you to my beta reader, Georgia, for making this book the best it can be. The people who have checked in on me during my rock bottom while writing this book, you have made a woman feel loved and worthy more than you will know. Thank you for letting me express myself through Lana's story.

ABOUT THE AUTHOR

Monica Shantel has always had an interest in artistic and creative hobbies of sorts. At the age of twelve, she began building stories to escape reality and find hope in life. Her debut novel is Beauty of a Crimson Soul. Her style can be described as pushing limits and striking emotional responses. She takes the time to touch on dark topics and aims to shed light on the impact trauma can have on people. In the same breath, she also offers hope with the romantic and platonic side of things as a way to keep her head up even in the worst of times. When life lets us down, her goal is to give people a piece of ambition.

Keep up with Monica:
Instagram: @lxstinneverland
Backup Instagram: @authormonicashantel

For more information, visit:
www.monicashantelbooks.com

www.ingramcontent.com/pod-product-compliance
Lightning Source LLC
Chambersburg PA
CBHW020339310726
48979CB00015B/2436/J

* 9 7 8 1 9 6 0 6 9 6 1 4 4 *